Praise

"Mehl begins her new RYLA... thriller that blends modern-day Christianity with razor-sharp suspense."

—*Booklist* on *Cold Pursuit*

"Nancy Mehl never fails to deliver a complex, nail-biting story. With flawed characters who exhibit genuine emotion, this story is sure to leave you breathless from the thrill of the ride. Hold on tight, it's about to get exhilarating!"

—Lynette Eason, bestselling, award-winning author of EXTREME MEASURES on *Cold Pursuit*

"I love Nancy Mehl's books. Guaranteed to captivate with characters you care about, plot twists you won't see coming, and pacing that will keep you reading long into the night. Best of all, every one of her stories is filled with depth and authentic faith elements. Anyone looking for a clean read and a page-turner can consistently trust Nancy Mehl to entertain and uplift."

—Tosca Lee, *New York Times* bestselling author on *Cold Pursuit*

"Nancy Mehl's *Cold Pursuit* sucked me in from the first riveting page and pulled me deeper into an intricate, danger-filled plot. Unexpected twists and turns along with the terrifying threat of a killer closing in kept me chained to this gripping story and holding my breath until the satisfying end."

—Elizabeth Goddard, bestselling author of *Cold Light of Day*

"The relentless pace will keep readers glued to their seats. . . . This pulse-pounding romantic thriller is a wild ride."

—*Publishers Weekly* on *Free Fall*

"Mehl's rip-roaring inspirational hits the mark."

—*Publishers Weekly* on *Fire Storm*

COLD
VENGEANCE

Books By Nancy Mehl

ROAD TO KINGDOM
Inescapable
Unbreakable
Unforeseeable

FINDING SANCTUARY
Gathering Shadows
Deadly Echoes
Rising Darkness

DEFENDERS OF JUSTICE
Fatal Frost
Dark Deception
Blind Betrayal

KAELY QUINN PROFILER
Mind Games
Fire Storm
Dead End

THE QUANTICO FILES
Night Fall
Dead Fall
Free Fall

RYLAND AND ST. CLAIR
Cold Pursuit
Cold Threat
Cold Vengeance

RYLAND & ST. CLAIR | BOOK 3

COLD VENGEANCE

NANCY MEHL

BETHANYHOUSE
a division of Baker Publishing Group
Minneapolis, Minnesota

© 2024 by Nancy Mehl

Published by Bethany House Publishers
Minneapolis, Minnesota
BethanyHouse.com

Bethany House Publishers is a division of
Baker Publishing Group, Grand Rapids, Michigan

Printed in the United States of America

All rights reserved. No part of this publication may be reproduced, stored in a retrieval system, or transmitted in any form or by any means—for example, electronic, photocopy, recording—without the prior written permission of the publisher. The only exception is brief quotations in printed reviews.

Library of Congress Cataloging-in-Publication Data
Names: Mehl, Nancy, author.
Title: Cold vengeance / Nancy Mehl.
Description: Minneapolis, Minnesota : Bethany House, a division of Baker Publishing Group, 2024. | Series: Ryland & St. Clair ; 3
Identifiers: LCCN 2023055219 | ISBN 9780764240478 (paper) | ISBN 9780764243165 (casebound) | ISBN 9781493446568 (ebook)
Subjects: LCSH: Private investigators—Fiction. | Serial murderers—Fiction. | Missing persons—Investigation—Fiction. | LCGFT: Detective and mystery fiction. | Christian fiction. | Novels.
Classification: LCC PS3613.E4254 C67 2024 | DDC 813/.6—dc23/eng/20231201
LC record available at https://lccn.loc.gov/2023055219

Scripture taken from the New King James Version®. Copyright © 1982 by Thomas Nelson. Used by permission. All rights reserved.

Scriptures marked NIV are taken from the Holy Bible, New International Version®, NIV®. Copyright © 1973, 1978, 1984, 2011 by Biblica, Inc.® Used by permission of Zondervan. All rights reserved worldwide. www.zondervan.com. The "NIV" and "New International Version" are trademarks registered in the United States Patent and Trademark Office by Biblica, Inc.®

This book is a work of fiction. Names, characters, places, and incidents are the product of the author's imagination or are used fictitiously. Any resemblance to actual events, locales, or persons, living or dead, is coincidental.

Cover by Studio Gearbox, Christopher Gilbert
Cover images from Shutterstock

Baker Publishing Group publications use paper produced from sustainable forestry practices and postconsumer waste whenever possible.

24 25 26 27 28 29 30   7 6 5 4 3 2 1

I dedicate this book to Carolyn Parks-Williams,

a faithful book reviewer, reader, and most of all, my dear friend.
I will miss you until we meet again, but I know that
you are now dancing before the Lord, full of joy and
free from a body that held you back in this life.
I love you.

"Precious in the sight of the Lord
is the death of His saints."
PSALM 116:15

He uncovers deep things out of darkness, and brings the shadow of death to light.

—Job 12:22

PROLOGUE

Her will to fight was fueled more by fear than resolve, but it was all she had left. She stumbled down the dark hallway, fingers fumbling along the wall, searching for a way out. There was still a flame burning in her soul, willing her to battle for freedom. How could this have happened? Who had betrayed her? Forced her into this nightmare? Was anyone coming for her? She whispered a prayer to a God she wasn't sure was listening. Would He save her? Or had He abandoned her?

A sound from the other end of the hallway caused her to stop. She pressed herself against the wall as if the action could make her invisible. The floor beneath her rolled like restless waves on a deadly sea that was attempting to pull her under. She laid her cheek on the cool plaster, forcing herself to concentrate on its firmness rather than her unreliable surroundings. She waited for what seemed like hours but could only have been a few minutes. Silence. She finally began to creep forward again, using her hands to propel her farther down the hall.

She squinted, trying to clear her clouded vision. That's when she saw it. Bright red letters. *EXIT.* That was it. What she'd been praying to find. This might be her last chance. Her only chance. She moved away from the wall and tried to run, but she stumbled and fell. On her knees, she crawled toward the red letters that seemed to be flashing out a different word. *Deliverance.* But as she finally pulled herself up and pushed against the door, hands grabbed her from behind. She felt the sting from the needle jabbed into her arm, and she melted into a darkness that began to overwhelm her. The last thing she felt were the tears that coursed down her cheeks as she resigned herself to her fate.

CHAPTER *ONE*

Waiting for her to return to town had pushed his desire for her death to its breaking point. He could have killed her before this, but he had planned her demise to the finest detail and had no intention of altering things in any way. It was perfection. It was vengeance.

River Ryland's time was almost up. And he could almost taste victory.

"WHY ARE YOU staring at me?"

River's question jarred Tony. He didn't realize he'd been looking so intently across the office at his partner. There was something on her mind. Something she wasn't saying, and it worried him.

"Sorry. I was thinking about something and just happened to be looking your way. It's nothing creepy, I promise."

Even though River had been quiet, and clearly tense since they'd returned from visiting his family in Iowa before Christmas, she laughed lightly. "I didn't say it was creepy, although I have to admit it's making me a little nervous. I was beginning to wonder if I'd forgotten my makeup or something."

"No, but you don't wear that much anyway. Not sure if I'd know the difference."

It was true. A little blush and mascara were all she used—and all she needed. River had a natural beauty. Creamy complexion, captivating green eyes shaped like her Vietnamese mother's, and the kind of full lips other women got injections to achieve. Of course, River didn't believe she was beautiful, which made her even more alluring.

"Not really the point," she said. "You're worried about the Strangler's little friend, aren't you?"

A serial killer they'd profiled when they worked for the FBI's Behavioral Analysis Unit had been caught and convicted, but much to their surprise, they'd discovered after he was sent to prison, that he'd been working with a partner. This man had threatened to finish the job the Salt River Strangler had failed to accomplish—the death of River Ryland, the only woman to survive him. They'd become aware of his protégé's existence after they'd moved to St. Louis and opened a private detective agency. Now, they were trying to get their business off the ground with a deadly threat hanging over their heads. Tony had done everything he could think of to protect them. Cameras in the office and in the hallway, as well as the assistance of his friend, the police chief of St. Louis. Of course, he and River were armed. Always. Tony was aware that this wouldn't protect them from a long-range assassin's bullet. He pushed that thought from his mind. This guy wouldn't do it that way. He'd want to be up close and personal. It was the only way he would enjoy killing her. Tony was confident he'd picked the Mississippi River for River's final resting place since they were no longer in Arizona, where he and his mentor had focused their reign of terror.

Tony took a deep breath before saying, "Look, I know something's wrong, River. Why won't you talk to me about it? I thought we could discuss anything. I'm really starting to worry."

She looked away from him and bit her lower lip, a sure sign she was hiding something. He knew it . . . and so did she. Their expertise in reading body language meant that it was almost impossible to disguise their feelings from one another.

"I guess waiting for our stalker to strike is making me antsy."

Although it was the right thing to say, and it was exactly what he'd been wondering, for some reason her response struck a wrong chord in his gut.

"Surely you're not thinking about what my sister said."

When they were in Iowa, helping Tony's father with a cold case, his sister, Aimee, had accused River of putting Tony in danger because of the Strangler. At one point, River had wondered if she should get far away from Tony until the man was caught. But in the end, everyone had agreed, even Aimee, that they were both safer together. That splitting up could make them easier targets. River had concurred—or at least she'd said she did.

"No," she said, shaking her head. "I told you I wasn't going anywhere. Why would you even bring that up?"

Even though her body language seemed to match her words, an alarm went off in Tony's spirit. "Listen," he said, getting up from his chair and walking over to her desk, "promise me that you won't even think about leaving me. It's the wrong decision, River. You might think you're protecting me, but you're not. Confronting us both is a lot more intimidating. Sacrificing yourself for me could kill us both."

Her eyes widened at his declaration, and he felt sick inside. It confirmed his worst fear. She really had been thinking about taking off.

"Aimee made a good case . . ." she said, her voice faltering.

"No she didn't." He spoke more harshly than he meant to. He breathed in and out slowly, trying to control the rapid beating of his heart. "Aimee is my sister and she loves me, but she doesn't have the training we do. She spoke out of a concern for me—not from any kind of knowledge or experience. Please tell me you understand that." He pulled a chair up next to her desk and sat down. "We've got to trust the Lord . . . and each other, River. If you left . . ." His voice broke, and he was horrified to feel tears fill his eyes. What would she think? If she knew how he really felt, would that concern her? Make her rethink their friendship? They'd skated around their feelings for each other for a while now, but neither one of them had come out and said the three words that couldn't be taken back.

Rather than looking repulsed, she reached out for his hand. After a brief hesitation, he put his hand in hers.

"If I ever did anything that put you in danger again, I couldn't live with myself," she said softly.

"But if you left and something happened to you, I couldn't live with that."

River sighed deeply. "You have a way of making things more complicated than they should be. But in the end, you always seem to be right. I . . . I guess we should stick this out together."

He nodded and withdrew his hand. Then he went back to his desk, trying desperately to contain his emotions. With his head turned, he quickly wiped his eyes with his fingers and sat down. He was still trying to compose himself when the door to their office opened and a young man stepped inside. He was short but athletic looking with longish blond hair and wide blue eyes. He wore jeans and a Tommy Hilfiger quilted jacket. He seemed nervous and looked back and forth from River to Tony, as if unsure which one of them he should address.

"Can we help you?" Tony asked, hoping to ease his discomfort.

"Yeah. . . . I mean, I hope so," he said. "I . . . I need help finding someone." He blinked several times. "I thought she might be dead, but now I think it's possible she could still be alive. Do you think you could help me?"

TWO

R iver stood up and motioned to a chair near her desk. "Please, have a seat," she said. "Can we get you a cup of coffee? Or a bottle of water?"

"No, thank you." Before he sat down, he stuck out his hand. "I'm Nathan Hearne."

"River Ryland, and this my partner, Tony St. Clair."

"Nice to meet you." After shaking hands with each of them, he slipped into the chair and rubbed both of his legs with his hands, a nervous habit people used when trying to soothe themselves. River could see that this meeting was incredibly important to him and that asking for help wasn't easy. She could also see that he hadn't slept much lately. There was a blue tinge to the skin under his eyes, which were slightly bloodshot. His clothes said he had money, but a couple of stains on his jeans made it clear he wasn't taking very good care of himself.

"How did you hear about us, Nathan?" River asked.

"I'm friends with Hannah Baum. She used to work for you?"

Hannah had been her mother's caregiver before she hired Mrs. Weyland. Hannah had quit when she found out she was pregnant.

"How is Hannah?" River asked.

"She's doing very well. They just found out that they're having a girl."

"That's wonderful." River made a vow to call Hannah soon. Although Mrs. Weyland was a blessing, she missed Hannah.

"Tell us what we can do for you," Tony said.

"It's about my girlfriend," he said. "April Bailey. She went missing almost seven months ago. I need you to find her for me."

"Seven months ago?" River said. Nathan's words didn't fit the physical clues she was seeing. She looked at Tony, and he frowned at her. He'd obviously noticed the same things.

Nathan nodded.

"You don't act like someone whose friend has been missing that long," River said. "It's clear something has recently happened that concerns you."

Nathan looked surprised. "How could you tell . . ." He shook his head. "Never mind. I don't care. I just want to find her."

"Can you tell us more about it?" Tony asked.

Nathan reached into the pocket of his jacket and pulled out an envelope. "I was already certain she hadn't left on her own, and I'd started to wonder if I'd ever see her again. I'd begun to believe she might be . . . dead. Then this came in the mail yesterday. I . . . I'm not sure what it means, but it frightens me."

River looked over at Tony, who got up and took out two pairs of gloves from a drawer in the filing cabinet. Tony handed one pair of latex, powder-free nitrile gloves to River, along with a plastic bag. The gloves were the kind made especially for collecting crime-scene evidence. They wouldn't contaminate the evidence, and they were thick enough so that they were harder to pierce in case crime-scene techs came in contact with blood or deadly substances.

She slid the gloves on. It was probably too late to find fingerprints from the envelope since it had been touched by so many people, but just in case Nathan was the only person who had handled the letter besides the author, it was smart to be careful. There wasn't any return address, but the postmark was from St. Louis.

She cautiously pulled out the folded piece of paper and opened it. Someone had written, *Don't give up. She needs you. I'll try to contact you with more information as soon as I can.* The writing was in longhand, smudged and shaky, as if written hastily and under duress.

"How do you know this is about your girlfriend?" she asked Nathan.

"I don't, but what else could it be? Why would anyone send a message like this if it isn't about April?"

It was a good question, but if April had been missing for months and she hadn't left on her own, then Nathan's fears were justified. She was most likely dead. So why the note? River glanced at Tony again. He nodded slightly. He wanted to hear more and so did she.

After taking a picture of the note with her phone, she carefully put the envelope and the note into the bag. "So, tell us about April."

Tony pulled his chair over to River's desk and sat down next to Nathan, who took a deep breath. This was incredibly important to him. Everything she saw told her that he was absolutely sincere and very worried about his friend.

"First of all, explain why you brought this note to us instead of the police," Tony said.

"I did talk to the police," Nathan said. "They took my report, but I'm not family. If her family doesn't think she's actually miss-.ing, there's not much they can do. I came to you because I need someone who will listen to me. Take me seriously. Besides, even if her father thought something was wrong, with the amount of crime happening in St. Louis now, I doubt April would be a priority with the police."

Actually, Nathan had a point. Fifty years ago, ninety percent of murders were solved, but today, a third went unresolved, the murderers walking around, unimpeded. Most of it was because of increased crime, less law enforcement personnel, and gang activity that was out of control. The situation seemed almost unbelievable because law enforcement now had better tools to fight crime. DNA testing and databases like the Integrated Automated Fingerprint Identification System, or IAFIS, and the Violent Criminal Apprehension Program, or ViCAP, should make criminal arrests more successful, but unfortunately, these tools weren't being utilized the way they could be. When it came to most crimes, law enforcement had no choice but to prioritize cases based on solvability. This was determined by witness cooperation, DNA, behavioral profiles, known suspects, and physical evidence. In many cases, all investigators needed was for one witness to come forward, but many times, no one did. This was especially true in neighborhoods with violent gang activity. Residents were afraid of retaliation.

"We understand your frustration," River said, "but why isn't her family worried about her?"

"Her father thinks she ran away."

"But you're convinced she didn't?" Tony asked.

"I'm certain of it. The police officer I talked to asked if I had any evidence that a crime had been committed, and I don't." He met River's eyes. "But I'm telling you that I know April. She wouldn't just disappear. She . . . we . . . we got engaged just a couple of weeks before she went missing. She was really happy, and so was I. And she left her cat behind. She loves that cat. She would never do that on purpose. I . . . I'm taking care of him now. I know she'd want me to."

Tony cleared his throat. "Did you two have a fight before she left?"

Nathan's face reddened. "No, not really, but . . . well, her father wasn't thrilled about our engagement. He held some trust fund over her head, but she told him she didn't want the money. I tried to talk to her about it, but she got upset. Told me not to worry about it. I just wanted her to think carefully about walking away from all that money." His smile was sad. "She insisted that all she wanted was me. That the trust fund didn't matter. Neither did her father's opinion."

"Has it occurred to you that maybe April left because she decided she wanted the money after all?" River said. "Maybe she wasn't being honest with you."

Nathan leaned forward in his chair and looked directly at her, his gaze unflinching. His actions meant that he was getting ready to tell the truth. "There's no doubt in my mind that it had nothing to do with the money. We loved . . . I mean, we love each other. I make a decent salary, and she did okay too. It's not like we'd be destitute. Besides, like I said, she wouldn't leave Mr. Whiskers behind—or her purse and her clothes."

"She left her purse behind?" Tony asked.

That was significant. Most women wouldn't take off without their purse. "Did she have a cell phone?" River asked.

Nathan nodded. "I found it in her apartment, along with her laptop. She would never abandon that either. She used it for all of her cases."

"Cases?" River asked. "What are you talking about?"

Nathan sighed deeply. "I'm sorry. I should have explained that. I'm so worried I'm not thinking straight. April has a podcast. *Hot Coffee and Cold Cases.* She investigates cases that the police have given up on."

River looked at Tony, who was obviously surprised.

"That fact is rather important," Tony said, a hint of annoyance in his voice.

"I know. Again, I'm sorry," Nathan said. "To be honest, I'd almost given up on ever seeing her again. But then the note came. The idea that she's still alive . . ." His eyes filled with tears.

"It's okay," River said, attempting to comfort the distraught young man. She was trying to digest this new information. Was April missing because of one of her cold cases? Did she get too close to the truth? Had someone kidnapped her . . . or worse . . . decided to shut her up?

Suddenly, this missing-person case had turned interesting— and potentially very dangerous.

CHAPTER
THREE

Where is April's laptop now?" River asked, hoping Nathan still had access to it.

"I have it. I didn't want her father to take it. April didn't want him to know about her podcast. But he has her purse and her clothes. I went through her purse before he had time to take it, just in case there was something important in it."

"And was there?" Tony asked.

"I don't think so. It's just a purse."

Nathan took a deep breath. He was under a lot of stress. River felt badly for him.

"Besides the phone and her laptop, I also have her notebook. She had notes about her cases, along with phone numbers, contacts she'd made while investigating. I thought it might be important."

"You realize that her parents could accuse you of theft for taking her personal property, right?" Tony asked.

Nathan shrugged. "I don't care. April wouldn't want her dad to have them. In fact, she told me once that if anything ever happened to her, she wanted me to take anything that had to do with her podcast." He shook his head. "We were just . . . talking, you know? Neither one of us actually thought that day would come. So, once she disappeared, I did what she'd requested. But I left her regular phone behind, as well as a second laptop that she used for other things besides the podcast. And it's just her father, by the way. Her mother died a long time ago."

"Where are April's things now?" Tony asked.

"In safekeeping at my place. I wanted to see if you'd take my case before giving them to you. As you can imagine, I don't want anything to happen to them."

"If you want us to proceed, we'll need them. As well as your phone and laptop."

Nathan's eyebrows shot up. "Mine? Why would . . ." His eyes widened. "I didn't hurt her."

"Actually, we believe you," Tony said. He brushed a lock of curly black hair from his forehead. "But we have to make certain there's nothing to tie you to her disappearance. If you don't have anything to hide . . ."

"But I need my phone and my laptop. I use them for work."

"What do you do?" River asked.

"I'm a graphic designer for an advertising firm in California. I work out of my apartment."

"Can we get them from you after work so we can go through them?" River asked. "We'll get them back to you in the morning. We may have some questions concerning what we find, but we can make notes and talk to you when we're done."

They could actually clone the cell phone onto another device, but since it could be tricky with certain models, going through it manually would probably be easier. They would copy the files on the laptop to a USB drive.

"I . . . I guess that would be all right."

"A warning though, Nathan," Tony said solemnly, "if we find

that you've deleted anything before you give them to us, we're done. Do you understand?"

The young man nodded. "Look, I have no plans to hide anything from you. I just want to find April. I pray with every fiber of my being that she's still alive. But even if she isn't, I need to know the truth. So does her father. Even though he believes she's alive, he's really upset. I've tried to stay in touch with him for April's sake, but he blames me for her disappearance."

He sighed. "Sometimes I've wondered if I should just walk away from him, but I feel like April would want me to help her father if I can. Even though they argued before she disappeared, they love each other." He hesitated a moment before saying, "There's something else. I'm not sure if I should share this. At the time I believed it was April's imagination, but I feel like I should tell you everything. April loved what she did, investigating cold cases. She thrived on interviewing family and friends of the victims and asking the public for help. She felt as if she was doing something good. Something noble." For the first time since he'd walked through the door, his smile was genuine. "Believe it or not, she actually helped solve two different cases since she started the podcast a couple of years ago. An arson and a murder. I was so proud of her." His smile slipped and his expression became serious again. "But sometimes she got spooked, you know, by the details of a crime, or by thinking the person behind the crime was after her. Thankfully, it was never real."

"So, was she *spooked* about one of her cases in particular before she disappeared?" River asked.

"Yeah."

"So, she believed she was in danger and then she went missing?" Tony said. "It didn't occur to you that the two things might be related?"

Tony's frustration was showing. River felt the same way, but alienating Nathan by making it seem they blamed him for April's situation wouldn't help anything.

"This wasn't the first time she'd felt that way down through the years," Nathan said, his tone somewhat defensive. "It never turned out to be real. I assumed this was the same thing."

"Can you tell us about the case?" River asked calmly. "It's possible her state of mind is important, even if there wasn't any real threat. How she acted in the days up to her disappearance could reveal something that might help us."

She frowned at Tony, who seemed to take the hint. He leaned back in his chair and nodded at her.

"I can't be certain which case was bothering her," Nathan said. "She wouldn't tell me. I'm not sure why, but since she'd been wrong before, she might not have felt confident enough to share her concerns. In the months before she went missing, she was trying hard to focus only on the facts. She wouldn't move on anything until she had solid leads. I think her mistakes in the beginning made her cautious. So, this is just a guess, but the case that was taking up most of her time was the Castlewood Casanova. Two teenagers—a guy and a girl—were reported missing. Their bodies were found in Castlewood Park in Ballwin, near the river. It was assumed that they went there to make out."

Tony frowned. "Why use the word Casanova?"

Nathan shrugged. "April named most of her cases, but this one had already been given a title by a newspaper reporter. I think it was because the young man involved had a bit of a reputation. I have no idea if it was deserved or if the reporter just wanted something that started with a C. You know, because of Castlewood Park."

"And they never found a suspect?"

"They interviewed several people, ruled them all out. But April felt there was one man who could have done it. She also suspected that he'd killed before. She didn't talk much about it, but I could tell those murders really bothered her."

"Are there any notes on her laptop about that particular case?" River asked.

"Yes, some. But she kept most of her notes in her notebook. She was kind of old school when it came to that. She'd take that notebook with her wherever she went so she could write down things that occurred to her when she wasn't home. Look, she was working on seven cases when she disappeared." Nathan frowned. "I don't want to steer you in the wrong direction. The Casanova case might not have been the one she was concentrating on when she disappeared. April was . . . is . . . the kind of person who doesn't know how to let go of something. She could have been super focused on any one of her cases."

"We need to go through the items we asked for," River said. "If we have questions about them, we'll let you know when we see you. After we're through, we'll talk about our next steps. Is that okay?"

He nodded. "I'll do anything I can to help. I need to go home and get back to work. Where can I meet you to give you everything?"

"What time do you quit working today?" Tony asked.

"Around six."

River looked at Tony. "Why don't we come by your place? We'll pick up your phone, April's phone, both laptops, and the notebook."

Nathan nodded. "That's fine. Then you'll bring my phone and laptop back in the morning?"

Tony nodded. "Around eight?"

"That's perfect. I never get calls from my boss before nine." Nathan recited his address and River wrote it down on the notepad on her desk.

"Can we find April's podcast by searching for *Hot Coffee and Cold Cases*?" River asked.

"Yes, but here's a card with the URL." He stood up and reached into his back pocket, taking out his billfold. He opened it, took out a card, and handed it to River.

"Okay. We'll see you around six," Tony said.

"Do I need to give you a retainer or something?"

"Why don't we take a look at April's things first?" Tony said. "Then we'll tell you if we think we can help you."

Since their past cases hadn't made them much money, River decided to tell Nathan the amount of their retainer and how much they would charge each day the case extended beyond the initial amount if they took his case.

"That's fine," Nathan said, not reacting at all when River mentioned the totals.

Rather than walk toward the door, he stood where he was, shifting from one foot to the other. Something else was bothering him, but River had no idea what it was. Had she read him wrong? Was he actually concerned about the retainer? "Are you certain our fee isn't a problem for you?"

He shook his head. "I earn quite a bit, and I inherited some money when my father passed away. Like I said, I have money."

He was pretty young to have lost his dad. "I'm sorry about your father."

"Thank you. We were shocked when he died. A sudden heart attack."

"That's rough," Tony said. "My condolences."

"I miss him every day. I wish he were here to give me advice now." He blinked away tears. River felt empathy for Nathan. First he lost his father, and then the woman he loves disappeared? Compassion made her really want to help him, but would they be able to? This case really was cold. When it came to a missing person, those in law enforcement believed the first forty-eight hours were crucial. After that, it was likely they would only recover a body. The note had brought April's disappearance back to life, but was it real? If April's podcast had a lot of followers, could one of them have sent it for their own reasons? People did strange things. As behavioral analysts, she and Tony had seen individuals take actions that were hard to explain—even with their training. Was there actually a reason to hope they could find the answers Nathan was looking for?

"Is there anything else?" Since their fee didn't seem to bother him, why was his body language telling her that something was on his mind?

"Look, I hadn't planned to bring this up. I love April. With all my heart. But loving someone doesn't mean you think they don't have flaws. April wasn't perfect. I'm not perfect. Even though she had her . . . problems, she was . . ." He sighed. "Is . . . the best person I've ever known."

He was trying hard to keep April in the present tense, but it was obviously difficult even though Nathan desperately wanted to believe she was alive.

"What are you trying to tell us?" Although Tony was attempting to be patient with the young man, it was clear he was exasperated with the way Nathan was dispensing information in dribs and drabs.

Nathan didn't respond. He just stared down at the floor.

"Nathan, you have to be completely honest with us if you want us to help you," River said sternly. "No hiding anything. Even if something doesn't seem important to you, it might be vital to us. If you don't trust us, this isn't going to work."

"All right, all right," he said, shaking his head. "I don't want you to think April was unbalanced—or paranoid. She was . . . is . . ."

"I realize you're struggling to believe she's still alive," Tony said. "We understand that. Don't worry about how to talk to us about her. We get it, okay?"

"Thank you. I want to believe I'll see her again. Life without her is so . . . nothing." He looked up at them, his eyes shiny with tears. "Please . . . please don't give up on her, okay?"

"Tell us what you don't want to tell us," Tony said. "Trust us."

Nathan took a deep breath. "Before she disappeared, she told me that . . . she wondered if she might be putting me in danger. She talked about leaving so she could be certain I was safe."

FOUR

River suddenly felt cold. Nathan's revelation rocked her to her core. It mirrored her own feelings about Tony. She wanted to respond, but she couldn't seem to find any words. Thankfully, Tony took over.

"It isn't just that you don't want us to believe April was paranoid," Tony said, "you were afraid we might think she left on her own, right?"

Nathan didn't say anything, he just nodded.

River took a deep breath, willing herself to calm down. "If it helps," she said, "I understand." River offered him a small smile. "There is good reason to believe that's not the case. If it were true, she would have packed all of her clothes and taken her phone, laptop, and purse. Most importantly, she would have taken her cat. My mother has a cat, and it means the world to her."

"Is that it, Nathan?" Tony asked, his voice steady. "Is there anything else you're hiding from us?"

"No, I promise. I've told you everything I know. Please believe me when I say I'm certain she didn't just walk away on her own."

"We do," River said. "Don't worry."

"Go home," Tony said. "We'll see you around six."

"Okay. Thanks."

"And Nathan," Tony added, "be careful. We don't know what we're dealing with yet. Just keep your eyes open, watch your back, and don't let anyone into your apartment that you don't know."

"You really think I'm in danger?" he asked, his eyes wide.

"I seriously doubt it, but it never hurts to be careful," Tony said. "Until we get an idea of what April was into, it's just best to err on the side of caution."

"Okay . . ."

River didn't want the kid to worry, but Tony was right. Nathan needed to be careful, just in case.

After he left, River leaned back in her chair and met Tony's gaze. "So? What do you think?"

"I don't know. Before I render an opinion, I want to see April's laptop. And I'm especially interested in her notes. If . . . and that's a big if . . . she wasn't being paranoid, she's either dead or in real trouble."

"I told Nathan she wouldn't have left without her purse, her laptop, and her phone, but that's not necessarily true. I'd really like to know what was in her purse."

"You're thinking she may have left decoys behind and taken her real credit cards and identification with her?" Tony said.

River nodded. "We've seen it before, but why would she want to frighten Nathan and her father? I tend to doubt she would have done that. Why not just tell them she's going away for a while? It would have been a lot less dramatic, and it might have stopped them from looking for her. And I meant what I said about her cat. That fact alone makes me believe she didn't leave of her own accord."

"I've never had a cat, but I'd never leave Watson behind. He's family. I'd like to look at her bank accounts and credit card statements. See if she's still using them."

River frowned. "Her father would have checked that, right? Just to make certain she's okay?"

"I don't know. Even if he'd believed she's really missing, most adults don't give their parents their bank account information."

"Maybe April had access to funds no one knew about."

Tony's right eyebrow shot up. "Like another credit card? But payments would show up on her checking account . . . unless she opened a new one and didn't tell anyone."

River could see his mind working.

Finally, he sighed. "You know, if her father believed she was in trouble, this thing would be a lot easier."

"Maybe. I keep thinking that April seems to be particularly savvy. I think she could have created another identity if she'd wanted to. I doubt seriously she would keep using her credit cards or her checking account if she was trying to hide."

Tony grunted. "You're probably right." His eyes locked on hers. "You think she's still alive?"

"I don't know. Until we know more, I don't want to speculate."

"So, what does that note mean? Who could have sent it?"

"That's exactly what I'm wondering," River said. "April wouldn't mail it if she wants to stay concealed. And if someone took her, or worse, they wouldn't send it. If this was some kind of killer who wanted attention, he wouldn't wait this long—and he'd be touting his own superiority, not making it sound like she was still alive."

Tony was quiet for a moment. "Is this case hitting a little too close to home for you? Is that going to be a problem?"

River was still a little unnerved by Nathan's revelation, although she didn't want Tony to know it. Even though this situation wasn't exactly the same as hers, River couldn't help but feel a deep connection to the missing woman. However, if she ever decided to leave, she wouldn't do it like this. She would never allow Tony to wonder if she'd been abducted. He would assume the Strangler's accomplice had taken her. She couldn't possibly do that to him.

"We need to keep ourselves out of the equation," River said, struggling to sound composed. "We really have no idea what's going on yet."

Tony gazed at her for several seconds, making River feel a little unsettled. Sometimes she could swear he was able to see right through her. Finally, he got up, retrieved the envelope with the letter, and took it back to his desk.

"Let me see if I can get any fingerprints from this," he said. "If I can, I'll send the images to Arnie so he can ask the lab to run them through IAFIS."

IAFIS maintained tens of millions of fingerprints. It even stored prints from crime scenes that were never matched to an individual in hopes that at some point they could be identified.

"It's protocol to send the letter to the police," River said. "Let them look for fingerprints."

"I realize that, but we're former FBI. Arnie won't care if we do it. They're so backed up, it could take them forever to get to it. After I send them the images, we'll turn the letter over."

"I don't know. What if this turns out to be important evidence?"

Tony shrugged. "The St. Louis PD will run the prints. No one cares who found the images. Arnie will make sure everything turns out okay."

River didn't say anything, but if this ended up being a vital clue, it might be inadmissible in a trial. She was also worried about going through April's things. They didn't actually belong to her father since April hadn't yet been declared dead, but at some point, it was possible they would have to be turned over to the police.

Tony put on a new pair of gloves and removed the letter from the evidence bag. Then he retrieved a fingerprint kit from his desk and carefully sprinkled dark powder on the white paper. With a small brush, he whisked away the extra powder.

River realized she was holding her breath and slowly let it out. A moment later, Tony looked up at her.

"I have prints, but they're probably Nathan's." He took out a roll of tape and nodded at River. "Could you get me a piece of printer paper?"

She got up and got another glove. Then she walked over to the printer and picked up a piece of paper using the glove to protect it from her own prints. She carried it back to Tony and laid it on his desk. He carefully placed a piece of tape over each fingerprint and transferred it to the clean paper. When he was done, there were six very clear prints and a couple of smudged ones.

"I'll call Arnie and let him know this is coming," Tony said.

River nodded. "I'll get online. I want to listen to April's podcasts."

"Good idea," Tony said. "Didn't Nathan say she was working on seven cases at the time she disappeared, including the Castlewood Casanova case?"

"Yeah," River said. "Just because she mentioned suspicions about that one, it doesn't mean it's connected. Or that any of them are."

"That one is close though," Tony said. "Ballwin's a little less than twenty miles from here. The others could be in different states. Less likely anyone connected lives close enough to be stalking her."

"Not impossible though. If she has listeners in other parts of the country, someone could still be worried if she's getting too close." River looked at the clock. "It's after eleven. Why don't you get us some lunch before I start researching? Once I get started, I hate to quit."

"Sounds great," Tony said, getting to his feet. "What are you in the mood for?"

River smiled. "Gyros?"

Tony laughed. "You're reading my mind."

The Gyro Company had become one of their favorite places to eat. From their gyros to their hummus and all their other great choices, River and Tony never tired of it.

"Grab some tiramisu too," River called out as Tony headed out the door.

"You didn't have to tell me."

After thinking about it, River decided she also wanted some hummus. She searched the top of her desk for her phone, but it wasn't there. She grabbed her purse and looked through it too, but no phone. Maybe she left it in the car. Hopefully she could catch Tony before he left the parking lot. She got up and hurried out of the office and down the hallway.

The other reason she'd suggested an early lunch was because she needed to clear her head. She couldn't stop thinking about April. Had she made the choice River had been willing to make to protect Tony? Did she leave to keep the man she loved out of harm's way?

As she jogged past the other businesses that lined the hallway on the second floor, River glanced briefly at a couple of the newer ones. The first was a graphic design firm called Art Attack Design. Cute name. There were two men and a woman working at computers who didn't look her way as she passed by. They'd said hello, though, when she'd passed them in the hallway before. They all seemed nice. The other new business, down at the end of the hall was called TSRS. Just one man working there. So far, they'd never spoken. He kept to himself. There wasn't anything on his door or on his windows to indicate what kind of business it was. The man looked up from his desk and saw her. He had dark hair, a mustache, a small beard, and thick black glasses. He smiled, and she returned his smile. As she hurried down the stairs, she realized she was breathing quickly. She always felt a little anxious when Tony was gone. Silly. She was a grown woman, armed, and trained by the FBI. As she tried to catch Tony before he left, she did her best to focus on their new case and not think about the Strangler's partner, who had threatened to carry out Joseph Baker's death sentence.

FIVE

After a great lunch, River made herself a cup of cappuccino and parked herself in front of her laptop. It had been a snowy winter so far in Missouri, but today was bright, the sun shining as if promising that spring would surely come. Still, it was really cold, with temperatures in the teens. The coffee helped to warm her up, but each time she brewed a cup, she couldn't help but think about the deranged man who had added a drug to some of the flavored pods they'd used in their single-serve coffeemaker a few months ago. These were new, and that man was gone, but the memory of that awful day still tickled her thoughts whenever she touched her lips to the rim of her cup. She pushed the uncomfortable memory back into the recesses of her mind and glanced toward the large windows at the front of their office. They looked out onto the hallway, which was also lined with glass that faced outside. Even though it didn't look like winter from her vantage point, she felt sad knowing that each day brought them closer to the end of her favorite season. She'd loved snow ever since she was a little girl. It had made her feel safe, as if nothing bad could happen when it snowed. Evil was frozen and covered with a blanket of white that kept it hidden from the world. But of course, that wasn't true. Evil flourished in winter just as it did in any other season. Their recent cases had proven that.

She turned her attention back to the matter at hand. It only took a couple of minutes to find a website for April's podcast, *Hot Coffee and Cold Cases.* River was surprised to see how many people followed it. Ads along the sides of the first page made it clear there were several sponsors connected with the site. She wondered how long they would hang on with April gone. River grabbed her headphones and plugged them in so she wouldn't disturb Tony as she listened.

The main page featured a picture of April. She was lovely— long brown hair and dark eyes. A smile that made it look as if she enjoyed her life and what she was doing, yet there was something in her gaze that caught River's attention. An echo of pain. Of fear. River recognized it because she'd experienced the same thing. That cloud following you everywhere, casting its shadow on every aspect of your life. She sighed. Had the cloud finally consumed this young woman? Was April really dead? Had she been killed by someone connected with one of the cases mentioned on her site?

River scrolled down the page and found links to several different cases. Each one had a title.

She located the two cases April had helped crack. Just like the others, they had rather silly titles, but both of them had a large red circle across the page with the words *Solved by Hot Coffee and Cold Cases* within its border. River quickly looked through them. Each case had pages that detailed the crime and how the killers were caught. Although they were interesting, both criminals were in prison and unlikely to be the reason someone might want to stop April from further investigation. She proceeded to the unsolved cases. April had added new cases every couple of months. There was a written description about each one, as well as the podcast that people could listen to. April also had a disclaimer stating that the identity of anyone contacting her with a tip would be kept confidential. Besides the actual podcast, April had recorded updates as things changed with each case. It would take a while to listen to the original recording as well as the updates. River grabbed her notebook and settled into her chair, determined to get as far as possible before they had to leave for Nathan's. Each one had an interesting title.

1. *The Case of the Missing Mother*
2. *The Case of the Railroad Rage*
3. *The Case of the Convenience Store Carnage*
4. *The Case of the Hit-and-Run Hitchhiker*
5. *The Case of the Virtuous Volunteer*
6. *The Case of the Disappeared Diabetic*
7. *The Case of the Castlewood Casanova*

The last case was the one Nathan had mentioned. River decided to listen to it first. She clicked on the link and a female voice began to talk. April. She had a soft, pleasing tone. River wasn't sure what she was expecting, but April sounded so . . . normal. Why was this young woman so interested in these violent cold cases? It was an important question. One she wished they'd asked Nathan when he was here. She paused the episode and then went back up to the top of the page, where she found a link to April's bio.

She selected it and found herself on a page with a different photo of April. The bio contained the usual things, where she was born, where she'd attended college, etc. It turned out that at one point, she'd been studying for a degree in English. She'd wanted to be an English teacher. River wondered why that hadn't happened. Had she dropped out? How do you get from wanting to be a teacher to investigating cold-crime cases?

Then she started on the second paragraph. When April was

a child, her mother was murdered. At one time, April's father was the prime suspect. River wasn't completely surprised. Family members are always looked at first. Most murders are committed by family or so-called friends. But after he was cleared, there were no arrests. It seemed that the case turned cold. April actually left college to investigate the murder herself. She was never able to figure out who killed her mother—nor could the police. It was now obvious to River why April began the podcast. She'd seen what can happen when murders remain unsolved. She obviously felt driven to help others who were in the same situation she'd been in. River couldn't help but feel sorry for April's father. He lost his wife, and now his daughter had disappeared. She could understand why he might suspect that Nathan was involved in some way. If River was in his shoes, it would certainly occur to her. However, if Nathan was guilty, he wouldn't come looking for someone to investigate his crime. He'd want it ignored. If she and Tony decided to take this case, they would want to talk to April's dad. Would he be willing to talk to them? Hopefully, he'd welcome the idea that someone was looking for his daughter, even if he believed she'd left on her own accord.

Following the bio, there was a Scripture. Job 12:22. "He uncovers deep things out of darkness, and brings the shadow of death to light."

For some reason, the Scripture made River shift in her chair. The words were so powerful, and they resonated with her. Is that what she and Tony were doing? Working with God to bring darkness into the light? River suddenly felt an even deeper bond with April. It was as if the cries of their souls were the same. From the time she was a young girl, River had felt called to battle wickedness. Her father's betrayal had awakened something inside her. His rigid standards and his commitment to pastoring a church he professed to care for wasn't enough to keep him from running off with the church secretary and abandoning his wife and children.

River had watched her mother disintegrate and had felt her father's rejection. It made her angry, even vengeful. It had also given her a deep understanding of right and wrong as well as a desire to see justice done. As crazy as it sounded, her father's treachery was the impetus that led her to becoming a behavioral analyst for the FBI. A dream had died when her father left—and a dream had died when April's mother was killed. Yet both she and April had developed a quest for righteousness. Of course, once she came face-to-face with a loving and merciful God, River finally realized that He wasn't the God her father had preached about. God was love, and although River was still driven to eradicate criminals from society, her desire was no longer based in hate.

River heard a muffled noise and looked over at Tony. He gestured toward her headphones, and she took them off.

"You okay?" he asked.

"Sure. Why do you ask?"

"You were making odd noises."

She frowned at him. "What kind of odd noises?"

He smiled, the corners of his gray-blue eyes crinkling. "Hard to explain. Kind of a cross between sighing and humming."

"Humming? I don't think I . . ."

He shook his head. "Not like humming a tune. You kept saying *hmmmm* over and over."

This made River laugh. "That makes more sense. I don't see myself as the *humming* type."

"Definitely not." He appeared to study her for a moment before saying, "Something interesting?"

"Yes. I was reading April's bio." She quickly filled him in on what she'd discovered.

"Wow. I guess we know why she was so interested in solving crimes."

"Sorry about the sighing and humming."

"Not a problem," Tony said. "While you were busy making

noises, I called Arnie. Sent the fingerprints to him, but as we suspected, he wants the actual letter."

"Why don't you take it to him?" River said. "I've got quite a bit of work to do here."

"I . . . I don't want to be gone that long," Tony said. "A trip to pick up lunch is one thing, but . . ."

"It's been almost a month since the Strangler's little friend sent that Christmas card," River said. "We haven't heard a peep since then. Could you be overreacting?"

"He bugged our offices, River," Tony said sternly. "We can't just blow that off. He's been in here."

"Calm down," she said. "I understand what you're saying, but I'm tired of letting this guy control us, aren't you?"

"Yeah, I really am. But we have to keep our guard up until he's behind bars." Tony frowned at her. "He helped Baker kill all those women, and if he didn't kill Jacki himself, he most surely murdered David."

David Prescott was the man who just happened to be walking near the Salt River the night Baker shot Tony and threw River into the water. David called the police, and they arrived just in time to pull River out before she drowned. He testified at Baker's trial and helped to put the serial killer behind bars. Then a few months ago, he disappeared. Law enforcement hadn't been able to find him.

"I don't want to sound like a grump," Tony continued, "but I really don't want you to leave this office again when I'm not here. Even to chase me down because you want to add something to your lunch order."

"Tony, that's ridiculous. It's daytime. We're surrounded by people. The building even has a security guard. With all the cameras, no one would try anything here." She pointed her finger at him. "Besides, aren't I safer with my phone? What if I needed to call for help?"

"It's a good point. So from now on, don't leave it in the car."

"Great idea," she said, her tone slightly sarcastic. "Why didn't I think of that?" She leaned back in her chair and stared at him. "We've done everything we can to stay safe in this building. You need to trust that."

"I'm not so sure," he said slowly. "I still wonder if we should move out of here."

"We talked about that and decided that this is the most secure place for us." She waved her hand toward the cameras mounted on the ceiling. "Look, I've been worried about our safety, that's true. But not here. Not in our office. Since installing the cameras, I feel we're very well protected. Better than anywhere else we could go."

He shook his head. "I know. Still, I'll be glad when that slimeball is in prison—or dead."

"Wow, where's all the 'love your enemy' stuff you said you believed? And where is your faith? I lean on your strength, you know."

Tony sighed loudly. "I do have faith, and don't preach my own words back to me. I pray for this guy, River. But I'm tired of this. How long do you have to live under the Strangler's influence?"

River just stared at him. It was a good question, and one that she couldn't answer. Tony was usually so strong. But he was a human being too, and it was clear that he was getting weary from the pressure. At that moment, a Scripture popped into her head. She was pretty sure it wasn't just her own thoughts. "Isn't there something in Isaiah that says, 'But those who wait on the Lord shall renew their strength; they shall mount up with wings like eagles, they shall run and not be weary, they shall walk and not faint'?"

Tony stared at her for a moment, and the tightness in his face relaxed. "Yes. Yes, there is. Isaiah 40:31." He sighed. "If anyone had told me a couple of months ago that you would be encouraging me with Scripture, I wouldn't have believed it. But here you are. You've come a long way in a short time."

"I told you that I read the Bible when I was younger, and my father quoted verses a lot. I heard it. I memorized it. But he used God's Word as a weapon. Thanks to you, those Scriptures he parroted have finally come alive. I've learned the Bible is full of hope, faith . . . and love. Now it's powerful. Real. I'm seeing it in a whole new light." Her voice caught as she choked out the next words. "And it's because you just . . . cared about me. Kept being an example of what Christians should be. I don't know where I would be . . . without you."

He nodded and turned his head, but she'd seen his expression. It wasn't one of just friendship. It was something more. Much, much more. River put on her headphones and tried to concentrate on April's podcast . . . but all she could think about was the man sitting at the other desk and how much he meant to her.

CHAPTER
SIX

Tony had been convicted by River's words. He was supposed to be a good example, yet lately he'd allowed his fear to crowd out his faith. To be honest, he'd always seen himself as someone with great faith. But this situation had pushed him into something . . . different. Even though he tried to ignore it, he was frightened. He wanted to believe that the Strangler's partner wasn't going to move past threats, yet he knew they couldn't count on that. In fact, something inside him seemed to be warning him that River was in real danger. The problem was, he couldn't be sure if it was worry talking . . . or if it was the Holy Spirit whispering to him. If he wanted to protect River, he had to get himself in a place where he could clearly hear from God. Right now, in the face of the panic he felt, the heavens seemed like brass.

"I've got my headphones on," River said. "I'll try to keep my sighing and humming down."

Tony looked toward her and smiled. "Thanks. I'd appreciate that. It's very distracting."

She stuck her tongue out at him and went back to April's podcast.

Tony's mind drifted to Joseph Baker. There were four main types of serial killers. The visionary, who kills because he believes he is being commanded by God; the hedonistic killer, who takes lives for the sake of personal pleasure; mission-oriented killers, who believe they are saving society from a particular group of people that deserve to die; and the fourth type, the power-and-control killer, who wants to exhibit total control and dominance over his victims. Ted Bundy was a power-and-control killer, and so was the Salt River Strangler. He wanted to dominate his victims. He needed to feel that their lives were in his hands.

Tony realized with a start that Baker was succeeding. Even though he was in prison, Tony was allowing Baker to control his thoughts . . . his peace of mind. Was that Baker's plan? To use his minion . . . his partner . . . to terrorize River? And through that also manipulate Tony's life? Baker was an evil man, and God had won the battle over evil a long time ago. So why was this so hard for him? Why was he struggling so much?

He forced himself to concentrate on something else. While River was listening to April's podcasts, he'd dig a little more into April herself. He began to pull up social media accounts. First, he checked Facebook. Sure enough, he found her. Two pages. A personal page and a public page for *Hot Coffee and Cold Cases.*

The podcast page was interesting. She had quite a few followers. Over ten thousand. He began to read back through her posts and the comments. Most of them were positive. There were a few people who seemed to believe that April was stirring up people's pain as a way to grow her numbers. They were convinced that she should leave murder investigations to the police. The truth was, getting the public involved in cold cases had proven to be quite useful in some situations. Then Tony began to find idiotic posts by scammers claiming they'd tried to friend her but couldn't and asking her to contact them. These lowlifes set up fake pages, trying to establish relationships. Then they'd use that as a way to get personal information so they could steal from the people they targeted. Since he couldn't find any of these messages earlier in the threads, it was clear to him that, at first, April had been blocking these knuckleheads and erasing their posts. Since she'd disappeared, their comments remained while her followers' posts went un answered.

As he scrolled through the comments made before April quit replying, he found something troubling. There were several remarks from someone calling themselves Lamont Cranston. His comments had a harsher tone than any previous posts by people who felt April's podcast was inappropriate. The first remark read "You're an amateur who has no idea what you're doing. You could be causing damage to innocent people. You need to stop!" A week later, the same poster said, "You have no right to interfere in the lives of others. The police need to put a stop to you!" This comment puzzled Tony. The person who wrote this mentioned law enforcement. Usually, someone who had something nefarious on his mind wouldn't mention the police. He would be hiding from them. It was interesting to see that after both comments, followers of the page went after him. Although Tony couldn't be sure the poster was a man, the verbiage and the strong tone suggested a male. Even though he was attacked by people who liked April and her podcast, he didn't respond to them. He clearly didn't care about them. He also had no interest in defending himself, which spoke to his razor-sharp focus . . . on April.

Just a few days before she went missing, there was this. "You haven't listened to me. You'll be sorry for that." After that, Lamont Cranston stopped posting. There were several more comments from people, asking where April was, wondering why she wasn't responding. Then there was a comment from Nathan letting them know that April was missing and asking them to look out for her. Immediately after that, the page exploded with notes of concern. Eventually, they petered out, although occasionally, someone would post a message, asking if April had been found. There was no response. It seemed Nathan had no desire to step in again and update April's worried followers. He probably felt he'd posted enough on the page and didn't see a reason to continue. It was at this point he'd probably started to give up seeing April again.

Tony flipped over to April's personal page. The comments were set to "Public," which wasn't unusual when someone wanted to point people to a blog, a podcast, or some other kind of business. This made it easier for Tony. If the page had been set to "Friends" he wouldn't have been able to see all the comments, although it was possible Nathan could have let him in.

Lamont Cranston hadn't commented on this page. Here, April attempted to be friendly and welcoming, but her posts were stilted. Sometimes awkward. Several people who'd responded at first eventually drifted away. One other thing stood out to Tony. None of her "friends" appeared to be people with whom she actually had personal contact. They lived in other areas, and although they seemed to like April, there wasn't any attempt to connect in real life. April didn't invite that kind of response. Although the podcast was mentioned on this page, she'd tried to steer the page toward other topics as well. Tony could tell that she wanted to relate to people, but she didn't have the necessary social skills to do it. He and River had seen this before. People who were obsessed with something had a habit of pushing people away, not because they didn't want personal relationships, but because their main interests lay somewhere else. The podcast was obviously the most important thing in April's life, and although it was evident she wanted friends, she was unable to invest the time or the emotional commitment to make that happen.

Before he put any more time into the case, Tony had a question. He found Nathan's number and called him. The phone rang several times before Nathan picked up. He was probably working, but Tony needed to know something before he proceeded.

"Hello?" Nathan said, his voice a little tight.

Tony apologized for interrupting him and asked about Lamont Cranston. "His posts are rather disturbing."

"Yes, I know. I contacted Facebook about him, but they didn't really care. I checked him out as well as I could on my own, but all his personal information was fake. The police might do better than I did, but unless they get involved, there's not much we can do."

Tony made a mental note to ask Arnie if he could find out anything about Lamont Cranston.

"I noticed you said something about April's disappearance, but you didn't post again after that. Can you tell me why?"

A deep sigh came through the phone. "There's a part of me that wanted to keep her page going, but April was so good at what she did. I couldn't possibly follow in her footsteps. Besides, with my job, I just don't have the time to invest in it. Sometimes I feel like I'm letting her down."

"I don't think you are. Just because you don't feel capable of continuing the page, it doesn't mean you aren't interested."

"I felt like my part was to listen to her, and I did. I tried to be there for her, you know? She used me to bounce ideas off of. I think she appreciated it." His voice caught. "Anyway, I hope she did."

"I'm sure she did," Tony said. "We'll see you at six."

Tony hung up and stared at his laptop. Lamont Cranston was hiding his identity. He chose a name from an old radio show called "The Shadow." Obviously, he was hiding in the shadows. This information bothered Tony. Whoever this was knew what he was doing, and he'd gone to a lot of trouble to make certain he couldn't be found. But why? Could he be the reason April was missing?

SEVEN

It was almost four o'clock when River took off her headphones. She'd made notes about every episode. Even though the Casanova case seemed to be the one they should focus on first, each podcast April had recorded was compelling. The behavioral analyst in her wanted to profile all of them, but she wasn't sure it was necessary. She looked over at Tony and noticed that he was staring at her.

"Did you get through all of them?" he asked.

She nodded. "I think April had good instincts. Each of these cases make me want to dig in and look for solutions. Of course, some seem more likely to be connected to April's disappearance than others."

"That's good, because I'm not sure we have time to investigate them all."

"Yeah, because we're so overloaded with work," River said dryly.

Tony laughed. "I hear you, but I'm talking about doing what we can for Nathan." He frowned at her. "That's if we *can* help him. What do you think?"

"Why don't you let me run these active cases past you? I'd like to see what you think."

"All of them?"

"Yes. I mean, we can concentrate on the Casanova case first, but since we're not certain it had anything to do with April's disappearance, we should look at each one, don't you think?"

"Yeah," Tony said. "Until we see April's notes, we won't have a clue which case might be connected to her disappearance. Or if any of them are."

"That's what I was thinking." River stood up. "Want a cup of coffee?"

"Sure." Tony got up from his chair and carried his cup over to the counter next to the coffeemaker. River didn't even need to ask what kind he wanted. She took his cup, put it under the spout, and added the pod. Black coffee. Always plain black coffee. She brewed his coffee and then handed it to him.

"Thanks," he said. "You really don't need to make my coffee, you know."

"I realize that, but I was taught to respect my elders."

Tony grinned. "You're only a year and two months younger than me."

River shrugged. "Sorry. I forgot. I guess it's because you look so much older."

"Very funny."

He headed back to his desk while she looked through the pods and picked a favorite—Southern Pecan. As she waited for the coffee to brew, her mind ran over the cases she'd listened to. She could understand why Nathan thought the Casanova case was the one that might be connected to April's disappearance, but River wasn't certain. There were a few of them that concerned her. She wondered if Tony would see the same thing she did.

"Hello? You still with us?"

Startled, River realized she was staring at her cup, but it was already done. She picked it up. "Sorry, just thinking. It's hard to listen to April's voice and not feel like I know her. I understand her interest in all of these cases. To be honest, I think I would have picked them too." She sat down at her desk.

"So, you think the two of you are alike?"

"Yeah, I do. I think we could be friends. I . . . I really hope this isn't going to end badly."

Tony stared at her for a moment, then said, "River, you know the chance that we'll find April alive isn't good. Unless she purposely left her father and Nathan behind, she would have contacted one of them by now."

"I know. We're used to seeing the worst outcomes. But there's a part of me that can't stop hoping that someday we'll get that fairy-tale ending, you know? It's not impossible."

"But . . ."

River held up her hand. "You don't need to protect me. I understand the situation."

Tony smiled. "You amaze me. You've survived a nightmare most people couldn't. But here you are, holding out hope for this girl."

"With God, nothing is impossible."

He nodded. "You're right. But the Bible also tells us to guard our hearts and minds."

"Point taken."

Tony took a sip of his coffee, then said, "So, what can you tell me about these cases? We don't have much time. We need to leave around five-thirty so we can get to Nathan's by six."

"First of all, let's divide the work. You want the laptop, the phone, or the notebook?"

Tony sighed. "I can download the laptop and go through the phone. Why don't you take the notebook? Since you identify with her, you might get more out of it than I would."

"Exactly what I was going to suggest."

"Great minds think alike," Tony said with a grin.

River took a sip of her coffee and then picked up her own notebook. Like April, she liked to write her thoughts down on paper. It was what she was used to. Besides, writing something down helped her remember it.

"I guess we should wait before going through the cases in detail. We just don't have time now. I can at least tell you what she called them. Like I said, there are seven different cases. Okay, first up, we have what April called the case of the Missing Mother. After that, there's the case of the Railroad Rage, followed by the case of the Convenience Store Carnage."

"They all have titles like this?"

"Yes," River said. "I guess she needed to call them something."

"Not sure I'm a fan of cutesy titles for crimes where people lost their lives."

For some reason, River felt a little defensive. She realized that she needed to disconnect herself from April. Seeing the truth in situations where murders had been committed needed a certain detachment—the ability to see things clearly and without emotion. Her bond to April could cause her a problem she didn't need.

"After that, we have the case of the Hit-and-Run Hitchhiker, the case of the Virtuous Volunteer, the case of the Disappeared Diabetic, and finally, the case of the Castlewood Casanova."

"Are these in any particular order?"

River shook her head. "I thought maybe she'd list the older cases first, but I don't see any rhyme or reason when it comes to how they're listed. I do want to say that even if you don't like the titles, I'm very impressed with her ability to detail each one. What's on her podcast is for the public. I'm interested in what she's done regarding background research and any tips she may have received. There are some updates following some of the original podcasts. We'll need to listen to all of them at some point—if we take this case."

"Sound good," Tony said. "Hey, I've got nothing in my fridge. I'd like to get something to eat before we go over to Nathan's."

"How can you be hungry?" River asked, a look of bewilderment on her face.

"I just have a faster metabolism than you do."

River shook her head. "You should weigh four times more than you do. I don't get it."

He looked at the clock. "We could run by that pizza place you like so much."

"I thought you didn't like it because they serve froufrou pizza."

Tony shrugged. "Pizza should have red sauce and lots of pepperoni and sausage. White sauce with eggplant and chicken?" He shivered dramatically. "No thanks."

"They do have red sauce and fatty meats. You'll be fine."

"I guess so. I'll just pretend it's the only thing they serve."

River laughed. "You really are fragile, aren't you?"

"No one should mess with pizza."

River was about to make a snarky comment when the door to their office opened. It was the building manager, Dustin. "I'm sorry to bother you folks, but something was delivered to my office that I think you should see."

He walked over and handed a large manila envelope to River, whose desk was closest to the door. She took it and thanked him. Instead of leaving, he stood there, looking distinctly uncomfortable. What was going on? River looked at the front of the envelope. There was nothing written on it.

"You opened it?" she asked him.

He nodded. "Someone slid it under the back door of my personal office. My security guard saw it when he was making his rounds and brought it to me. Whoever left this found the one exterior door in the building that doesn't have a security camera covering it."

River looked over at Tony and frowned. He got up, grabbed a

pair of gloves, and brought them to her. After putting them on, she reached into the envelope and pulled out what was inside. It was a rather fuzzy photo printed onto paper, but it was clearly a picture of Nathan Hearne walking out of the building. Written across the bottom were the words *Stay away from April Bailey, or you'll be sorry!*

EIGHT

Tony grabbed a glove and took the picture from River. After looking it over, he addressed Dustin, who was still standing there.

"There's nothing else you can tell us?"

"No, like I said, there isn't a security camera back there. Across the street, there's a small parking lot for the office supply company's employees. They don't have a camera there either, but you might wanna ask them if anyone who works there saw anything."

"Thanks," Tony said. "We appreciate you bringing this to us."

Instead of leaving, he stood there, shifting his weight from foot to foot.

"Is there something else?" River said.

"Look," he said slowly. "I'm not tryin' to make trouble, but the landlord isn't gonna like this. After what happened a couple of months ago . . ."

"You mean when my partner was attacked in this office . . . by the man you hired to clean the building?" Tony knew he sounded angry, but for this guy to be threatening them right now made his blood boil. They'd spent their own money to put the cameras up, and now he was upset because someone was trying to intimidate them?

The man held his hand up. "I'm not gonna tell the landlord . . . this time. But I'm jes tellin' you that he's kicked people out for less. I like you people, and I don't wanna see that happen."

"We appreciate that," River said quickly. Tony knew she was trying to keep him from another angry retort.

The man nodded and left, closing the door softly behind him.

"I really don't want to get thrown out of here," River said.

"I'm sorry. It's just that after what you went through . . ."

"I know, I know," River said softly. "But he didn't mean anything by it. He was trying to help us."

"Maybe." Tony took a deep breath and let it out slowly. "I guess I shouldn't have reacted like that." He pointed at the picture. "So, what do you make of this?"

"We need to take it to the police and have them check for fingerprints."

"I can . . ."

River held up her hand. "Let's let them do it this time. I don't want to push it."

"Okay, okay. If you really think it might jeopardize evidence, we'll do it your way."

River frowned. "You're believing Arnie will investigate April's disappearance—even though her father didn't file a report?"

Tony nodded. "I'm sure he'll look into it. Maybe we're not family, but with our background, he'll take our concerns seriously."

"Good," River said. "I think we need to check with the office supply place. Then we could run by the police department. You can give the letter and the photo to Arnie and let him know what's going on. After that, we'll go to Nathan's and then get you some pizza—if you can survive that long." She could tell that Tony was already invested in Nathan's case, even though they hadn't gone through the phones, laptop, and notebook yet. The photo made it clear to them both that there was something suspicious about what happened to April. She didn't say anything to him about it, though. They'd decided to wait until tomorrow to tell Nathan if they wanted to pursue the case, so she felt compelled to follow through.

"I guess I'll have to. If I faint from hunger, just open my mouth and shove something in, okay?"

River laughed. "I can do that. I think I have an old granola bar in my desk. . . ."

"Uh, never mind." He grimaced and shook his head. "But before we go, I'd like to take just a second and talk about what's written on the picture."

River sighed. "I guess we should. I think I'm getting used to being threatened."

"Yeah, I know. Didn't happen this much when we were with the FBI."

"It never happened when we worked for the FBI. Well, except that once . . ."

He grinned. "You mean when the crazed serial killer tried to murder us?"

River nodded. "Yeah, this seems much milder than that."

"Thankfully. As you know, most killers don't warn their victims first. The Salt River Strangler's protégé likes to mess with his victims. He's a narcissist. He gets some of his jollies by causing fear before he strikes. But this is . . . nothing. I don't think this is someone who really intends to hurt us. Why would he warn us first? Unless he thinks we're wimps and we're going to back off because of something like this."

"Then he doesn't know us very well, does he?"

"No, he doesn't," Tony said.

River stood up. "The thing that bothers me is that he obviously followed Nathan and took a picture. That shows some commitment."

"True." Tony was quiet for a moment before meeting her gaze. "I'm not sure what to think. Why was he following Nathan? And why warn us?"

"Good questions. I don't know the answers." She sighed. "Let's get going."

She grabbed her purse and coat and waited for Tony to join her. Once he shrugged on his coat, they walked out of the office and locked the door behind them.

When they got downstairs and stepped out of the building, the cold January air hit them like a punch in the face. River pulled up her coat collar and put her head down. The wind fought against them as they made their way to the car.

Their trip to the office supply company yielded nothing. No one saw anything, and as Dustin had said, there weren't any cameras outside the store.

Next, they went by the police station to drop off Nathan's letter and the photo they'd received. For once, Tony didn't kick up a fuss about River waiting in the car for him. No one was dumb enough to come after her in the department's parking lot. She watched Tony walk to the door. Once he got inside, she took out her phone and pulled up April's Facebook pages. Tony had seen them, but she wanted to look at them herself. She'd been going through them for several minutes when the driver's side door opened, causing her to jump.

"Sorry, didn't mean to startle you," Tony said as he got into the car.

"You're fine. I was concentrating."

"I realize that takes a lot out of you," Tony said with a grin.

"You're a laugh a minute. What did Arnie say?"

"He was in a meeting. I left the envelope with a brief message and said I'd explain about it later."

As Tony drove out of the parking lot, River sent up a silent prayer for help. For some reason she felt a sense of urgency. If, by some miracle, April was still alive, and if the person who had her knew that Nathan had come to them for help, it could mean that keeping April alive was becoming too risky for them.

CHAPTER
NINE

After checking in with the guard positioned at the gate to Nathan's complex, they finally located Nathan's unit.

"There it is," River said suddenly, pointing toward a row of numbered residences. It was a nice complex with attractive townhomes.

Tony pulled up in front of Nathan's place, then he looked around. "Pretty fancy," he said. "Guess he was telling the truth about having money."

"At least if we take this case, we should get paid."

"Well, my dad did send us a nice check," Tony said.

"Which we returned. We can't accept money from your father. We helped him because he's family."

"You know I feel the same way, but he wasn't too happy about it." Tony laughed. "You watch. He'll find some way to give the money back to us. He's pretty sneaky."

"Well, we're pretty cagey ourselves."

"Yes, we are. Hopefully, we're cagey enough to find out what happened to April Bailey."

River sighed.

Tony frowned at her. "You think this case is a dead end?"

"Interesting choice of words," she said. "I just hate thinking that if we find April, it will be too late. Nathan will be devastated."

Tony had been thinking the same thing. Nathan seemed to really care about April. Confirming that she was dead would be incredibly difficult. That was part of the job they'd never had to deal with when working at the BAU. However, the photo with the warning scribbled at the bottom of the paper irritated him. Even before going through April's things, he'd already decided he wanted to follow this through to the end. No matter what.

"Let's see what we can find out from her stuff," Tony said. He smiled at her. "I know we're both leaning toward taking this case. I just think we need to be sure."

"Are we going to tell him about the picture?"

"I believe we have to," Tony said. "The threat was leveled at us, but the picture is of him. I don't want to make him paranoid, but this person knows about April. Now, they seem to be focused on Nathan. They must be following him for some reason."

"If he'd been warned to drop it, he would have told us, I guess."

Tony nodded. "I think so." He shook his head. "I have a feeling about this case . . ."

"I'm glad you said that. I feel the same way. As if we're looking at the surface, but there's a lot more going on that we can't see."

Tony had been a Christian long enough to know that listening to those odd feelings was important. Besides that, their training had kicked in more than once, making them look more closely at something that might otherwise have seemed inconsequential. He just prayed that his concern for River wasn't messing with his ability to see what was important when it came to Nathan's case.

"Maybe after reading April's notes and seeing what's on her laptop we'll be able to figure out what's really going on here," he said.

"If she's not alive, why would someone send Nathan that note? And make sure we saw the photo?"

Tony shrugged. "I don't know. Maybe they killed her, and they don't want us to find them. But that leads to another question. Why is someone following Nathan? And how would they know he was coming to this building to see us? And that it was about April?"

"Good question," River said. "He didn't mention telling anyone that he was planning to talk to us, but we should probably ask him about that."

"Good point. We might be able to use that to narrow our search." He grinned at her. "Ready?"

"Come on, Watson. The game is afoot."

"Hey, wait a minute. Why are you Sherlock?"

River tossed her hair and laughed. He not only enjoyed the sound of her laughter, he loved it when she did that with her hair.

"I'm Sherlock because I thought of it first. Besides, you have the dog named Watson. That settles it."

Tony sighed dramatically. "That doesn't make any sense."

"Sorry. Suck it up, my friend."

They got out of the car and together they walked up to Nathan's front door. River rang the doorbell and, a few seconds later, the door swung open. Nathan motioned them inside.

If Tony had been impressed by the outside of Nathan's townhome, he was even more amazed by the inside. Tony had expected a casual, messy dorm-room type of vibe, but Nathan's apartment was stunning. Clean and modern with real wood floors and an open-concept living room that led to a gleaming white kitchen with hanging lights and modern appliances. It confirmed Nathan's claim that he could afford to pay them. Not that they were doing it just for the money, but Tony was relieved that if they decided to take the case, it wouldn't be pro bono. They really needed to bring in some income if they wanted to keep their agency afloat.

"Have a seat," Nathan said. "Can I get you something? Cup of coffee? Iced tea?"

Tony looked at River, who shook her head. "We're good, but thanks. We have a lot of work to do tonight, so we'll take what we came for and get going."

"Sure." Nathan walked over to a coffee table and picked up a tote bag with a *Hot Coffee and Cold Cases* logo. "Everything's here. Remember, though, I really will need my phone and my laptop in the morning."

"Don't worry. We promised we'd bring it back to you," Tony said, taking the bag. "I need to reiterate that if we find you've deleted anything, we can't help you."

"I understand," Nathan said. "Most of what you'll find on my laptop is from work. I've backed it up, but please be careful."

"We will," River said. She looked over at Tony, who nodded.

"April's notebook is pretty big," Nathan said. "It might take a while to go through it. You don't need to return any of her things until you're finished with them. I don't have any use for them." He hesitated a moment. "I added something else that might not have anything to do with her disappearance, but . . . I don't know. It's rather disturbing."

"What is it?" River asked.

"Ever since April was young, she's been plagued by something. She had nightmares as a child and when she got older, she began drawing pictures of . . . of what she saw in those dreams. I didn't think to mention this when we talked earlier, but April's mother was murdered when she was young. I think she was projecting her mother's murder into these drawings, yet they don't match the facts of the crime. Her mother was found in a parking lot, not far from their house. She'd been robbed and shot in the chest. April's drawings are of a woman who was stabbed and left under a tree. The figures don't have a face, but the hair is dark like her mother's."

"I read about her mother when I looked over her site," River said. "Is it possible April saw someone else's body under a tree when she was young?"

Nathan shrugged. "I doubt it. Her father surely would have known about it. He told her that what she saw in those dreams never happened. He thinks it's her way of processing her mother's death. She never saw her mother after she died. Maybe she saw something on TV or just imagined the image."

"She didn't see her mother at the funeral?"

Nathan shook his head. "Her father didn't think it was good for her to be there. He especially didn't want her to view Katherine's body. He was afraid it would traumatize her."

"How old was she when her mother died?"

"Nine."

River sighed. "So, her mother just disappears and never comes back? No wonder she was obsessed with cold cases. She was trying to make sense of something she never had closure from."

"Look, Nathan, this showed up at our office today," Tony said. "It's a warning directed at us, but someone's taken your picture. They may be following you. We feel you need to know."

Tony handed him the copy they'd made of the photo.

When Nathan looked at it, his face turned pale. "I don't understand. Why would anyone do this?" He looked back and forth between them. "Doesn't this mean that April may still be alive? I mean, why would anyone care enough to do this unless they were trying to protect a secret? What else could it be except that they don't want her found?"

"It could also mean that someone doesn't want us to identify them and find out that . . . that they hurt her," Tony said.

"Maybe," Nathan said, "but I won't give up. I just can't."

"We hope this will turn out the way you want," River said gently. "If we decide to move forward, we'll do our very best to find out what happened to April."

"You thought I'd want to give up because of this picture?" Nathan asked. "I live in a gated community, and I work from home. You don't have to worry about me."

"Do us a favor," Tony said. "Don't leave here. Have your food delivered. Can delivery drivers leave your food at the gate?"

"Yeah, as long as I've paid for it ahead of time."

"Are you stocked up on other things?" River asked.

Nathan nodded, "Just went to the store a couple of days ago." He frowned at them. "Do you really think I'm in danger? I mean, if someone's trying to tell you to back off, maybe you're the ones who need to be careful."

"We were both trained by the FBI," Tony said. "We're not worried. We know how to take care of ourselves." Tony sounded confident, but with the Strangler's apprentice still out there, another threat made him wonder if they were biting off more than they could chew right now.

"Should . . . should I get a gun?"

"Not at this point," River said. "You seem to be pretty well protected here. Arming yourself should be a decision you make under normal circumstances. Not under duress. Besides, you should never buy a gun without learning how to use it first."

"Okay," Tony said. "That's it for now. We'll be back in the morning. Don't forget to give the guard our information."

"I'll remember."

Tony gazed into Nathan's eyes. "I want to ask you just once more before we leave. You're absolutely sure you want to move forward with an investigation if we decide to take your case?"

"Yes." Nathan's body language and expression made it clear that he was determined to see this through. "I have to know what happened to April. Like I said, this . . . picture hasn't changed my mind."

"All right," Tony said. "We'll let you know our decision in the morning."

"I'll have a check ready for you."

Tony and River said goodbye and walked out to their car. Once they were inside, River said, "I hope we find something that will give us direction in those seven cold cases April has on her site. If we don't, this could take a while."

"You're trying to find a nice way to tell me we don't have time to get pizza."

River didn't say anything, just smiled at him.

Tony shook his head. "Fine, but if the police call you in the morning and tell you they've discovered my emaciated body lying on the floor of my apartment, I want you to remember that you could have saved me."

"I'll try hard to get over it," River said, laughing. "Besides, you pass that great hamburger place you like on the way home. I think you can pick up something and eat while you work."

"You're a slave driver, but I guess that would work. I'd better get you home so we can get started," Tony said. "Call me if you find anything."

"When are you going to stop driving me around?"

"When the Strangler's accomplice is behind bars or under-ground. Until then, you have a chauffeur. Get used to it."

River sighed. "Why do I get the feeling he's laughing at us? I still wonder if his only plan was to stir up trouble and make us worry."

"Frankly, that would be great, but my gut's not telling me that—and neither is yours."

River was quiet as Tony drove to her mother's house. He was getting tired of worrying about the threats from the Strangler's friend, and he knew River was too. But if they lowered their guard, they would put themselves squarely in his sights, and they couldn't afford that.

TEN

After checking on her mother and Mrs. Weyland, River took April's notebook to her bedroom and sat down at her desk. Tony was going to download the files from the laptops and manually go through both of the phones. River had offered to take one of them, but when she saw the size of April's notebook, she decided Tony was right. This was going to take a while. It had a soft leather-like cover and two hundred pages, with other notes and sheets of paper stuffed into a pocket in the back. Thanks to Nathan's willingness to let them keep April's things, she wouldn't have to go through all of it in one night.

She began by looking through the pages at the front of the notebook. First of all, there were notes about a couple of cases that had been solved by police work. Then were the two mentioned on April's podcast that had been closed through the tips and information that had been sent to her. River had seen them on April's site, but she hadn't listened to them yet. Right now, they were more interested in the cases that April had been working on when she disappeared. River was impressed by April's notes and the information she'd collected from people who either listened to her podcast or followed her on Facebook.

She chose the Castlewood Casanova case first. The information was the same as that on her podcast but there was also a list of people who had contacted April with supposed information pertaining to the murders of the teenage couple. April had crossed off most of their suspects' names. There were four names that she was investigating, according to her notes. One was marked *credible*. River wrote the information in her own notebook as a safety measure. No matter what happened, she and Tony would still have what they needed.

She'd planned to move on to the next case, but she wanted to do a little research on this one first. Nathan felt as if this was the case April was worried about. Was it really connected to her disappearance?

"Nathan could be wrong," she muttered to herself. "Keep an open mind. You need to look through everything." She sighed. "Of course, her disappearance might not have anything to do with any of this." She rubbed her eyes. She was tired and not in the best mindset to think too much about anything she read tonight. Sharing her findings with Tony would help. He often brought clarity to situations.

Going over April's notes about the Castlewood Casanova case, it was clear that April was interested in a man named Oscar Hemmings. He lived in the same apartment complex as the girl who had been killed. The apartment manager said that Hemmings had acted inappropriately toward her. April noted that the police had checked up on him but had ruled him out. River wondered why he'd been eliminated. Next to the notation about the police investigation, April had added a question mark.

"Interesting," River said softly.

April had noted that four years earlier two teenagers in a park in Illinois were killed in a similar manner. Brian Janko and Terri Gillespie. Both shot. One in the car, one outside on the ground.

Murdered just like the other teenagers. Both crimes had occurred in the winter. Not many people around to witness the shootings. The parks were basically deserted. Two different guns, but for some reason, April seemed to think the killings were connected. River couldn't find anything to explain why she believed that, though. Seemed as if she was trying to pull them together without much proof. River wondered how she was able to find out what kind of gun was used. That's not something the police usually share with civilians. She began pulling up articles about the incident, but there was nothing that definitively connected the two killings. However, as she continued to read, she felt as if she were going over the same articles that had been written about the deaths in Castlewood Park. Clearly, she was getting tired. She needed to look over the information again once she'd had some rest.

River began quickly flipping through the other pages when some of the papers in the back fell out. She picked them up and began to sort through them. Most of them were just sheets with more notes, but there were also pictures and articles from different news sources that April had printed out. Somehow, she'd acquired a couple of photos from the crime scene in Castlewood Park. They were disturbing. The victims were both so young. They'd had their whole lives ahead of them, but on that night, someone malevolent, someone vile, had robbed them of their futures. River was grateful she could still feel anger and sorrow when seeing the aftermath of evil. So many in law enforcement had created, out of necessity, a hardened shell in an attempt to protect their hearts and minds. However, in many cases, those shells eventually cracked, and the lives of those sworn to defend the innocent died by their own hands.

She yawned several times and found herself blinking as she tried to clear her bleary eyes. It was time to stop. She was too tired to make sense of what she was looking at.

As she slid the papers and the photos into the pocket at the back of the notebook, she noticed a different newspaper clipping about the earlier murders. One she hadn't seen before. The photographer had captured pictures of the victims, probably without the police realizing it. The bodies echoed the scene at Castlewood Park. Out of the car, one lying in the snow, in the same pose. Her interest rekindled, she began a search on her laptop and started pulling up articles about that incident. Again, many similarities, but nothing that proved they definitely were connected. If this was a serial killer, where was his signature? Why wasn't he taking credit?

She had just closed both notebooks and her laptop when there was a knock on her door.

"Come in," she called out.

Her bedroom door swung open, and Mrs. Weyland stepped inside. "Am I bothering you?" she asked. The gray-haired woman was what some people called pleasantly plump. The wrinkles at the edge of her hazel eyes made it clear that she loved to smile. She exuded kindness. River was so thankful she'd come into their lives.

"Of course not," River said with a smile. "Is everything okay?"

Mrs. Weyland softly closed the door behind her. "Your father called today."

"I don't want him speaking to my mother when I'm not here. I'm afraid it will upset her."

"He didn't call for her. He called to talk to me. I guess you told your brother about me?"

River nodded. She'd emailed Dan, wanting to keep him up to date with what was going on with their mother. She felt obligated to do so.

"I . . . I don't understand," River said. "Why did he call?"

The elderly caregiver walked over and sat down on the edge of River's bed. "Your father wants to visit, River. He wants to ask for forgiveness from your mother . . . and from you."

River's brother, Dan, had already mentioned that their father wanted to make the trip to Missouri. The woman he'd left them for had taken off once her father's money ran out. Big surprise. Was her father's request connected to that? Did he want money? Or was she being too suspicious? River had learned a lot about forgiveness over the past couple of months. She'd come to realize that God had paid an unbelievable price for her sins. How could River not try to forgive the man who had destroyed their family? Yet even thinking about him made her feel nauseated.

"I need some time to think about it," she said. "I'm not sure how this would impact my mother." She frowned. "Does she know about it?"

Mrs. Weyland shook her head. "Your brother might have said somethin' about it a while back, but I don't believe Rose remembers."

"You spend more time with her than I do," River said. "What do you think?"

Mrs. Weyland took a deep, slow breath before saying, "I honestly don't know, honey. She's mellowed quite a bit over the last few weeks. She asks me to read the Bible to her every day. I think she's tryin' hard to find her way back to God. It's possible that your daddy askin' for forgiveness might mean the world to her. It's also possible . . ."

"It could cause her to flip out."

Mrs. Weyland nodded. "She's at the point where it's hard to know just what she'll do next." She paused for a moment and stared down at the floor. When she raised her head, River was surprised to see tears in her eyes.

"What's wrong?" she asked.

"When I took this job, I told you I'd be honest with you."

"Yes, you did."

"This disease is cruel," Mrs. Weyland said slowly. "I wish I could keep it from hurtin' you, but that's not possible."

River felt her stomach tighten. "Just tell me."

"When you left the kitchen after supper, your mama . . ." She took a shaky breath. "Your mama asked me who you were."

Even though River had been mentally prepared for what she knew was probably coming, Mrs. Weyland's words felt like a punch in the stomach. She tried to respond, but she couldn't seem to catch her breath.

"Oh, honey, I truly didn't want to tell you about it, but I felt I had to. She's your mama, and my job is to take care of her and keep you updated on her progress."

"No, it's okay," River said, unable to keep her voice from quivering. "It just took me by surprise."

"If it matters, she's in her room now, watchin' TV, and she asked me to tell you to come and say good night before you go to sleep."

"So, she only forgot me for a little while . . ."

Mrs. Weyland nodded. "Yep, just for a couple of hours, but in most cases, if this disease takes it's natural course, it will happen more and more." She leaned forward and gazed at River intently. "The biggest mistake we can make is to forget about Jesus in all this. He's a healer, honey. I don't want to strip away your hope. Let's believe for the best, okay?"

"I will. Thank you. And let me think about this thing with my dad, all right? It sounds like a good thing, but I don't want to jump into it too quickly."

Mrs. Weyland rose to her feet. "I'll pray that God will give you wisdom about it. Good night, honey."

"Good night."

After Mrs. Weyland left the room, River just stared at the open notebook in front of her. She couldn't really make sense of the words scribbled on the pages. All she could think about was her mother . . . and the father she'd once claimed she'd never forgive. What was more important here? Her mother's stability or her father's need for absolution?

ELEVEN

He drove past River's house. The lights were on. They were all awake. River's time was running out quickly. He would make his move soon, but as he waited for the perfect time, he'd started to believe that a reminder that he was watching her, planning her demise, was needed.

He had to be careful. If his action was too violent, River and St. Clair might pull up roots and put themselves out of his reach. But until their destined meeting, he had to make her wonder if he was still here. Still stalking her.

Whatever he decided to do, it would be soon. River Ryland was facing extinction—and he was her executioner. He wanted her to remember that. Then, when it happened, she would recall that he warned her. That knowledge made him smile.

RIVER WAS GETTING READY to head to her mother's room when her phone rang. It was Tony. She picked it up.

"Hey there, what's going on?"

"Just wondering how you're doing. I've gone through Nathan's phone. Calls from work and to work. A few calls to family and friends. I'll check out the names a little more, but there's nothing that makes my inner alarm go off. As far as April's phone, there aren't any recent calls listed, but there are several numbers in her phonebook. I'm writing them down. They don't mean anything to me, but they might be somewhere in April's notes."

River sighed. "Well, her notebook is interesting, but it's going to take me a while to go through it. She took really good notes. Lots of them."

"What about the Casanova case?" Tony asked.

"I was just looking at it. April believes it was connected to two other murders four years earlier."

"Anything that makes you think she was right?"

"Photos of the crime scenes look very similar, but she wasn't able to prove a connection," River said. "I was thinking about the possibility these kids were killed by the same person, but if they were, we're missing something important."

"No one took credit for it?"

"Exactly," River said. "As we know, serial killers are narcissistic. They want people to know who they are. What they've done. I can't find anything that makes me think the killer got attention for himself. Also, I'm not finding a signature. Except for the way the teenagers were killed, where the bodies were found, and the time of year they died, nothing else links them. And killings in parks during the winter certainly isn't unusual. It happens because they're usually deserted. Oh, and the killer didn't use the same gun."

"But if these murders are related and we wrote a profile for them, what would we be looking at?"

River paused a moment before saying, "This may be a waste of time, but let's give it a go." She thought for a moment before saying, "Okay, the killer would have to be a younger man since he was able to overpower these teenagers. He probably presented himself as someone non-threatening. These parks were basically empty of people or traffic. Perhaps he told them he worked for the park. Like a security guard. Or he could have been dressed like a police officer who was there to tell them they needed to move on."

"Like Dennis Rader," Tony interjected. "He was a city compliance officer. That made it easier for him to get close to his victims."

"Exactly." River couldn't stifle another yawn, but she wanted to keep going. She and Tony had worked on a lot of profiles for the FBI. It was a part of her. She couldn't help but think along those lines.

"He's probably white since most serial killers are Caucasian. My guess is he chose young lovers probably out of some kind of jealousy."

"Which means he may not be that attractive," Tony said. "Or he has something that makes him feel inferior. A disability? Perhaps he's a stutterer? We've seen that combination before."

"Possibly," River said. "Honestly, we may be reaching. I couldn't find much to convince me these cases are related. We can talk about it more tomorrow. I've just begun to look through everything. April's notebook is pretty big. Every page filled, plus notes, articles, and photos stuffed into the sleeve in the back. Like I said, this will take some time."

"Well, I copied the files from both the laptops to a USB drive."

"Good. So, I guess I'll see you in the morning."

There was a short pause before Tony said, "Yes. Are you still upset about having your own personal chauffeur?"

"I know you're trying to be careful, but why do I have this picture in my mind of being eighty years old and waiting for you to take me to get my blue hair permed?"

"You plan to have blue hair?" Tony said. "Not sure that would be a good look for you."

River sighed loudly.

"Look, once the Strangler's accomplice is behind bars you can drive anywhere you want," Tony said, his tone firm. "But until then . . ."

"I know, I know. Big Brother is watching out for me."

Tony chuckled. "I think the phrase is 'Big Brother is watching.'"

"I edited it. Fits my situation better."

This time, he laughed out loud. Tony's laugh erupted from somewhere deep inside him and then bubbled up to the surface. River hadn't laughed a lot before she met him. Even when they were working at the BAU, he had the ability to break the tension of the job with a dumb joke or by kindheartedly teasing someone in a way that would make everyone laugh. He was able to bring a touch of healing to the horror they faced on a day-to-day basis. River had never really poked fun at anyone before Tony taught her how. Now, she felt free to tease him whenever she wanted to. There was no way to explain the joy he'd brought into her life, or how he'd helped her find her way to a God she'd never really known.

"I need to go," she said. "My mother wants me to come by her room and say good night. After that, I'm going to look through this notebook a little longer. As long as I can stay awake, that is. April could have worked in law enforcement. Her instincts were excellent. She was a natural."

"We can talk about it more in the morning," Tony said. "Breakfast before or after we go by Nathan's place?"

"If we have to be there by eight o'clock? After, please."

"I second that." Tony yawned, which made River do the same. "Good thing you yawned. I'm always watching people. If someone yawns and anyone around him doesn't . . ."

"You decide they're most likely a psychopath?"

"Yep."

It was River's turn to laugh. "Side effects of the job. I'll see you about seven-thirty?"

"I'll be there."

River disconnected the call. Training as a behavioral analyst came with certain side benefits. Or maybe disadvantages. Being able to interpret physical reactions was a blessing since they could tell if someone was lying to them. But watching to see if people yawned when another person did was . . . nuts. Yet, it was a known fact that most of the time psychopaths didn't yawn in response to the same reaction in someone else. They lacked empathy—couldn't connect to other people. It worked with emotional responses as well, like crying or laughing. Some psychopaths learned to laugh or pretend to cry. But it was much harder to pretend to yawn.

River got up from the desk in her bedroom and went to her mother's room. She knocked softly on the door.

"Come in." She could barely hear her mother's thin, thready voice. Sometimes it felt as if everything about Rose Ryland was slowly disappearing. Her memory, her voice, and even her body. Rose was naturally thin, but lately her cheekbones had become more pronounced, accenting her Vietnamese features. Her mother had always been a beautiful woman, but even though her dark hair was peppered with silver, age had only given her a more ethereal look. As if she were closer to heaven than anyone around her.

River opened the door and found her mother in bed, her small TV turned on. She picked up the remote and turned down the sound. There were two bookshelves in her room. Rose had always loved to read, but River couldn't remember the last time she'd seen a book in her mother's hands. Was it because the words no longer made sense? Although River had an urge to ask her about it, she had a feeling the answer might break both their hearts.

"Mrs. Weyland said you wanted me to say good night," she said.

"Yes, dear." Rose patted the bed next to her.

For a moment, River was stunned. She couldn't remember her mother ever asking her to sit on her bed. Even when River was a child. Rose was always concerned she would mess up the covers.

She walked over and gingerly lowered herself next to her mother.

"You need to get some sleep, *tình yêu*. Why are you up so late?"

River was surprised to hear her mother use a Vietnamese term that meant *love*. Rose had called her *tình yêu* when she was very young. But not after her father left. She forced herself to respond to her mother's question.

"Just trying to get some work done," she said. "I'll go to sleep soon."

"Good. You need to get plenty of rest before school tomorrow."

River opened her mouth to remind her mother that she wasn't in school any longer, but then she remembered Mrs. Weyland's admonition not to correct Rose when she was confused.

Just go with her wherever she is, she'd said. *If you try to straighten her out, it will confuse and frighten her.*

"You're right," River said, fighting back sudden tears. "I'd better get back to bed, *Má*." It felt odd in one sense to use the Vietnamese term for *mother,* but River was certain that in this moment it was exactly the right thing to do.

Rose leaned over and took River's face in her hands. Then she kissed her forehead. "Don't forget your prayers. I love you."

"I love you too." River left the room, shutting the door behind her. Then she hurried to her bedroom, closed the door, leaned up against it, and slowly sank to the floor, where she covered her face with her hands and cried until her tears finally stopped.

CHAPTER
TWELVE

When the alarm went off at six-thirty, River reached over and turned it off. She wasn't asleep. In fact, she hadn't slept much at all. Her mind kept going back and forth from the information in April's notebook to what had occurred with her mother. She forced herself to dismiss her thoughts and concentrate on getting ready to meet Tony. She headed down the hall to the kitchen to start the coffeemaker before getting dressed. She was surprised to find Mrs. Weyland already there. She usually got up around eight.

"Why are you awake?" she asked. "Did my mother have a tough night?" From time to time, Rose had restless nights and Mrs. Weyland would go in to check on her, but when it happened, River almost always heard them. Last night the house was quiet.

"No, but I knew you were gettin' up early. I wanted to make sure you had coffee and ate somethin'. Goin' out without breakfast isn't good for you." She carried a dish over to the table that held bacon, a cheese omelet, and toast.

"You really didn't need to do this."

"I heard you tossin' and turnin' last night. You need to eat."

River laughed softly. "First of all, I don't think it's possible to hear someone tossing and turning from two doors down. And besides that, I'm not sure food will make it better anyway."

The elderly woman put her hands on her ample hips and stared at River. "No arguin' this mornin', missy." She pointed at the table. "You sit down and eat this breakfast I fixed for you."

River wasn't used to being ordered around. If it had been anyone else, she probably would have mentioned that Mrs. Weyland wasn't actually her boss. In fact, it was the other way around. But she knew in her heart that this lovely woman, this incredible blessing in her life and in her mother's, was truly concerned for her. Rather than getting angry, she was moved by it.

River smiled at her. "Yes, ma'am," she said as she slipped into her chair. River really didn't like eating a large breakfast. Sometimes it made her sleepy. But the food looked and smelled delicious. She was surprised to find that she really was hungry. She noticed something sitting on the table and picked it up. A newspaper.

"Is this yours?" she asked Mrs. Weyland.

"I just transferred my subscription here. I love readin' the newspaper, and I think it might be good for your mother too. Readin' is a good way for her to exercise her brain. She asked a question about somethin' the other day that made me think she might be willing to read it if it was in the house." She smiled. "I know most people read the news online, but I like havin' a real paper in my hands. One of these days, they might not be around anymore."

"That's a wonderful idea," River said. "Please let me reimburse you."

Mrs. Weyland waved her hand toward River. "Not necessary, honey, but I appreciate it. Like I said, it's my subscription."

"Okay, but if my mother does read it, how about we split the subscription price?"

Mrs. Weyland chuckled. "All right, but let's not worry about it now. Let me pour you a cup of coffee."

River prayed silently over her meal and looked up to see Mrs. Weyland carrying two cups over to the table. She put one in front of River and then sat down with the other one.

"Where's your breakfast?" River asked.

"I'll eat with your mother. She's not too bad off yet, but my husband actually forgot how to chew and swallow at one point. I found that eatin' with him helped. He just copied what I did."

"So even though my mother isn't at that point, you're preparing her for it?"

Mrs. Weyland nodded. "I'm usin' everything I learned so I can help your dear mama." She paused for a moment while River ate. Why was it that some people could make a dish you'd eaten many times before, but the way they prepared it tasted so much better? This breakfast was a great example.

"I'm really sorry for everything you went through," River said. "Did you have any help? Was there a Mrs. Weyland in your life?"

The question made the older lady smile again. "No, unfortunately, we had no children, and his family lived out of state. Henry had a sister, but she didn't want to help. She was married to a wealthy man, and they had a very active *social life*."

River didn't miss the emphasis. "So, what you're not saying is that she's a big jerk?"

Mrs. Weyland chuckled softly. "I won't say anything against her, 'specially since she's passed on. But you won't hear me arguin' with what you just said."

"I'm really grateful you're here with us," River said. "I don't know what we'd do without you."

"Oh, honey. I feel the same way. After Henry died, I had no idea what I was gonna to do with my life. You've given me a home and a reason to live. I feel useful again. You've done more for me than you could ever know."

Mrs. Weyland tried to blink away the sudden tears that filled her eyes.

River reached over and put her hand on the older woman's arm. "Boy, who knew breakfast could be this emotional?"

They both laughed at the same time.

"You have a busy day today?" Mrs. Weyland asked.

"Actually, we do. We have to drop some things off at a new client's place, and then we need to start looking into his case."

"You have a job? That's wonderful!"

Although she and Tony hadn't talked about whether or not they were going to take Nathan's case, River was certain Tony was on board. Especially after the picture showed up. If that hadn't been enough, she still would have wanted to keep going because of all the notes April had kept. As River peeled back layer after layer, April's disappearance was becoming more and more fascinating. April was smart and intuitive. So how could she just suddenly go missing? Why didn't there seem to be any trace of her? It just didn't sit right with River.

She finished eating and quickly got dressed. She hadn't allowed extra time for breakfast, so she wasn't ready when Tony pulled up outside. Thankfully, he only had to wait a few minutes.

"Sorry about that," she said when she opened the car door.

"You usually gripe at me for running behind," he said, grinning, as she slid into the car and closed the door.

"Not my fault. I was tempted above what I was able to withstand."

"I think God promised He'd provide a way of escape if we were ever tempted that much."

River laughed. "Okay, I was weak. Mrs. Weyland got up before I did and prepared an incredible breakfast for me. I couldn't say no."

Tony put the car in gear and started down the street. "I thought you didn't like breakfast."

"I didn't think I did. But she changed my mind."

"Okay. I forgive you for not waiting for me."

"Oh, Tony, I forgot. We were going to have breakfast together. We can still stop. I'll drink coffee and watch you eat."

"Wow, that sounds relaxing. I'll just grab some doughnuts on the way into the office."

"If you're sure."

"I am." He glanced down at the car's beverage holder. "I picked up your favorite coffee from that coffee house you like. Cinnamon dolce latte."

"Now I feel even guiltier."

"Good," Tony said, grinning. "I'm avenged."

"You're silly." River picked up her cup and took a drink. "Yum. Thank you."

"So, are we taking this case?"

"I'd like to," she said. "I need more time to go through the rest of April's notebook, but I feel a connection to her, and I'm interested. I really want to find out what happened."

"I agree. I'm not sure we can find her, but I'd like to try."

River turned the radio up a little bit. One of her favorite Christian bands, Casting Crowns, was playing a song that really ministered to her. When it was over, she turned the volume down. "My father wants to visit," she said.

"You told me he'd asked if he could come," Tony said, "but you didn't sound very positive about it."

"I wasn't, but then you started talking to me about forgiveness. I think you ruined all my arguments."

Tony smiled. "I'm not sure I can say I'm sorry."

"You shouldn't." She sighed. "I haven't decided what to do. Not because I'm not willing to forgive him, but I'm not sure what his visit might do to my mother."

"I assume Mrs. Weyland knows about this request?"

"Yeah, she talked to my father yesterday. He told her."

"What does she think?" Tony asked.

"She's not sure either. She says my mother is trying to find her way back to God, and that this might go a long way toward that. But it could also go really wrong. It could set her off. I know she'd hate it if she said or did anything in front of my father that might cause her embarrassment."

Tony picked up his coffee and took a drink before putting it down. "I guess you have to weigh those two outcomes against each other."

"What do you mean?"

Tony looked over at her. "I can't tell you what to do, River. This is your decision. You need to pray about it."

"I understand, but I'd really like to hear your opinion."

"I guess I'd shoot for the chance your mother and father could forgive each other over a temporary upset she may experience. Does that make sense?"

River thought about his response for a moment before saying, "Yeah, it does. And maybe I could tell him I've forgiven him too. It might mean a lot to him, and it could also help me to finally let go of the anger I've held against him for so long." She was quiet for a moment. "It sounds like the benefits could far outweigh a possible temporary disadvantage."

Tony shrugged. "Like I said, it's not my business, but I think you're right."

River had expected this reaction, but for some reason, she'd just needed to hear him voice it. Maybe she didn't trust herself enough to make the final decision.

Tony turned onto the road that led to Nathan's apartment complex. He pulled up to the gate and rolled down his window so he could speak to the guard. It was a different man, but it stood to reason that the person who watched the gate at night wouldn't be the same one assigned to the morning schedule.

"Can I help you, sir?" the man said with a smile.

"We're here to see Nathan Hearne," Tony said. "River Ryland and Tony St. Clair."

As soon as Tony mentioned their names, the man's expression changed. "I'm sorry," he said sternly. "I'm not supposed to let you in. Mr. Hearne asked that you give me the items you're supposed to drop off. He left this letter for you."

Tony took the letter and frowned at River. He slid the letter out of the envelope. Then he read it and passed it to River.

I've decided not to go forward with this investigation. Please return everything I gave you, including all of April's belongings. I need my laptop and phone this morning. April's laptop, phone, notebook, and drawings need to be dropped off with the guard by 5:00 p.m. today, or I'll contact the police. Nathan Hearne.

"What in the world?" River said. "What should we do?"

"I'll tell you what we *don't* do." He turned and smiled at the serious-faced guard. "You may tell Mr. Hearne that we can't return his items to you. If he wants them, he knows where to find us."

With that said, Tony put the car in reverse and drove back toward the street, leaving River to wonder what could have possibly caused Nathan to suddenly do a 180 and abandon his search for the woman he claimed to love.

THIRTEEN

River and Tony went back to the office and waited.

"I hope you did the right thing," River said. "You told him to stay inside for his own safety. I also hope he doesn't really call the police. I mean, this *is* his stuff."

"I'm guessing that whoever forced him to write that note is the same person who left us the photo. If I'm right, he needs our help."

"What if the person who threatened him is watching the apartment?"

"I've been thinking about that," Tony said. "One of the things we learned during our time at the FBI is that dangerous people rarely warn their victims. They just take action. If whoever this is wants to stop Nathan, why didn't they just take him out instead of taking his picture? And why send the original threat to us and not to him?" That tells us that they aren't committed to hurting him."

"I see your point," River said, "but it doesn't always work out the way we think it should. Are you sure you didn't act too hastily?"

Up until that moment, Tony had been convinced he was right, but had he made a mistake that could put Nathan in danger?

"Look, that note was ridiculous. The threat about calling the police is absurd. First of all, he can't file charges against us since he gave us this stuff. That, combined with the photo, makes me feel something else is going on here. I want him to come here so we can talk. It was obvious we weren't getting inside. It was the only thing I could come up with." He sighed loudly. "If he doesn't show up soon, I'll call the police and ask them to check on him." He looked at her. "You know I act too quickly sometimes. Why didn't you stop me?"

"So now it's my fault?"

"Maybe if I'd had breakfast . . ."

River shook her head, but he saw her lips twitch. "You really are a pill. So, what do we do if he really is in trouble?"

"If he's truly being threatened, I'll call Arnie. They can move him somewhere safe."

"He'll need clothes and personal items. Of course, we can't call him because we have his phone . . ." Even though River's tone was sarcastic, Tony was convinced she understood his decision to keep Nathan's phone and laptop even if she didn't agree with his method.

"I don't think clothes are his problem right now, do you?"

"Maybe not, I just . . ."

The door to their office swung open, and Nathan stepped inside. He didn't look angry. He looked scared.

"I need my stuff," he said. "And April's. I left a message for you."

Tony took a deep breath and let it out quickly, relieved to see Nathan and thankful he hadn't put him in danger.

River got up and went over to Nathan. She put her hand on his shoulder and looked into his eyes. Tony was amazed at the way she was able to immediately establish a connection with him. His taut expression and his stiff shoulders began to relax. At the same time his eyes filled with tears.

River gently led him over to a chair. He slumped down into it and put his hands over his face.

"You need to tell us what happened, Nathan," River said. "We can't help you if you don't tell us the truth."

Tony stayed in his chair and kept quiet. River had the young man where she wanted him. He didn't want to break the spell.

"I . . . I can't," Nathan said, blinking away his tears. He was clearly embarrassed by his emotional reaction. River and Tony both knew that people didn't always cry because they were sad. Almost any strong emotional reaction could cause a human being to weep. Fear, remorse, even anger.

River pulled another chair up close to him. "It's just us here, Nathan. No one else will ever know what you tell us."

Nathan looked down at the floor for a moment, cleared his throat, and then raised his face to meet River's gaze. It was at that moment Tony knew Nathan was going to tell them what had happened to cause his abrupt turnaround. River was amazing. Tony was convinced that he wouldn't have been able to get Nathan to trust him the way River did. She had a special way with people. Of course, in many situations, men tended to trust women more than men. It had something to do with the strong connections boys usually had with their mothers. It wasn't always true, of course. Boys abused by their mothers had the ability to react violently toward women. As behavioral analysts, they'd seen this trait displayed through serial killers trying to murder their mothers because of the emotional pain they'd caused them, but Nathan wasn't a serial killer, and River was definitely getting through to him.

Nathan reached into his jacket pocket and pulled out an envelope. Tony almost sighed audibly. What was the deal with all these envelopes? In this day and age, corresponding through snail mail was almost unheard of. This was definitely unusual. Of course, sending an email usually made it easier to track the sender. A typed or handwritten letter handled correctly could make it impossible to locate its origin.

"This was dropped off at the guard gate last night after you left." He handed the envelope to River. She looked over at Tony, who got up and grabbed two sets of gloves. He was beginning to wonder how many gloves they had left.

"If you receive any other notes, Nathan," he said, "please handle them with caution. We may be able to find fingerprints that could help us. But if you get yours on the paper, it could actually keep us from getting a clean print."

"I noticed how careful you were with the other note I received. I didn't think about it at first, but after I opened this envelope, I used a paper towel to hold the note inside."

"Good. Thanks."

Tony handed one pair of gloves to River, who put them on. Tony did the same with the other pair. When River was ready, she slid the folded piece of paper out of the envelope. Then she handed the envelope to Tony. Someone had written Nathan's name and apartment number on the front in block letters with black ink. Obviously, they were trying to disguise their handwriting. The letters were written just like the printing on the picture of Nathan. Although he could be wrong, Tony suspected that the same person had sent both messages.

After reading the note inside, River passed it to Tony. In the same block lettering, someone had written *Stop talking to the PIs or she will die. Then you will be next. No police or you both die.*

"You said the envelope was given to the guard at the front gate last night?"

Nathan nodded. "He came by my apartment to tell me someone had dropped off a delivery." He frowned at them. "He tried to call me first, but I didn't have my phone."

"You should have called us," River said.

Nathan shot her a look.

"You could have asked the guard to use his phone."

"To be honest, I was afraid to. Especially after this note. I only ventured out this morning because the laptop you took has work on it that I need. I had no choice." He shook his head. "I made one stop on the way here and bought another phone. I guess it pays to have two."

"I keep a spare," River said.

For a moment, her comment confused Tony. Then he remembered the extra phone she'd bought as a backup in case she was in trouble and couldn't get to her regular phone. River believed that if she'd had an extra phone when she was attacked by the Strangler, who'd taken the phone in her pocket, she could have gotten help sooner. She liked to call the second phone her *boot phone*. Anytime she felt she might be facing a dangerous situation, she planned to put it in her boot. He'd forgotten all about it. She hadn't mentioned it in a long time.

"You realize that this confirms that April is alive, right?" Nathan said.

River shook her head. "Not really. They may be saying this because they're trying to control you. The one thing it does tell us though, is that whoever wrote this knows about April. They might very well have something to do with her disappearance."

"Why can't you believe she's alive?"

Tony could tell he was frustrated.

"Look, for now, let's talk about you," Tony said. "I know you're afraid. I think we need to err on the side of caution. I believe we should move you to a more secure location." Even though he found the continued warnings problematic, Tony had no intention of taking another chance with Nathan's welfare.

"I live in a gated community," Nathan said. "I should be okay at home."

"But whoever left that note knows where you live," River said. "The guards at the gate aren't law enforcement. They're people.

People who have to use the bathroom—or who can be bribed. Or even fooled by someone pretending to be with a utility company."

"Actually, they're planning on adding an electric gate," Nathan said. "It will take a code to get inside the community."

"But that gate isn't up yet, and you need security now," River said. "Besides, the code can be shared by anyone living in the complex. A gated community is safer than living in a regular neighborhood, but it isn't totally secure. If someone wants in, they'll figure out a way."

"What's the name of the guard who was on duty last night? The one who called you about the note?" Tony asked. "I'd like to talk to him."

Nathan frowned. "I only know his first name. It's Kevin."

"Surely they have some kind of video camera at the guard shack," River said.

"I think so. I mean, I remember noticing something mounted underneath the small roof that covers the building where they sit. I assume it's a camera."

"Okay." Tony looked at River. "We need to get the guard's full name and number." He turned his attention back to Nathan. "Do you know the guard who's working today?"

"Yes. His name is Darrell. He's the friendliest guard. I think he likes me."

"Good," Tony said. "Can you call him and see if you can get Kevin's last name and his telephone number? And when you talk to Kevin, ask him for a description of the person who dropped off the envelope." He paused for a moment. "If we want to see the video, we'll have to bring the police in. They can get a warrant. We can't."

"But the note said no police," Nathan insisted.

"If they were watching you this morning, they already know you came here. Believe it or not, bringing the police into the situation will actually keep you safer. These people are afraid of the police because they know they're vulnerable now and it's harder to get to you."

"I'm not worried about me," Nathan said. "I don't want them to hurt April."

"We were trained as behavioral analysts with the FBI," River said gently. "What some people call *profilers*. If whoever took April has kept her alive for several months, they're most likely not going to kill her now. Bringing law enforcement into the situation may actually cause them to let her go so they won't get caught—or if they do, at least they won't be charged with murder."

River was telling the truth, but Tony had very little hope that April was still alive. In fact, he was fairly sure she'd been dead for quite some time.

FOURTEEN

When Nathan got off the phone, he said, "Darrell couldn't give me Kevin's number. He wants to help, but if he told me how to reach Kevin, he could lose his job. But he did say he'd call Kevin and ask him to phone me."

"Great," River said. "When Kevin calls, ask him to describe the person who dropped off the note. And don't forget a description of the car."

"Sure. Do you suppose you could give me back my phone now?"

"Oh, sorry," Tony said. "I guess that would help." He took Nathan's cellphone and laptop out of the tote bag where he'd placed them. He handed both items to Nathan.

Nathan took his new phone and put it on the edge of River's desk. "I guess we wait," he said.

"I'm going to call Arnie and let him know what's going on," Tony said. "Although right now, we don't have any proof of a crime. I'm not sure what he can do."

"Well, we have a threat," River said.

"True. Hopefully, that will be enough." Tony got up and walked out into the hallway. River was certain he didn't want Nathan to overhear the conversation.

"How about a cup of coffee?" River asked Nathan.

He sighed deeply. "Thank you. I didn't get time to make any before I left." He frowned. "I've got to get on my laptop and contact my employer. I'll tell them I need a sick day. It won't be a lie. I really do feel ill."

"Look," River said as she went over to the coffeemaker, "I've learned that most of the things we worry about never happen. Worry can be a huge waste of time and energy. Let's relax until we know we can't, okay? Tony and I both believe that whoever wrote that note is just trying to intimidate you. If he really wanted to hurt you, he would have done it without warning you first."

"That actually makes sense," Nathan said. The tightness in his face loosened a bit.

"What kind of coffee do you want?" River read off the different flavors of pods they had.

"I think straight black coffee for now," Nathan said. "Maybe after I wake up a bit more, I might try a mocha latte. But honestly, at the moment, all I want is caffeine. As you might imagine, I didn't sleep much last night."

"I wish we'd suggested you pick up a cheap cell phone last night," River said. "It never occurred to us."

Nathan's laugh was almost like a moan. "I thought it might be nice not to have a phone for one evening, you know? I tend to look at mine too much. I convinced myself it would be restful." He looked at her and raised his eyebrow. "It wasn't."

In spite of herself, River laughed. "No, I guess it wouldn't be." She gazed at him for a moment before saying, "Nathan, I know things seem scary, but Tony and I aren't going to leave you alone. We're with you in this. We won't let anything happen to you."

He grinned. "I guess this means you're hired again."

"Let's not worry about that right now. We just want to help

you." River was committed to protecting this young man from whoever was trying to frighten him. It made her angry, and she was certain Tony felt the same way. All she cared about was Nathan and finding the truth about April.

River carried a cup of coffee over to him and put her own cup on her desk. She looked up as Tony opened the door and came inside the office.

"Arnie says the police will be happy to send someone down to take Nathan's statement. They'll want the note. As far as the other things we gave them, the copy of the photo has no fingerprints. There was a trace of powder on one edge meaning whoever sent the picture wore the kind of gloves that have talcum powder. Most people buy those. All that tells us is that the person who took the picture probably isn't in law enforcement. There were fingerprints on the envelope with the photo, but only one set besides ours. I'm sure they're Dustin's. As far as the note Nathan got originally, there was a discernible print on the note. Nothing in the system, but they can tell it's either from a young boy or a woman due to the size of the print. As we suspected, the envelope was so covered with prints, they couldn't pull anything off of it that was usable."

"Could the fingerprint on the note I got in the mail be April's?" Nathan asked.

"No, actually, she was in the system," Tony said. "When she was eighteen, she worked for a daycare center. All employees were fingerprinted as a requirement for the job."

"She told me about that job," Nathan said. "She didn't mention that she was fingerprinted."

"It's required in almost every job or volunteer position where children are involved," River said. "People are much more cautious now. The world isn't as safe as it used to be."

"I believe it," Nathan said. "April said the same thing more than once. It makes us both sad. April's a Christian. She's convinced that we're in the last days and that evil is growing stronger." He shrugged. "I don't know if that's true, but it would certainly explain a lot. Of course, April spent a lot of time looking at evil. I'm sure it affected her outlook."

"What about you, Nathan?" River asked. "Are you a Christian?"

He looked a little uncomfortable. "I went to church several times with April. I've never gone up to the front and prayed for . . . salvation, or whatever . . . but I've thought a lot about it." His smile looked a little sad. "When she went missing, I got mad at God. I haven't been back to church since."

River was a little startled by his response to her question. She completely understood how he felt. Maybe at the right moment, she could talk to him. Share her story. Whether April was alive or dead, she wanted Nathan to know God. She started to say something else when Tony's phone rang. He picked it up and looked at it.

"It's Arnie," he said, frowning. He answered and then listened silently for what seemed like a long time. Finally, he said, "Okay. I get it. We'll wait here for someone. And thanks."

When he put the phone down, River could tell something was wrong. "What's going on?" she asked.

"This case has changed," he said, his face tight. "The police just found the security guard, Kevin Bittner. He's been murdered."

FIFTEEN

... I don't understand," River said, stunned. "How ... I mean, how did Arnie know to call us?"

I told him the whole story when I spoke to him a few minutes ago," Tony said. "And I mentioned where Nathan lives. We'd just hung up when he got word about the murder. He saw that the victim was a security guard at Nathan's complex and put two and two together."

River glanced over at Nathan. His face was white as a sheet. "How was he murdered?" she asked.

"He was shot. Arnie said his body was discovered this morning in his backyard. His wife found him. She woke up and realized he wasn't in bed, so she went looking for him. When she couldn't locate him inside the house, she stepped out onto their back porch. That's when she saw him. The police haven't been able to talk to her much. She's understandably upset."

"He's . . . he's dead because of me," Nathan said, his voice shaking.

River shook her head. "No, Nathan. That's not true. He's dead because someone really bad killed him. None of this is your fault. Don't let thoughts like that get into your head."

"Arnie's sending a couple of officers over to take Nathan somewhere safe," Tony said. He looked at Nathan. "Until the police know what's going on, they don't want to take any chances with your safety."

"But what exactly does that mean?" Nathan asked, looking worried.

"The police will take you to a secure location and keep a close watch on you until they can find out who killed Kevin and why. Right now, they're not sure if you're a target."

"How could they not be sure? Kevin's dead."

"We understand how you feel," River said, "but the police are just now getting involved with your situation. As it is, the police chief is taking our word that you might be in danger."

Nathan swallowed hard. "Okay. Will . . . will I be able to see you?"

"I think so," Tony said. "We'll have to get clearance, but I don't think that will be a problem."

"So, you think whoever threatened me killed Kevin? And now they could be after me?" Nathan shook his head. "This is nuts. Why is this happening?"

"We're not sure yet," River said. "It could have something to do with April's disappearance, or it could be connected to one of her cold cases. Right now, we have no idea. You're going to have to let the police investigate—and we'll be doing what we can too."

"What about work?" Nathan asked. "I can't afford to lose my job."

"That's something the detective in charge of your case will have to decide," River said. "You can't do anything that might lead whoever killed Kevin to your location." She swung her gaze to Tony. "What do you think?"

"I have no idea. Unless Kevin's killer has access to Nathan's emails or his laptop, I don't see why he can't work. But if our killer knows who Nathan's employer is, that might be a way for them to locate him."

Nathan frowned. "No one really knows who I work for. I mean, they're in another state. I'm not sure even April could have told you who they are."

"Ask the detectives assigned to your case if you can continue to work, but whatever you do, don't tell your employer what's going on."

"I won't." Nathan shook his head. "To be honest, I'm not sure I could. This is really confusing." He stared at them for a moment before saying, "So, you'll help me, right? Look for April and try to find out what's going on?"

"The police will be working on your case now," Tony said. "You probably won't need us."

Nathan shook his head. "No, you're wrong. They won't be looking for April, will they? Not the way you could. I don't want her to get lost in the shuffle. I'd feel better having you for backup." He swung his gaze toward River. "I know you said you didn't care about being paid, but I don't agree. April used to quote some Scripture about a workman being worthy of his hire. I'm not sure what it means, but I think it's saying that if you work, you deserve to be paid. So please, take this." He reached into his jacket pocket and pulled out a checkbook. "I brought this from home in case I needed it." He quickly wrote out a check and handed it to River. Then he asked, "Are you going to turn over everything I gave you?"

"Yes, if they want it. But we have copies of all of it," River said. She looked at Tony. Nathan was probably right. The police would be looking for Kevin's killer. Searching for April would probably be put on the back burner. Maybe she and Tony could look into April's cases and turn over anything that might relate to the police investigation. Tony looked a little confused, but he gave her an almost imperceptible shrug.

"Please," Nathan said. "The police have a lot of cases, but you can make mine a priority."

The truth was the police were inundated with crimes while she and Tony could devote all their time to Nathan. River sighed. "All right. We'll take this retainer, but if we feel we're just duplicating what the police are doing, we won't charge you anything else."

"That sounds fair. I still think the answer will be found somewhere in those cold cases April was working." He put his checkbook back in his pocket. His expression became serious. "The note says April's still alive. That's two different messages that say she's not dead." Nathan didn't ask a question, but it was implied.

River took a deep breath before responding. The last thing she wanted to do was to shatter Nathan's hope, but she and Tony knew the statistics. Why would anyone who felt threatened by April still be keeping her alive? It didn't make sense. Before River could say anything, Tony spoke up.

"Look, Nathan," he said, "the chances that April's alive are slim. But she's a Christian, and all things are possible with God." He smiled at River. "I've seen God do great things. Even save people from death. So, of course it's possible. But the thing you need to understand is that even if she isn't alive in this world, she's definitely alive in the next. Let's go forward as if this is a rescue. River and I just don't want you to be crushed if this doesn't turn out the way we all want."

Nathan stared at him for a moment before saying, "So you believe in all this heaven stuff?"

Tony smiled at him. "I'm betting my whole life on it. You know, Nathan, some people act as if believing in God is just some kind of giant speculation where you hope you'll guess right and end up in heaven. They call it faith, and in a way it is. But God is knowable. He still talks to people today. I know He's real. He speaks to me, and He's answered my prayers. I'm not guessing."

Nathan studied him for a moment. "You can actually hear His voice?"

"Sure. Sometimes it's a voice that comes up inside me—like a knowing. Sometimes it's a whisper. Of course, the main way He speaks to me is through His Word. The Bible is more than just a book. It's alive and full of God's Spirit."

"On rare occasions, God does speak audibly," River interjected. "As loud and clear as the way you hear me now. Although, I wonder sometimes if He's just done that for me because I was so stubborn. Like Tony says, the Bible helps me to really know Him—to hear Him. But no matter how he speaks to you, He makes sure you know you're not alone. And He really does answer prayers. Things happen that would never happen just by accident. You know it's Him."

"But the most outstanding thing about God?" Tony said. "The way He changes people completely. There's no belief system or so-called god in this world who can change people from the inside out. Watching people turn into completely different human beings is . . . well, it's a miracle. I've seen it many, many times. Drug addicts set completely free. Alcoholics instantly delivered. People full of anger turning into loving, caring human beings. Only God can do that."

"April said a lot of the same things. I guess if we find her alive, I would finally believe."

River was wondering if she should say anything else or just leave it alone. Pushing people too hard could cause them to back off. But her decision was made for her when the door to their office opened, and two uniformed police officers stepped inside.

"We're looking for Tony St. Clair," one of them said.

"That's me." Tony stood up and walked over to them.

"Chief Martin sent us to pick up a Nathan Hearne? We're supposed to take him to a secure location."

"I thought he'd send detectives," Tony said, frowning. "Hold on just a moment."

Tony picked up his phone and punched in a number. River was still impressed that he had a direct line to the chief of police in St. Louis. And Arnie, as Tony called him, always picked up. As usual, Tony got right through.

River glanced over at Nathan, who looked scared. She was sure that Tony's concern worried him, but it was just a precaution. It was always best to be careful, just in case anything happened that investigators weren't expecting.

"Just a minute," Tony said. He walked up to the officers and looked at their badges. "Yes," he said, "that checks out." He listened for a moment more, then he thanked Arnie and hung up.

"The detective in charge will meet you at the secure location and get some information," he said to Nathan. "These officers will escort you there." He picked up Nathan's laptop and handed it to one of the officers. "Nathan uses his phone and laptop for his job," he said. "Once detectives go through everything, it would be great if he could get back to work. We'd hate to see him lose his job over this thing."

"We'll have to leave that up to the detective in charge," one of the officers said. "But we'll make sure he knows about it."

River got up from her chair and walked over to Nathan. "You'll be fine. We'll keep in touch. Don't worry. Is your new phone activated?"

Nathan nodded.

She looked at the officers. "Nathan bought a new phone on the way here. Let me get that number, okay? That phone should be completely safe."

One of the officers nodded at her, so she grabbed her notebook and quickly wrote down the number Nathan read off to her. She'd just put her notebook down on her desk when Nathan suddenly moved forward and hugged her. It startled River, and she almost pulled away. Her parents weren't huggers, so she wasn't used to physical affection. However, she realized Nathan was afraid and needed comfort, so she hugged him back. The action made her feel even more committed to helping him. When he let her go, she could see that he was a lot more relaxed than he'd been when he came into the office.

"Everything will be okay," she said, not completely sure it would be. But for his sake, she prayed it would.

"Okay." He put his hand out and shook hands with Tony, then he turned and went out the door with the officers right behind him.

"Do you really think he'll be all right?" she asked Tony.

"I don't know. I certainly hope so." He shook his head. "I have a bad feeling that this case has just started, and it's only going to get worse. One thing that really worries me?"

"Just one thing?"

"Good point. Kevin's wife obviously didn't hear a shot. Neither did his neighbors." He looked at her and frowned. "If our killer used a silencer, he could be very dangerous. He might be a professional. And he may not be through."

Although River wanted to challenge him, she couldn't because she was afraid he was absolutely right.

CHAPTER SIXTEEN

He watched as police escorted a young man to their squad car. He was certain this was the same kid who'd visited River and Tony before. What was going on? For just a moment, he thought about following them. Find out where they were going. The kid wasn't handcuffed, so he wasn't under arrest. At the last second, he decided to let it go. He couldn't get sidetracked from his ultimate goal. River Ryland was his target. Whatever was going on in this guy's life wasn't his business, nor did it really interest him.

He had everything planned down to the last detail. His only regret was that he wouldn't be able to watch the life drain from her eyes. It was the best part of taking a life. But he'd experienced that quite a bit. No, he wanted her to die in terror. Even if he couldn't see it, he could envision it, and that would bring him great satisfaction.

He wasn't certain why he hated her so much. It wasn't her fault she'd survived the first time. Not at all. But there was just something about her. Something that repelled him. Seems she believed in God now. Maybe that was it. He believed in God too. He just didn't bow down and degrade himself at His feet. He worshipped no one but himself and fully embraced the hate that fueled him. It was that hate that strengthened him. Hate had taught him to kill from the very beginning. His mother had been his first victim, and her death had taught him that he was the one with the power. Not her. He'd shoved that horror of a human being down the basement stairs when he was eight years old. Then he'd gone outside to play. No one ever suspected him. His big sister had raised him, and he never endured the beatings and the torture again. Natalie had done her best, but he'd already learned true dominance. Real power. He'd waited patiently until he could move out and use his new power to prove his superiority. Then he'd met Joseph Baker. He'd never known anyone else who understood him the way Joe had. They were the same. Forged in the same fires of destruction. Scores of dead human beings lay in their wake. And no one suspected he was part of a team. Until it was too late, that is. River Ryland had been his last victim, but she was still alive. He wasn't going to allow that to continue.

However, the next time, no one would step up to save her. He smiled to himself and went back to pretending to be busy. The words he typed on his laptop were repeated over and over.

River Ryland is going to die screaming. River Ryland is going to die screaming. River Ryland is going to die screaming.

"SO NOW WHAT?" Tony asked after Nathan left.

"We get back to work," River said. "Why don't we go through April's cases together?"

"Sure," Tony said. "Should we get lunch first?"

"Fine with me, but can we go out? I'm getting a little claustrophobic. Between work and home, I haven't gone anywhere lately. We haven't gone out to eat for quite a while, even though we've planned to."

"We drove over to Nathan's twice," Tony said, trying not to sound snarky.

"Yeah, that was great fun. But that's about it since we got back from seeing your parents."

"By the way, I talked to my mom last night. She told me to tell you hello and asked when you could visit again."

River sighed. "I'd love to see them, but I guess that won't happen until we solve this case."

"I know. After this is done, and when the Strangler's friend is caught and put away forever, we can go back if you want to."

"I'm surprised you let me leave town last month," River said, rolling her eyes.

"And maybe I shouldn't have." Tony looked away. "I wanted to help my dad, and I knew you needed a break. Maybe it was too risky."

"If it had been I wouldn't still be alive. I realize we owe it to Nathan to stay here and look for April before we leave town again, but we have no idea when the Strangler's partner will be caught. I don't want to live sheltered from life forever."

Tony met her gaze. "The problem is that the longer he waits, the less time we may have. He won't hold off forever." He scowled at her. "I can't believe you considered leaving me for one second. You would have walked right into his path. How could you . . ." He was surprised and embarrassed when his voice broke. When he'd found out what she'd been thinking, he was horrified. How could she have considered something so reckless? He knew his sister had planted the notion, but he was still shocked that River had fallen for it. River's expression made him look away. He struggled to regain his composure.

"Tony, you know why I thought about getting away. I was afraid . . . am still afraid . . . this guy will hurt you. Don't you think you've given up enough for me? Your health? Your career? I can't have you give up your life as well."

The look on her face almost made him lose it again. He struggled to keep his tone steady. "I can protect you . . ."

"I know you believe that, and like I told you, I'm now convinced that we're stronger together. But sometimes I think you forget that I was trained by the FBI just like you were. And I'm a better shot than you are."

Tony was able to laugh lightly. "Not so fast. We need to go to the range. You'll have to prove that."

Although they had a friendly competition, the truth was, she really was a better shot. He didn't care. He loved it anytime he saw that old spark in her eyes. She was so much better now than she'd been right after her encounter with the Strangler. When she let God back in her life, healing had begun. She was still on a path to total freedom, but Tony was convinced she'd get there. She was determined, and so was God. He never gave up on His children.

"You've got a deal," River said. "So how about lunch? In a real restaurant?" She shrugged. "I'm armed, so if we're attacked by anyone, I'll just take them out. You know how much I hate having my meal interrupted."

"I'm sure the other customers would love that," he said dryly. Tony wanted to grant her request. They'd eaten out before, usually on the way to work or on the way home, but the past few days, he'd felt an impending sense of unease. He wasn't certain if it was his own fear, or if it was something else. He believed the Holy Spirit warns His children and leads them away from danger if they listen. He sent up a quick silent prayer about going out for lunch, but he didn't feel any check in his spirit.

"We can go somewhere and get a fast meal," he said, "if you really think it's the right thing to do. We need to jump on Nathan's case as soon as we can."

"I feel like getting out of here for just a bit will give me a new burst of energy," River said with a smile.

He loved her crooked smiles. They made him feel happy. He suspected that she knew that and from time to time used them to her advantage. He sighed. "Okay, so where do you want to go?"

"The new Chinese place down the street?" she said. "Their General Tso's chicken is so good."

"I was just thinking the same thing," Tony said, chuckling. "But we can't stay too long." He started to stand up but then stopped. "First, I think we need to talk about April's stuff. I want to be certain we have everything we need. I have a feeling we'll have to hand all of it over to the police before long."

"Have you downloaded all the files you took from her laptop and Nathan's to your laptop?" she asked.

He shook his head. "Not yet, but I've got the flash drives, so it won't take me long to do it. By the way, I looked up the numbers on April's phone. There were some calls to certain police stations. I'm assuming she called them in an attempt to get information. There were also some business numbers like fast-food restaurants, her father's phone number, Nathan's . . ." Tony shook his head. "What I couldn't find were calls to friends and other family. I think she was so focused on her podcast, there wasn't much time for anything else."

River sighed. "That's sad."

Tony frowned at her. "Does that sound like anyone else you know?"

"I have friends."

"I meant here. Since we moved to St. Louis."

"Tony, that's not fair. I've been focusing on my mother and starting our agency. I'll make friends when I can."

"I hope so," he said.

"Back to this case. . . . The pictures I took of April's notebook are on my phone so they're safe. And her podcast is online so that's not a problem."

"What about the notes you've made?"

She picked up a notebook and waved it at him. "It's all here."

"You might think I sound paranoid, but let's take April's stuff with us. I don't want to leave anything we have about this case lying around. It makes me nervous." He reached behind his desk and grabbed April's tote bag that read *Hot Coffee and Cold Cases.*

"Good thing this wasn't where anyone could see it," he said. "The police might have asked for it."

"I don't think the officers who picked up Nathan would have known the name of her podcast."

"But Nathan did," Tony said. "If he'd seen it, he might have said something and that could have caused a problem." He frowned at her. "Am I being paranoid? Taking this stuff with us?"

"I don't think so," she said. "We've seen what people will do to protect themselves."

Tony added her notebook to the tote bag. Then they both grabbed their coats and headed out the door.

While training at the FBI Academy, agents were taught to keep their head on a swivel when entering a possibly dangerous situation where guns may be involved. Tony felt like that now. He was usually just concerned about the Strangler's accomplice, but now there was someone else to worry about. It seemed that Nathan was the target, but they couldn't forget the picture that showed him entering their building. Did the person who was trying to keep his or her identity secret know that they had April's information? He didn't see how. Surely Nathan hadn't told anyone. As they went downstairs and headed for their car, it began to snow lightly. It reminded him of the case they'd worked for his dad. Snow, which he and River both loved, now seemed a little sinister. Tony was suddenly sorry he'd agreed to go out for lunch. It was possible they were being watched. Was this a mistake?

As his training kicked in, he kept a close watch around them and made sure his hand was near his gun in case he suddenly needed it.

SEVENTEEN

Lunch was great, but Tony had been nervous the entire time. Although River felt the need for some freedom, she knew his concern was valid. Although they'd believed the person who'd threatened Nathan wasn't actually planning to kill him, Kevin's death forced them to rethink their assumption. River glanced over at Tony, who was sitting at his desk, downloading the files he'd copied from April and Nathan's laptops. She couldn't help but wonder if they were in danger from whoever killed Kevin. Frankly, the killer's actions didn't make sense. It was almost like there were two different people involved. Was that possible? She didn't want to make the same error they'd made with the Strangler. They'd profiled him as someone acting alone. If there was more than one person watching Nathan, that made it much more dangerous. It was easier to predict the actions of one unknown subject than it was two. A second unknown subject, or UNSUB, might decide to color outside the lines. Even though Nathan was keeping his interaction with Tony and her secret, River was certain whoever had threatened him knew he'd been visiting them. Sure, the picture had only shown him coming out of the building and was taken from the parking lot.

114

But whoever had threatened him and killed Kevin wouldn't be upset if he was visiting an insurance office or some other kind of business. They were the only private investigative agency in the complex.

River watched as Tony finished the downloads. Then he picked up the information Arnie had sent about the murder. This was now a police investigation. Arnie could have told them to back off, but he hadn't. Arnie had confidence in Tony and was convinced he wouldn't cross the line between their investigation into the murder of Kevin Bittner and the search for April.

The most important thing they could do now was to find out exactly why someone was so concerned about Nathan coming to see them. River's gut reaction was that the answer could be found in one of April's cold cases. With April missing, the cases were really cold. Nathan's visit might make them worry that new eyes were looking them over. It seemed to River that someone was determined to keep that from happening. She started to bring up *Hot Coffee and Cold Cases*. She'd gone through all of the cases as thoroughly as she could in one night, but she wanted to listen to everything with April's notebook at hand. But at the last second, she decided to check out April's Facebook page first to see if there were any new messages.

There was one from a woman named Mary who was concerned about April, but nothing else. No new messages from Lamont Cranston.

"Tony," she said, "I just thought of something."

He stopped what he was doing and looked over at her.

"We need to tell Arnie about our man in the shadows, Lamont Cranston. Nathan said he wasn't able to find out anything about him, but maybe Arnie can find a way to do a more thorough search."

"Good idea," he said.

"Anything interesting in the information Arnie sent?"

"Kevin was killed with one shot to the back of the head," Tony said.

"We were right," River said. "This was an execution."

Tony leaned back in his chair. "Kevin saw them. They don't want to be identified so Kevin had to go."

"He had a family," River said. Anger at the killer boiled inside her. Killing Kevin was cruel and unnecessary. They could have found another way to deliver a message to Nathan. Something occurred to her. "Why not just call Nathan?" she asked Tony. "Why deliver an envelope to someone they'll have to eliminate? Seems . . . sloppy."

"What else could they do? If they'd called Nathan, their number could have been traced. Of course, they could have used a burner phone—except most of them now have GPS tracking. Not like the old burner phones."

"True, and maybe they felt they had to move quickly." River shrugged. "Of course, they wouldn't have gotten through to him last night since we had his phone. But he didn't receive any calls, so it's clear they didn't even try."

"Maybe they didn't have his number."

"That's possible," River said. "I hope they were captured by the camera at the guard station, although most professional killers would think about that."

"I don't know. I'm sure the police have gotten the footage." He picked up his phone. "I'm going to text Arnie about Lamont Cranston and ask him about the camera footage. He may not want to share it with me. I just want to know if they got a good image. I need to be careful and not push him too much. Friends or not, Kevin's murder isn't our case, and Arnie is really busy."

"He's never acted like you were bothering him," River said.

"Still, I don't want to take advantage of our friendship."

River watched as he entered his text and then sent it. Hopefully, the camera would yield something the police could use to catch the UNSUB. Once he was finished, River said, "Ready to go through April's cases now? The key to our killer could be here somewhere. However, I have to admit that, so far, I'm not seeing it. Four of these cases are in other states. My first reaction is that the man who committed this murder is close by. He moved on Kevin quickly."

"I tend to agree with you, but it's still not impossible that Kevin's murder is tied to a case from out of town," Tony said. "April's podcast is listened to by people all over the country. Maybe he hired a local professional to handle things."

"I'm still wondering how someone knew why Nathan visited us. Either Nathan told someone or . . . could his apartment have been bugged?"

"I don't know, but the police need to check that out." Tony frowned at her. "We certainly know it happens."

Tony was about to say something else when his phone buzzed. A text. He picked up his phone. "Arnie," he said. He read the text. He picked up a pen and made some notes.

"He gave me the number of the lead detective on the case. Arnie isn't directly involved, and like I figured, he's swamped with other things. He mentioned the other day that he's dealing with a lot of pressure from city hall. He needs more officers and funds, but the mayor is trying to please his voters who think defunding the police is a good idea. I wouldn't want Arnie's job."

"Me neither."

"One thing he did say—the camera at the guard house didn't give them anything helpful. The person who left the envelope was wearing a cap and he kept his face down the entire time. He knew where the camera was. The car he was driving was found not long after he left the apartment complex. It was stolen a few hours earlier. They don't have much hope of getting fingerprints since the video showed the man wearing gloves. Arnie said he's passing the Lamont Cranston info on to the lead detective, Armbruster.

They've actually been going through Nathan's apartment. They had the same thought we did, but so far, they haven't found any bugs. They're going to keep looking though. Nathan's phone is clean. At least we know no one was listening in." Tony stood up and stretched. Then he said, "Okay, so let's start going through these cases. But first let me get a cup of coffee. I think I'm going to need it." He walked over to their coffee maker. "You want anything?" he asked.

"I'll take pumpkin spice."

Tony's eyebrow shot up. "Pumpkin spice? That's new. I know it came in that big collection of flavors my parents gave us for Christmas, but I figured it would sit in the drawer and turn to dust."

River shrugged. "I'm feeling a little sad now that the holidays are over. I really enjoyed being with your parents, even though we didn't actually spend Christmas Day with them. Your mother made it seem like Christmas every day we were there. It was perfect. The best Christmas I've ever had, in fact. Well, except for the crazed serial killer part."

Tony's loud laugh made her smile.

"I can understand that," he said, still chuckling. "Maybe this year we can celebrate the holidays without the threat of death."

"That would definitely be a holiday miracle."

"Something to shoot for, forgive the pun."

"My arm is still sore from the last encounter, thank you."

While at Tony's parents' house, River had been shot in the arm, trying to protect Tony. Thankfully, it was more of a grazing wound than a penetrating one. Although it was still healing, the pain had lessened considerably.

He brewed her coffee and brought it to her. It smelled so good. Just like Mrs. Weyland's pumpkin pie. It was the best she'd ever tasted. River had even eaten a slice for breakfast until it was all gone. She wondered if asking the elderly woman to bake another pie would be out of line. She'd already made several.

"You're thinking about that pie Mrs. Weyland makes, aren't you?" Tony asked suddenly.

River's mouth dropped open. "Quit reading my mind. It's disturbing."

"If you don't stop asking her to make more pies, we'll need to get you a larger desk chair."

River stuck her tongue out at him. "I haven't gained an ounce. I know how to keep my servings small."

"I'm just teasing you. My mother's a great baker, but I have to admit, Mrs. Weyland's pumpkin pie is the best I've ever had." He pointed at her. "If you talk her into another one, you've got to bring me some, okay?"

"We'll see. If you help me come up with whoever killed Kevin Bittner, I'll get Mrs. Weyland to bake you your very own pie."

Tony finished brewing his own cup of coffee and carried it to his desk. Then he pulled up a chair. "You just made me an offer I can't refuse. Let's get busy."

River punched a key on her keyboard to bring up the image of April's site. At first, she thought she'd made a mistake.

"Is something wrong?" Tony asked.

"Wait just a second," she said, clicking the keys underneath her fingertips. Finally, she stopped. She couldn't believe what she was seeing. Or rather, what she wasn't seeing. She turned to meet Tony's eyes. "It's gone," she said. "All of the episodes on April's podcast are gone."

EIGHTEEN

Tony's mouth dropped open. "How could that happen? Who would be able to do that besides April? They'd need her sign-in information."

"I can only think of one other person," River said.

"Nathan? It can't be."

River leaned back in her chair. "I'm trying to wrap my head around this. Before we accuse Nathan, we need to see if the electronic-crimes task force can figure out who removed all those episodes."

"So now what do we do?"

River smiled at him. "Repeat after me. My partner . . ."

Tony looked confused. "Not sure why you're smiling, but I'm a little frightened."

"Do what I asked," River said.

"Okay, okay. My partner . . ."

"Is the best partner in the world."

Tony crossed his arms and stared at her. Finally, he said, "Is the best partner in the world."

"Because . . ."

His eyes widened. "You have all the information from her site, don't you?"

"Well, not all of it, but quite a bit." She picked up her notebook. "I already told you I took pictures of all the pages and notes in April's notebook, but I also took pictures of the podcast pages. Of course, they only contain a general description of the case. But I listened to each podcast and made additional notes. I just felt like the way things were going, it was best to make sure all the information stayed with us. I'm pretty sure we have everything we need."

"You really are brilliant," Tony said. "You know what this proves, right?"

"I'm not sure."

"It proves that no one is smarter than I am since I picked you as my partner."

River laughed. "You're ridiculous."

"I know, but I'm really cute, so that makes up for it."

"Yes, yes. You're adorable." River got up and grabbed her notebook. Then she brought it over to her desk. "We can go through my notes, and anything I didn't get, we can see on my phone."

"Before we do that, let me call the detective in charge of the case and tell him about the podcast."

"I'm not sure what they can do," River said. "Can they actually tell us who removed the episodes? Wouldn't whoever did it have to have access to April's login information?"

"Sure. That's why the first person I'd look at is Nathan. Supposedly, April wasn't close to her father, and she didn't want him to know about the podcast. I'm pretty sure it couldn't have been him." Tony picked up his phone and made a call.

While he talked to the detective, River began looking through her notebook. She had a lot of notes from the Casanova case. She even found some scribbles she couldn't decipher. It wasn't the first time she hadn't been able to read her own writing. She quickly pulled up the pictures she'd taken with her phone. She planned to send them to her laptop so they'd be easier to read, but she hadn't done that yet. She also grabbed April's notebook out of the tote bag and brought it over to her desk. As she looked through the pages, she saw something written in a margin that had to do with the Casanova case. This was the first time she'd noticed it. April had written the name Brent Wilkins. Who was that? Although she had no idea, something about the name struck a chord with her. As if she'd seen or heard the name before. Could it be someone who phoned in a tip? Had the name been mentioned somewhere else in April's notebook? Or on her podcast? Of course, there were a lot of reasons it might seem familiar. Maybe River had known someone with a similar name. Hopefully, she'd remember at some point, but right now she couldn't pull up any connection.

"Everything okay?" Tony asked. "You're frowning."

"Yeah. Just a name April wrote down here. I have no idea why she thought it was important. No explanation. Maybe I'll find it somewhere else in her notes. So, what did the detective say about April's site?"

"He said they'd noticed it was gone, and they're already looking into it," Tony said. "He also asked that you send him the pictures of the site. The good news is that most hosting companies keep copies of the podcast for at least ninety days. The police can request those copies, but they have no idea how long that could take. For now, they want the information we have."

"I want to call Nathan," River said. "I need to ask him a question."

"Like whether or not he has the login information? After thinking about it, I realize it would be very difficult for him to do something like that with the police department watching him."

"You're right. I'll bet they already checked that out themselves. They may not be looking for April, but I'm sure they've come to the conclusion that what happened to Kevin could be connected to her disappearance."

River picked up her phone and called Nathan, not sure he'd actually answer. When he did, he sounded stressed. She couldn't blame him.

"Nathan, April's podcast is gone," River said.

"I know. The police already checked my laptop and my phone to make certain I didn't do it. To be honest, I don't even remember her sign-in information. I have enough trouble remembering my own passwords."

"Did she make a note of it somewhere?"

Nathan was silent for a moment before saying, "Yes. She kept a small planner with all of her account information. It had blue flowers on it. When I went through her apartment, I didn't see it. To be honest, until you mentioned it, I'd forgotten all about it."

"Could you have missed it? Could it still be there?"

"No, her father cleaned everything out and took what was left. He waited a couple of months before he did that. I think he was hoping she'd come home on her own. I couldn't blame him."

"Is there any way he'd delete her episodes?"

"No, he's not good with the Internet, and like I told you, he didn't know about April's podcast."

"Okay, thanks," River said. "How are you doing?"

"Well, they're letting me work, and at least I feel safe. Have you figured out what's going on yet?"

"Not yet. It will take a little time, but we're working on it. You just relax and stay positive. We're going through all of April's cases to see who might want to stop you from trying to find her—or who might be concerned about someone reopening her cases. When we have something solid, we'll let you know."

"Okay. I just . . . really want to go home."

"I know. Hang in there," River said, trying to sound positive. She felt bad for Nathan, but she and Tony were doing their best. "Hey, before we hang up, have you heard the name Brent Wilkins? April wrote it down in her notes. It sounds familiar to me."

Nathan was silent for a moment. "Sounds familiar to me too, but right now I can't place it. If I remember I'll call you back."

"Thanks, Nathan."

When she hung up, she told Tony about their conversation.

"So, Nathan didn't take the episodes down," he said. "Not sure what happened to the planner. Maybe Nathan missed it."

"Could the person who took April have also stolen the planner?"

"And left all her other belongings behind?" Tony asked. "Doesn't make any sense. Maybe it was still in the apartment and her dad took it. It probably wouldn't have meant much to him since he didn't know about the podcast."

River sighed. "It could be anywhere. Besides, if the person or persons who took April wanted her sign-in information, they could have gotten it from her."

"If she's still alive."

"Did Armbruster give you an email address to send the photos?" River asked.

"Yeah." Tony read it off while River wrote it down. "You know we need to tell them we have April's laptop, notebook, and phone. They may want to see them."

"I'm surprised they haven't asked for them yet. Maybe Nathan didn't tell them that he gave them to us. I know they're concentrating on Kevin's murder, but by now they've got to be looking at the connection between Kevin and April's podcast."

"I agree," Tony said. "We need to tell them the truth. If they don't want April's things, fine. Either way it won't impact our investigation since we have copies of almost everything."

"I'll send the photos to Armbruster and let him know about them. We'll leave it to him."

"Okay," Tony said. "I think that's the right move."

"We have a lot of work to do."

"Step by step," Tony said. "It's not a race. It's a marathon."

"I hate that quote," River said with a sigh. "Unfortunately, it almost always seems to be the case."

At that moment, her phone rang, and she answered it. Nathan.

"I just remembered where I'd heard that name," he said. "That's the name of the reporter who coined the phrase the Castlewood Casanova."

"Thanks," River said. "I'd hoped it was a suspect, but at least I can let it go now."

Nathan said goodbye and they hung up again. Although River wanted to forget about Wilkins, there was still something nagging at her. But what was it?

HE WAS GETTING TIRED OF WAITING. He felt as if he were dying of thirst, but he wasn't desiring water. He was longing for death. Her death. He needed to watch the light leave another woman's eyes. His patience was almost at the breaking point. Several times he'd come close to kidnapping another woman in an attempt to slake his craving. But if he did that and his offering was discovered, it would bring too much attention. Law enforcement would invade the area in full force, and River would be hidden away from him. As it was, she and her friend suspected he was near, but they couldn't prove it. They'd been provided protection, but he could still get to her easily. He couldn't risk losing her. Sometimes he wondered if his yearning to finish what had been started was foolish, but his longing for her overwhelmed him. River Ryland's death would be his most outstanding accomplishment. The crowning achievement of his existence.

He was even ready to give up his own life if necessary. River Ryland would most certainly die. And she would die crying out for help from a God that couldn't protect her.

NINETEEN

Tony and River settled down to go over the seven cases mentioned on April's podcast.

"I've combined information from the podcast and April's notebook into my notes," she told Tony. "So, I'll just read from my own notebook."

"Sounds good," Tony said. "Go ahead."

"Let's start with the case of the Convenience Store Carnage. Five years ago, in January, a man walked into a convenience store in Chicago. There were two women working there, both in their twenties, and another woman, fifty-three, who was paying for gas. The man pulled a gun on the women, turned the *Open* sign to *Closed*, and then forced one of the employees to open the register and give him the money. He only got around forty dollars. Then he made all the women go into the back room, where he shot and killed every single one of them. There was a camera in the store, but the killer wore a ski mask. He also wore gloves, so no fingerprints. He left on foot. Police believe he had a car somewhere close by, but no one reported seeing him."

"How busy was this store usually?" Tony asked.

"Not busy at all. It was on the outskirts of the city. Just a small operation owned by a large chain that didn't seem to care how profitable it was."

Tony frowned at her. "So why rob this place for such a small take? And if you're wearing a ski mask, why kill everyone?"

"Exactly the questions April asked in her notes."

"So, the police never arrested anyone?"

River shook her head. "Nothing to go on. From what I gather, they looked into the lives of all of the women, which they should have, but they didn't go very deep. They believed it was a violent robbery and basically wrote it off."

"So did April come up with anything?"

River read down a little farther. She'd gone through all of April's notes, but she'd been so busy copying them, she hadn't memorized everything. She was a little surprised by what she found.

"Seems she got quite a few tips, but she only took one seriously. One of the women who worked there, a Michelle Matisse, was supposedly having an affair with a married man. One of her friends said Michelle had given the man an ultimatum. The friend wondered if the man had killed everyone, trying to make it look like a robbery, so he could get rid of Michelle. Seems his wife had money. Maybe he was afraid of losing his golden goose."

Tony sighed. "When will people learn that betrayal and lies only lead to sorrow?"

River looked over at him. "Too many won't until lives are destroyed. If anyone understands that, it's me."

Tony's eyes widened. "I'm sorry. I wasn't thinking . . ."

"Don't be sorry. It's nice that you understand. I hate that people can be so selfish. I know the Bible says the devil is the one behind the evil in the world, but it's hard not to be angry with people who choose to hurt others."

"I know how much you were wounded, River," Tony said gently. "But we don't forgive people because they didn't do anything wrong. I think we all have the ability to deceive ourselves. Some more than others."

River sighed. "I'm sure you're right. This forgiveness stuff is tough." She met his gaze. "If I let my father come to visit, could you be there?"

"Are you sure?" Tony asked. "I mean, I'm not family."

"You are to me."

Tony looked away for a moment. Had she just made him uncomfortable?

Finally, he turned back and smiled. "Of course, if that's what you want."

She nodded. "Thank you, Tony. Now back to the case." River looked down at her notes again. "Anyway, the friend suggested that the man Michelle was seeing was the shooter." She looked back up at Tony. "I think this is a good tip, don't you?"

"What did April do with it?"

"Says here she contacted the Chicago PD, was transferred to a detective Amato. No notes after that. Looks like she talked to him shortly before she disappeared."

"That's interesting," Tony said. He started typing on his laptop. "You said the woman having the affair was named Michelle Matisse?"

"Yes." River spelled the name.

A few minutes later, Tony smiled at her. "Looks like April was right. The man, Barry Davis, was arrested and charged with the killings. He's serving life in prison."

"Wow. When did his happen?"

"This article was written two months ago."

"So, April never knew she'd helped solve this awful crime."

"Probably not," Tony said. "That's sad."

"Yes, it is." River was finding all these cold cases sad. All this death. All this grief.

"Next time I talk to Arnie, I'll tell him about this. It might make him even more determined to help us find April. Seems she knew what she was doing."

"We really are blessed that you and Arnie are such good friends," River said. "You told me that you two met at the academy, right?"

Tony smiled. "Yeah, we bonded there. He left before you joined. We worked hard, but we had fun. Arnie pushed it a little too far sometimes."

"I can't imagine that."

"You remember Hogan's Alley?" Tony asked.

Hogan's Alley was a training location on the FBI Academy's grounds, set up to look like a small town. Gunfights and robberies were staged there to help the agents in training learn how to handle real-life emergencies.

"Of course."

"One of our instructors was named Jared Newcum. Arnie took a picture of him and had it made into something that looked like the front page from a newspaper. Newcum's picture was on it, along with an article saying he was wanted by the police for cruelty and the harassment of trainees. When we met at Hogan's one morning, the page was up on the window of the post office. We thought it was hysterical. Newcum, not so much."

"Did Arnie get in trouble?" River asked.

"No. Newcum tried to find out who did it, but no one would turn him in. We all had to run around the training track until we were ready to drop. Still, no one ratted Arnie out. I think Newcum was actually rather impressed."

River laughed, but something Tony said stuck in her mind. A newspaper.

"What's the matter?" Tony said. "You look like you've just seen a ghost. My story wasn't that disturbing, was it?"

"No, that's not it." River stared at him for a moment. Then she grabbed April's notebook and pulled out the copies of the articles written about both of the Casanova killings. When she was done, she looked over at Tony. "Look, I may be way off here, but I think you need to ask Arnie to check on something. Remember when we said that the Casanova killer probably didn't kill the other teenagers four years earlier since it didn't seem like he was seeking attention?"

He nodded. "Sure, what are you thinking?"

"What if he was getting attention, but just not the way we assumed? What if he didn't need to see his name in the news as the killer because his name was already associated with the murders. Already in the media?"

"You've lost me."

"It's been staring me in the face all this time. Brent Wilkins is the reporter who came up with the name Castlewood Casanova. When I was reading through the newspaper articles about both of the murders, I kept thinking they sounded the same. I just checked. The reporter who wrote about both cases? Brent Wilkins. He covered the story in Illinois, where the first murders took place. And then here, in Missouri."

"Where he gave the killer a nickname," Tony said slowly. He shook his head. "It makes sense, but it's flimsy. Still, the police need to look into it. Check out this Wilkins guy." He wrote something down on the pad of paper on his desk. He smiled at her. "Now that would be something, huh? If we were able to help April solve this case?"

TWENTY

Shhh. Don't say anything."

  She felt someone's hand over her mouth and started to struggle. Then she realized that the voice was familiar, and she relaxed.

"I'm not going to give you your medication this evening," she whispered. "But you've got to stay still. Pretend to be asleep. When it gets dark, I'll come back. You've got to get out of here. I overheard the doctor talking to someone on the phone. I'm afraid they want him to make you disappear. Permanently. Someone might be trying to find you, and they can't allow that. If you understand, nod."

It took all her strength and concentration to move her head up and down. Was this real? Was someone actually going to help her? She'd given up since her last attempt to escape had failed. She felt a tear roll down the side of her face.

"Oh, hon. I'm so sorry this is happening to you. I want to call the police, but I can't risk it. I'm afraid he'll find out. Never mind. I'm giving you too much information. I just need to get you out of here. We don't have much time. Wait for me tonight. Don't let them know you're lucid."

There was a noise that came from somewhere down the hallway. The nurse withdrew a syringe from her pocket. For a moment she was afraid it was a lie. Just another way to torture her. Then the nurse stuck the needle into the mattress and pushed the plunger. After that she put the empty syringe back in her pocket.

"Don't worry. I won't let you down."

She closed her eyes and listened to the nurse's shoes slap against the cold tile floor as she walked away. Then the door closed, and she flinched as the deadbolt lock slid shut.

Was it possible? Was she really going to finally be free? She couldn't stop the tears. She'd actually given up. She prayed silently, asking God to keep her hope alive. She couldn't take it if she was disappointed one more time. She just couldn't.

But that probably wasn't a problem. If she didn't make it out this time, it sounded as if she'd never get another chance.

"READY TO GO OVER some of these other cases?" River asked.

Tony nodded. "I guess we have to."

River flipped through her notebook. "Okay, another case mentioned on April's site was the case of the Missing Mother. This happened almost ten years ago. It seems that Emily Smallwood left her house one night and never came back. She left her teenage son, Brandon, and her nine-year-old daughter, Stephanie at home. When she hadn't returned home by ten that night, Brandon called the police. They found her car in the parking lot at the grocery store. The car was locked, but Emily was gone. They've never found her. Her children are now in Colorado. Stephanie is living with Emily's ex-husband. Of course, the police checked out the husband, but it wasn't him. He had an airtight alibi. He was at work when Emily went missing. The police had no other leads, and the case went cold."

"Where did this happen?" Tony asked.

"In Michigan."

River frowned. "It's a long way away, but I guess we should still look into it."

"I agree. Did April get any leads?"

"Yes. A few months before April disappeared, someone who claimed to once be a friend of Brandon's called and told April that he thinks a couple of Brandon's friends killed Emily. It seems she was abusive. Stephanie had frequent bruises on her body. She told one of her friends that her mother beat her and burned her with cigarettes. It was never reported because Stephanie was afraid to tell anyone. The caller, who was anonymous, it seems, thinks Brandon had Emily killed to save his sister." She sighed. "It appears that Emily had recently inherited a nice amount of money from her mother after her passing. Emily had a little over a hundred thousand dollars in the bank, as well as a home that was completely paid off. Not long after she disappeared, Brandon turned eighteen, so when she was declared legally dead five years later, he inherited everything. She wasn't certain how much Brandon got when they sold the house, but she guesses it was at least three-hundred thousand dollars. It would seem like a fortune to those kids."

Tony shook his head. "First of all, I have to assume the police checked out all these leads. Killing for an inheritance is common. If the police had found anything, they would have arrested Brandon."

"But what if they didn't know about the abuse?" River asked. "I think it gives him an even stronger motive. It doesn't sound like the kids mentioned that. And if Stephanie never saw a doctor or was taken to a hospital . . ."

"Did April contact the police in Michigan?"

River shook her head. "Like I said, she got these tips not long before she disappeared. I don't think she had time. Besides, the tip came from someone who wanted to stay anonymous. She didn't have any follow up notes in her notebook, and there wasn't any update on her podcast."

"Okay, let's call the police in . . ."

"Walker. Walker, Michigan."

"Okay, we'll contact them and give them April's information. Then we keep looking." Tony prayed silently that they'd find something sooner than later. If April *was* alive, they needed to find her before it was too late. Someone was nervous, and Tony didn't want April's captors to decide they couldn't afford to allow her to stay that way. Going through her notes and reading the pages on her podcasts was rather surreal. If April was already dead, it was as if she was helping them crack cases from the grave.

TWENTY-ONE

River and Tony decided to look over one more case before calling it a day. River brought up the next entry on April's list, which she called the case of the Railroad Rage.

"I think we can mark this one off," River said. "I doubt it will ever be solved. A man was found along railroad tracks in Kentucky eighteen years ago. It looked like he'd been savagely beaten. The ME said he was somewhere in his thirties, ragged clothing, probably homeless. A police sketch artist put something together, but the face was in such bad shape he couldn't be completely sure how accurate the image was. The police looked through all of the missing person cases, but no one fit this guy."

River pulled out her phone and clicked through the pages she'd taken pictures of. "Here's a copy of the sketch." She handed her phone to Tony, who looked at it and gave it back to her.

"Pretty generic," he said.

"I know. The body was never claimed and was buried by a local church who took pity on the man."

"Nothing else?"

River shook her head. "No, sadly."

"I agree that we should cross this one off," Tony said. "Too long ago, and too cold. Did April get any tips?"

"Not really. A couple of people hoping it might be someone in their family who'd gone missing, but it doesn't look as if those leads panned out."

"Why don't we wrap it up and take another crack at this tomorrow morning?" Tony said.

River yawned. "I agree. I'm tired. Time to go home. Do you want to join us for supper?"

"Are you sure it won't be any trouble?"

River laughed. "You've got my mother and Mrs. Weyland wrapped around your little finger. In fact, when I don't ask you over, they get a little peeved with me."

Tony raised an eyebrow. "They're *peeved* with you, Grandma?"

"Oh, stop it."

"Where do you get all of these old expressions? Do you spend your down time dressing up like an old woman and chasing old men?"

"No, I spend my time reading books by Jane Austen and Charles Dickens. Great literature. You wouldn't understand."

Tony sighed loudly. "Sorry if my books are a little more manly. If anyone used the word *peeved* in a Creston Mapes or Steven James book, they'd be shot."

"Very funny. I love their books too. But I'm also able to appreciate the classics."

"I've got to call Watson's daycare and let them know I'll be late," Tony said. "And by the way, they'll be closed tomorrow. The owner's father passed away. I'll need to bring Watson to the office with me."

"I love it when he comes here," River said. "I'm so glad the landlord allows pets in the building. The graphic design guys have the cutest dogs."

"They do, don't they? Bulldogs. Although they do seem to drool a lot."

"That's just part of their charm," River said, laughing.

Tony had just started to say something when the door to their office opened and a man stepped inside. Late forties, early fifties, sharply dressed. The expression on his face was anything but friendly.

"Can I help you?" Tony asked. He got to his feet in case the guy tried something. They were both trained to size up threatening situations and respond quickly. They didn't know this man, and he was clearly angry. His expression and the way he held himself were dead giveaways.

"You certainly can," the man said. "You can quit trying to help Nathan Hearne. My daughter is missing, and I think he may have had something to do with it."

HE SIGHED AS HE WALKED into another antique store. How many of these places had he been to so far? Unfortunately, old trunks were becoming popular with people who liked to repurpose them. It was irritating.

"Can I help you, sir?"

He turned to find a young woman standing behind him. He felt his heart race. Brown hair. Green eyes. His usual prey. He hadn't hunted in a long time, and he felt as if his blood was boiling. But he couldn't do anything to lose River Ryland. She was his most important trophy. The prey he *had* to kill.

"I . . . I was looking for an old trunk. It doesn't have to be in perfect shape."

Her smile widened. "We have one over here," she said, waving her hand to her right.

He followed behind her. As he watched her walk, his heart beat loudly in his chest. Could she hear it? He had to be careful. If he did or said anything out of the norm, it could cause her to remember him.

"This trunk is from the 1920s," she said. "It's solid wood with a liner, a leather handle, and brass accessories. We also have a key for the lock. There's some water damage, but all in all it's in very good shape."

"How much?" he asked.

"We're asking two hundred."

He knew it was exactly what he wanted, but if he didn't haggle a bit, it might seem unusual.

"Would you take one-seventy-five for it?"

"I'm not sure," the girl said, although he was absolutely certain they had a deal. "Let me ask the owner."

He tried not to watch her as she walked away, but he couldn't help it. A couple of minutes later, she came back.

"The owner says you can have it for one-seventy-five," she said, as if this news was the best thing she'd ever heard.

"That's wonderful." He took a deep breath and looked into her eyes, so much like his mother's. "I don't suppose you have any others?"

Her eyebrows lifted, showing her surprise, and he thought he'd made a mistake. But thankfully, her expression wasn't shock, it was pleasure. She was obviously making a commission on her sales.

"There is one in the back," she said, "but it just came in a couple of days ago. We haven't had time to clean it up."

"Would you mind if I looked at it? I repurpose these and sell them. People love to use them to decorate their homes."

"Yes, they do," she said. "If you don't mind coming with me, I'll be happy to show it to you. As I said, it's still rather dirty—but I guess you don't care."

"No, I don't." He smiled at her. "Just part of the job."

When they got to the back room, he saw the other trunk. As the salesgirl, whose name turned out to be Megan, described the features of the old trunk, his only interest was in figuring out whether or not she would fit inside.

Ten minutes later, he had two old trunks in his van and Megan's business card with her personal cellphone number in his pocket.

"I'M SORRY," RIVER SAID. "You think Nathan had something to do with April's disappearance?"

"Of course. Everything was fine until he came into her life. From the moment I met him, I didn't trust him. I tried to get April to listen to me, but the more I warned her, the more she gravitated toward him."

"It generally works that way," River said, keeping her voice calm. "If you tell a child to stay away from someone, they usually find them more appealing." She was trying to connect with him. Get him to relax and not see them as the enemy. She wanted to know why he was here. And how he found out Nathan had come to see them. She knew Tony was upset about the vibe April's father projected, but she needed to stay focused on him and not allow Tony to distract her.

"You said Nathan had something to do with April's disappearance," Tony said. "What makes you think that?"

"Do you mind if I sit?"

River motioned toward the chair in front of her desk. April's father sat down and let out a deep sigh. It was as if he'd exhaled all the tension in his body.

"I'm sorry if I was rude. This isn't your fault. I've just been so worried. We lost her mother when April was young. It was a terrible, terrible time. And now April's gone. I don't know what to do." He shook his head. "I'm Jeffrey Bailey."

Jeffrey, not Jeff. That told them something about him. "Jeffrey, how do you know about us?" River asked.

"Nathan called and left me a message the day before he visited

140

you. I didn't find it until this morning. I don't check my phone very often." He frowned at her. "I think he's trying to prove to me that he's genuinely looking for my daughter."

"He didn't tell us that you knew he was coming here," Tony said.

Jeffrey shrugged. "You can ask him. And you might want to ask yourselves why he didn't let you know that. Maybe you can't trust him."

River looked over Jeffrey's body language. She couldn't see anything that made her feel as though he wasn't telling the truth. He seemed genuinely upset.

"Coffee?" River asked.

"Not this late, thanks."

"I'm not sure what you want us to do, Jeffrey," Tony said.

"I want to know what's going on," he said, his tone a little menacing.

River cast a quick look at Tony before saying, "Nathan is our client. I'm afraid there's not much we can tell you."

"I've tried to call him, but he doesn't answer his phone. I really need to talk to him. He only told me he was coming to see you, but he didn't tell me why he decided to seek your help after all this time. I'd like to know more."

"We certainly can't force him to respond to your phone calls," Tony said. River knew he was trying to match Jeffrey's forcefulness, but that didn't seem to impress the man. River was grateful all of April's things were in the tote bag behind Tony's desk, out of sight. If Jeffrey had noticed and recognized the bag, she felt strongly he would have asked for his daughter's property. Since Arnie wanted the items, they could say no, but she had a feeling this man could become even more unpleasant than he'd already been.

On a whim, River reached into her drawer and took out a copy of the picture someone had left for them. She got up from her desk and put it in front of him.

"Did you take this picture?" she asked.

His eyes widened. "Of course not," he said, angrily. "I don't need to rely on cheap tricks or threats to get what I want." He stood up. "Look, you need to look carefully at Nathan Hearne. He's the only person who gains from April's disappearance."

"What are you talking about?" Tony said, also getting to his feet.

"Oh, I guess he didn't tell you?" Jeffrey's laugh was nasty and spiteful. "April has a very large trust fund. She told me she didn't want the money because I disagreed with her engagement to Nathan. Of course, I knew that someday she'd change her mind. It was important to her mother. But Nathan kept trying to talk her into taking the money now and giving it to him. If she disappeared against her will, you should look at him." He removed a card from his wallet. He hesitated a moment before slapping it down on Tony's desk. "I'd like to know if you learn anything about what happened to my daughter. I was convinced that she left on her own, to get away from Nathan, but now I'm not so sure. I'm truly worried. I'm her father, you know. Nathan Hearne doesn't love her, and I do." Then he turned on his heel and headed for the door without another word.

TWENTY-TWO

After Jeffrey left, Tony sat down and sighed. "Did we miss something? Could Nathan really be behind April's disappearance?"

"Then why come to us?" River asked. "It doesn't make any sense. I think *Jeffrey* just doesn't like Nathan. Maybe he was jealous of their relationship. A lot of fathers have problems with their daughter's boyfriends."

"You noticed that he likes to be called Jeffrey too, huh?" He shook his head. "I don't see any reason for Nathan to come to us. I mean, kidnapping April so he can get to her money? How would that work? I'm just not buying it."

The door to their office opened again and a police officer came in. "Chief Martin sent me to pick up some evidence."

Tony got up and handed him the bag. The officer took out a piece of paper that Tony signed. Chain of evidence. Crucial when passing off items that could end up as evidence in a courtroom.

"Hey, hold on just minute, okay?" Tony said. He pulled his pad of paper over and quickly wrote something. Then he removed the paper and slid it into an envelope. He handed it to the officer. "Please give this to Chief Martin, okay?"

"Sure. Not a problem."

River watched Tony hand the envelope to the officer, but she was still thinking about Jeffrey Bailey's accusation. She had confidence in her ability to read people, but she wasn't perfect. Could Nathan have fooled them?

"River?"

She looked up to find Tony staring at her. The officer had left.

"You're still thinking about what Bailey said, aren't you?"

She sighed. "Yeah."

"I thought we already decided that Nathan wasn't involved in April's disappearance."

"You're right," she said. "Sorry. I just want to make sure we're not dismissing the possibility out of hand." She met his gaze. "Why did Nathan tell Jeffrey that he was coming here?"

"Didn't he say something about trying to keep in touch with April's father?" Tony asked. "I'm guessing he thought it was the right thing to do."

"I guess so."

"It's getting late. I don't want your mother and Mrs. Weyland delaying dinner for us. Did you let them know I was coming?"

River shook her head. "I'll do it right now." She frowned at him. "Did the note you sent to Arnie have anything to do with our case?"

"I'm not sure. I told him about the reporter Brent Wilkins and how he was connected to the Casanova case. I didn't want to call him again in case it's a waste of time. It really is a stretch."

"But according to our mini-profile, not out of the realm of possibility," River said.

"That's why I sent it. Who knows? Okay. I'm going to run to the restroom. Be right back."

On his way to the bathroom, Tony passed by some of the

other businesses on their floor. Some people were already gone for the day. One newer business, TSRS, still had its lights on. Just one guy worked there. When Tony walked by, he looked up and smiled. Tony waved at him, and the guy waved back. Tony wasn't sure what the guy did, but it looked boring. A lot of paperwork. A job like that would drive Tony nuts. When he was done in the restroom, he headed back to the office. Now everyone was gone, even the guy at TSRS.

He hoped they wouldn't get to River's house too late. He'd grown fond of River's mother and the kind and efficient Mrs. Weyland. Sometimes God sent angels in the form of people. Mrs. Weyland was one of those. Without her, River probably wouldn't have been able to partner with him in Watson Investigations. He couldn't imagine his life without her. Even with the specter of the Strangler's accomplice hanging over their lives, Tony was happier now than he'd ever been in his life. He loved working with River every day, and he also loved what they were doing. As behavioral analysts, they created profiles to help law enforcement narrow down their search parameters. But now, they were the ones looking for the bad guys, solving mysteries, and bringing justice. The only thing he still wanted was . . . River. For more than a friend. He wanted to tell her how he felt about her, but he wasn't certain if she was ready to hear it. They'd danced around it for a while now. But with the threat of the Strangler's partner hanging over their heads, was this really the time? He took a deep breath before opening the office door and then smiled when he saw her. "Ready to go?"

She nodded. "Part of me wants to keep digging into these cases."

"Me too, but I don't want the gal at the doggy daycare to stay too late. It was nice of her to watch Watson so I could have dinner with you."

"She's a saint to put up with your hours."

He laughed. "Maybe not a complete saint. She's in love with my dog. She took Watson home with her on some of those nights we worked really late. And she took care of him when I was in the hospital and while we were in Iowa. I think if I was willing to give him away, she'd take him in a second."

River frowned at him. "You'd never do that, would you?"

He shook his head. "Absolutely not. We're bonded. I couldn't live with the notion that he might wait for me to come back to him but I never did."

He was surprised to see River's eyes flush with tears. River wasn't comfortable with tears, although she was getting better. He'd known her for years before he ever saw her cry.

"I'm sorry. I didn't mean to upset you," he said.

"No, it's me. Watson's kind of grown on me."

He hesitated a moment before saying, "Maybe I should tell you that in my will, should anything happen to me, I left Watson to you."

She looked up at him in obvious surprise, her eyes still shiny. "What? I mean, what about your parents?"

"He doesn't really know them, and he's crazy about you."

"But your dog sitter . . ."

"She has several dogs," he said slowly. "Watson isn't the kind of dog that would do well around that many dogs on a permanent basis. He loves his time at doggy daycare, and he loves Sylvia, but by the time I pick him up there or at her house, he's had enough. He just wants to chill out with me. Get belly rubs and sit next to me on the couch while I watch TV. The only other animal I've ever seen him really connect to is your mother's cat. I think he's in love with Scutter."

River chuckled. "Scutter is crazy about him too. But let's not plan your demise for anytime soon, okay?"

He laughed. "I'm not planning on going anywhere for quite

some time, but after the Strangler . . . well, you can't help but think about the future."

"I know what you mean. And in that vein, I've left my mother to you in my will."

Tony stared at her for a moment, not knowing how to respond, until she burst out laughing. "You're a horrible person," he said, grinning. "A really horrible person."

"I know. Now, let's get out of here."

"Good idea."

As she put her coat on, River said, "I'm so excited that Watson will be here tomorrow. Don't forget his bed this time. Last time he was annoyed at you all day long."

"Yes, I know. He wouldn't even look at me on the way home." River laughed again.

They left the office and went downstairs. As they got close to Tony's SUV, he noticed the owner of TSRS near the large trash bin at one end of the parking lot. He appeared to be upset, swearing, and looking at something on the ground. River and Tony went to check on him and found him kicking at trash next to his car. It looked as if someone had purposely chucked trash out of the open container.

"Everything okay?" Tony asked.

The man looked up suddenly, and Tony got the impression they'd startled him.

"Sorry," he said. "I get irritated when I find debris near my car. I think some homeless person was dumpster diving and just tossed trash everywhere. I'm afraid of finding scratches on the finish." He stopped pushing trash away with his foot and sighed. "I feel badly for them, of course, but I'm also tired of having my car damaged. This isn't the first time."

Tony could understand his feelings. The same thing had happened to him, and he told the man this. "I finally quit parking over here. I know it's closer to the door on our side of the building, but taking my car to the body shop was getting to be a pain."

"I'll start doing that. Thank you. I'm Thomas Sullivan, by the way. I own the Thomas Sullivan Recovery Service."

Tony introduced himself and then River. "We've seen you in the building. You moved in not long ago?"

"Yes. I run a debt recovery company. Not a very popular business but important to my clients."

"I can understand that. Well, nice to finally meet you."

"You too. And you, Miss Ryland."

River smiled. "River's fine. We'll see you around the building."

"Yes." Thomas walked back to his car, and Tony noticed he had a slight limp. Maybe that was why he wanted to park closer to the entrance near their side of the building. Tony felt bad for him, but there wasn't much that could be done to change things. He wondered if his limp was a temporary injury. If it was permanent, he would probably have a disability tag, and he didn't see one on his car.

Tony and River headed back to his SUV, and he unlocked the passenger side door for River. When they got inside, he apologized. "Boy, it's cold."

"Yes, it is." She smiled. "So, we get a Jeffrey and a Thomas in the same day. I always wonder about men who use their formal names instead of the commonly used nickname. He doesn't seem like a Tom though, does he? And Jeffrey doesn't seem like a Jeff."

Tony started the car and turned on the heater. "With Thomas it's probably a business thing."

"Debt recovery, huh? So, he's the guy who calls people and threatens them if they don't pay back a debt?"

Tony laughed. "I guess so. He's not very intimidating."

River was strangely silent and looked away from him, out the window.

"You okay?"

"Yeah. After my father left, we had some people like that call our house. My mother had to handle them. My father was the breadwinner, and he left us with the bills. My mother started working two jobs to keep us going. Eventually, Mom took him to court and got back child support. She was finally able to drop one of those jobs."

"That's the first time you've told me that," Tony said. "You only mentioned that she was very shut down."

"She was. She worked, came home, and went to bed. That was it. No time for Dan and me." River sighed. "I don't think I gave her enough credit for what she gave up. Maybe I was too focused on my own pain."

"You were a child, River. That's normal."

"Yeah, maybe."

Tony didn't say anything else. It had been a tough day. She needed to process what she was feeling. She'd always been that way. Ever since he'd known her anyway.

They drove in silence the rest of the way to her house.

HE SAT IN HIS CAR AND WATCHED them drive away. He couldn't stop laughing. Here he was, so close to them, but they had no idea. Tonight, he would deliver the old trunk to the place by the water where River Ryland would face her final moments. The clock was ticking, and soon he would finish what had been started.

He'd made other plans as well. As soon as River was dead, he would take his next victim. The little brunette at the antique shop would follow River into the water. They had to be washed clean. The way his mother had tried to wash his sins away. But he wouldn't use scalding water the way she had. He still carried the scars from her cruelty.

Then after River and Megan had been dealt with, he would keep going. He would finally unleash the beast that growled inside him. And that monster would force St. Louis to cry for mercy.

He started his car and headed to the place of River's execution.

TWENTY-THREE

Dinner with Tony went well. River's mother was happy to see him. She seemed to be having one of her good days. They laughed at Tony's corny jokes, and Scutter tried valiantly to jump into his lap during dinner. Once they were finished, Tony picked up the friendly cat and stroked his golden fur, which Scutter loved.

Although Tony wanted to help with the dishes, River made him leave, knowing that Watson was waiting for him. Then she made Mrs. Weyland and Rose go to the living room so they could watch their favorite show. They loved watching reruns of NCIS. River suspected they both had slight crushes on actor Mark Harmon.

As she loaded the dishwasher, she couldn't seem to relax. She was unsettled, but she wasn't sure why. To distract herself, she kept running April's remaining cold cases through her mind. She felt strongly that her disappearance had to be tied to one of the people connected to her podcast. But which one? Which case should they focus on?

Once the dishwasher was loaded and River had wiped down the counters, she went to check on Rose and Mrs. Weyland. Her mother was already nodding off.

"I'll get her to bed," Mrs. Weyland said softly. "Then I'd like to talk to you for a few minutes. It won't take long."

"Sure." River headed to her room. She was tired tonight and just wanted to take a shower and crawl into bed. Instead, she sat down in the overstuffed chair in the corner of her room and waited for Mrs. Weyland. River leaned her head back and closed her eyes. When she heard the knock on her door, she realized that she'd fallen asleep.

"Come in," she said, trying to clear her head.

Mrs. Weyland pushed the door open and smiled at her. "I'm sorry to bother you, honey. I'm sure you're tired, but something happened today. You need to know about it."

"It's about my mother?"

"In a way."

River got up from her chair and motioned to the older lady to sit down.

"Oh, thanks, but I won't be here long. I just need you to know that your brother called again today. He talked to your mama for a while, and when she was done, she gave the phone to me. He and your dad plan to visit on Saturday. I told him he needed to talk to you about it first, but he reminded me that this is your mama's house. She told them to come, honey. Now, she may have felt that way today, but it doesn't mean she'll feel the same way on Saturday. I just wanted you to know that whatever you decide to do, I'll support you."

River knew this was coming, but she certainly didn't think it would happen so soon. She knew eventually she had to face her father. She wished her brother had talked to her about this first, but he was right. This really was their mother's house. Still, he had to know how traumatic this could be for her and for River.

"Thanks for telling me." She sat down again and stared at Mrs. Weyland. "How do you feel about this?"

She smiled. "Honey, it doesn't matter how I feel. You have to search your heart and listen to God. What does He want you to do? One thing I will say—if your mother's illness proceeds along a normal course—the sooner she faces your father, the better. Your mama thinks she's ready for this now, and I believe she is. But a few months from now . . . Well, it could be a different story." She sighed. "I'm goin' to bed now, and you should too. You sleep on it. Maybe by the time you wake up, you'll know what to do. That's worked for me many times. 'Night, honey."

"Good night."

When the door closed, River sat for a moment, trying to digest what the elderly caregiver had told her. It occurred to her that she hadn't been very accommodating to Dan. He was trying to bring healing to their family, but she'd been acting as if he were trying to cause harm. She felt the need to talk to him before he and her father showed up. Of course, Dan wasn't asking for permission to come, but at least she could let him know she wanted to see him. She and Dan had been close growing up, but he'd fled when he was eighteen to get away from their mother. River had felt abandoned. Even betrayed. But in truth, she couldn't blame him. Their mother had been very difficult to live with. River had blamed herself because her father left. It wasn't true, of course, yet River had felt guilty about it for years. She'd tried to be perfect, hoping her mother would finally forgive her. How strange that now, after getting Alzheimer's, Rose was finally showing love to her daughter. She credited Mrs. Weyland for much of her mother's transformation.

But even more than facing Dan, seeing her father again after all these years made her feel . . . what? Nauseated? She knew she was supposed to love him, but she didn't. She had forgiven him . . . told herself she had anyway. But there was still resentment. Her pastor had said once that love wasn't a feeling. It was a decision. When he said it, River had felt as if God was actually speaking to her. The revelation that her feelings didn't define her gave her a sense of freedom. She'd experienced such a sense of relief—and she was finally able to begin to let go of the guilt she'd felt. Her feelings toward her father were still negative, but she'd made the decision to forgive him, no matter how she felt.

A wave of weariness washed over her, and she took off her boots. Yet instead of preparing for her shower, she continued to sit there and think about the case. Things had turned deadly, and she was concerned that someone else could be next. She suddenly wondered if Jeffrey, April's father, could also be in danger. If someone was watching and they'd seen him come to their office . . . She found her phone and quickly called Tony.

"Hey, sorry to bother you, but have you wondered if we should warn Jeffrey Bailey to be careful? Nathan is in protective custody because he visited us, and now Jeffrey's been to our office."

Tony was quiet for a moment. "I don't know, but it's a good question."

"I think if something happened to him, we'd feel awful. Especially after today."

"Tell you what," Tony said, "I'll call him and let him know that someone may be targeting people who are looking into April's disappearance. I mean, you showed him the picture. I'll remind him about that. Maybe that will be enough to make him cautious."

"If he doesn't take it seriously, tell him about the guard, Kevin," River said.

"Should we tell him Nathan is in police protection?"

River thought for a moment. "No. The police are pretty secretive about things like that. If Jeffrey said the wrong thing to the wrong person . . ."

"Of course, you're right," Tony said. "Sorry. I'm tired. I'll just mention the guard's death and that we think it might be connected with April's disappearance."

"Sounds good," River said slowly.

"Something else on your mind?"

"Again, how do you know what I'm thinking? Stop it. It's weird."

Tony laughed. "Great minds, I guess."

"My father's coming to visit on Saturday."

Tony didn't respond immediately. Finally, he said, "How do you feel about that?"

"Well, according to Pastor Mason, I'm not supposed to worry about how I feel. Just decide to love him."

"I know it's hard, but I know you can do it."

"I guess we'll find out. Remember you promised to be there when I face him."

"I will," Tony said. "I promise."

River felt some peace for the first time since hearing about her father's visit. "Thank you. See you in the morning?"

"You bet. Good night."

"Good night."

River forced herself to gather her sweats and head to the bathroom for her shower. She continued thinking about the case so she could forget about her father for a while. But there was something else picking at her, trying to get her attention. It was as if it were just out of her grasp, yet she kept trying to reach it. Frankly, it was beginning to wear her down.

She'd just started shampooing her hair when it hit her. She quickly rinsed, got out of the shower, and hurried back to the bedroom, where she'd left her cellphone. As soon as Tony answered, she told him what she'd realized.

TWENTY-FOUR

Although the place he'd picked was largely deserted, he waited until the last car was gone and no one had come by for quite some time. Then he drove to the spot he'd scouted out earlier. It was perfect. A group of trees close to the river. He'd searched for a while before he'd found it. Spruces don't lose foliage during the winter, so pulling down some branches to cover the old chest wouldn't look suspicious. The last time River had faced the Strangler, the chest had been taken from the trunk of a car. It had taken too long. She'd almost gotten her hands on a gun and ruined the fun. This time, her coffin would be on site. Ready to go.

He turned off his headlights and took the chest out of his trunk. After that, he carried it to a spot beneath the trees, broke off several branches, and covered it up. Then he gathered up lots of dead leaves and placed them in any bare spots. After a few minutes, he walked a few feet away from the trees and gazed at his work. Perfect. No one would suspect anything.

He laughed softly. The clock was ticking on River Ryland's life and her coffin was ready. She would soon belong to him forever.

TONY PICKED RIVER UP EARLY, and they drove to the office. Watson was secured in the back seat by a special harness. The puggle seemed extremely happy to be going with them. River knew Tony didn't want to take advantage of the landlord's willingness to allow pets, but she wished she could spend more time around him. Watson was getting a little older and his once-blond snout was now flecked with gray. River didn't like to think about Watson's mortality. If anything happened to the small, friendly dog, Tony would be devastated—and so would she.

She'd tried to call Dan before she left, but she'd reached his voicemail. She almost left a message but at the last minute just hung up. She felt they needed to talk, and she didn't want their contact to become a series of voicemail messages.

When they reached the office, she waited in the car while Tony took Watson for a brief walk. Once Watson had done his business, they came back to the car and the three of them went upstairs. In the elevator, River kept reaching down to pet his soft head. He looked up at her with affection. He'd captured her heart long ago, and she wondered if he knew how much she loved him.

Once inside the office, Watson settled down into the soft dog bed Tony brought from home. Tony made a phone call, and when he was done, they talked about the situation that had arisen last night. They weren't completely in agreement on how to proceed, but River reminded Tony that no matter what else was going on, they had to concentrate on the cases left on April's list. A man had died, and they needed to try to figure out how to stop the UNSUB before he hurt someone else.

"We've got to focus on what's in front of us," she told him. "We have a client to think about. We'll work out the details of this other thing with Arnie. We've got the upper hand now. Remember that."

Tony was silent for a moment. "You may be right, but I don't like it. I think it's too dangerous."

"Duly noted. Now let me grab my notebook."

Tony sighed loudly and shook his head. "Okay, I guess I'll make coffee. But this discussion isn't over."

"Just black for me," she said, ignoring him.

Tony stopped in his tracks and turned to look at her. "Excuse me?"

"I'm flashing back to the time our coffee was tampered with."

"I don't think you need to worry about that," Tony said.

"I know. Just humor me."

He shrugged. "Black it is."

After he'd brewed both cups, he placed them on River's desk and then grabbed a chair. "When I talked to Arnie, he told me they weren't able to track down Lamont Cranston. His account is fake, and he used public computers when he posted. So that's a dead end."

"Exactly what Nathan said."

Tony nodded. "So back to April's cases."

River looked through her notebook, flipping the pages. Finally, she found what she was looking for. "This one is called the case of the Hit-and-Run Hitchhiker. According to April, three years ago, a woman named Cheryl Armitage was on her way home after drinking at a bar on the outskirts of St. Louis, in a rather isolated area." She looked up at Tony. "A case close to home." Then she went back to her notes. "After the bar closed, her car wouldn't start. Everyone had gone home except the bartender, who wouldn't open the door when she knocked. According to him, he wasn't allowed to reopen once he'd locked up." River glanced up once again. "I don't think he wanted to deal with her. He could have at least called someone to help her, even the police, yet he chose to ignore her."

"Maybe he thought she was just trying to get another drink."

"Possibly, but I'll bet he wonders now if he should have done something." River took a sip of her coffee then went back to her notes. "It seems she tried to phone her ex-husband, but he ignored her call because their divorce was rancorous. She then tried to contact her mother, but she was in bed and had turned her ringer down. She didn't discover the call until the next morning after she got up. After that, it appears she attempted to hitchhike home. A few people reported seeing her on the side of the road trying to get a ride, but they didn't stop to pick her up since she was so obviously inebriated. One person did phone the police, hoping they would help her, but before they could get there, Cheryl was struck by a car. The driver left her there in the road and drove away. Cheryl was taken to the hospital by ambulance, but the doctors in the ER couldn't save her. The police were never able to locate the driver." River sighed. "This is so sad. Would you have stopped for her?"

"That's a tough question for a man by himself," Tony said, "but if she was actually in the road? Yes, I'd have to. I couldn't just leave her there."

"That's because you're a good man," River said.

"Thank you. I know you would have stopped too."

"You're right. If just one person would have waited with her until the police came . . ." River sighed. "It's hard to believe that no one cared. I mean, sure, someone finally called the police, but they left her walking down a rather deserted road late at night."

"So did April have any responses to her podcast?" Tony asked.

"Yes, according to her notes, a few people contacted April. She'd asked her listeners to look for anyone with damage to the front of their cars around the time of the accident. There were some leads, but none of them panned out. The police followed up on all of them, but either the reasons for the damage were explained, or the drivers had solid alibis. In the end, the police had to move on. April refers to a Detective Porter here and underlined his name. He was the detective in charge of the case."

"This probably is a case of hit-and-run," Tony said, "but I'd like to know more about the ex-husband. Maybe he didn't answer his phone, but if she left him a message, he would have known where she was. Were there children? Any kind of custody battle? Could he have had a motive to kill his wife?"

River looked at her laptop where she had April's notes. "I don't think so. Not unless I missed something. And he had an alibi. He was out of town at the time." She looked over at Tony. "Hey, I told you about the notes she'd torn off and stuffed in a pocket of her notebook?"

Tony nodded.

"I looked them over, but not as closely as I should have. I see something I missed before. April made some additional notes about this case . . . and the ex-husband. She confirms that he had an alibi. But then she scribbled something. . . . It's hard to make out. I think it says that she spoke to an EMT who helped Cheryl at the scene and rode with her to the hospital. Before she died, she whispered something to him."

"And that was?"

River looked at him with a puzzled expression. "April's notes say that Cheryl said, 'Three little piggies.'"

"Did you say three little piggies?" Tony asked.

River nodded. "I may not be reading this correctly. Like I said, this note looks like it was written in haste."

"I would think someone's dying declaration wouldn't be part of a nursery rhyme." Tony frowned at her. "I'd really like to know more about this, wouldn't you?"

"Yeah. I guess we should talk to the police who investigated the accident."

"It just feels like there is more to this than meets the eye."

River stared at him for a moment before saying, "I'd have to agree."

TWENTY-FIVE

R eady for the next case?" River asked.

"Another cup of coffee first," Tony said. "You?"

"No, not yet. Do we still have any of those doughnuts we picked up on the way in?"

Tony smiled at her. "I've had two and you've had one. We bought half a dozen. What do you think?"

"I'm never sure. You've been known to scarf down four or five at a time." Tony's slim frame belied his love of food and how strong he really was. At least until he was shot. Since then, he'd experienced some weakness in his left arm and numbness in his feet. He hadn't mentioned it in several weeks, nor had he shown any signs of the aphasia he'd been left with. It had caused some memory loss. Nothing major, just forgetting the names of certain things. River wondered about it from time to time, but she didn't want to ask him. She was afraid that if she did, he'd think she was hinting that he wasn't at full strength. Tony was the best person she'd ever known, but he was proud in his own way. It wasn't conceit. It was that he didn't want her to think he was inadequate. Unable to keep her safe.

"Not this time," he said, grinning. "What would you like?"

"Any of the doughnuts with strawberry icing and sprinkles left?"

"Well, since you couldn't pay me to eat something like that, I'd say it's a safe bet there's at least one."

River laughed. "I know, if it's not chocolate, it's not worth your attention."

While Tony got up to get coffee and doughnuts, River flipped through her notes to the next case. "Ready?"

Tony sighed loudly. "Sure, but so far I haven't heard anything that makes me feel as if we've found something that would lead to Kevin's murderer."

"I know. We just have to eliminate everything we can and then look closely at the rest. I'm glad we're going to follow up on Cheryl Armitage's case.'"

"Yeah, me too." He put a pod in the coffeemaker and turned around to look at River. "Even if it isn't tied to April's disappearance or Kevin's murder, I think someone needs to listen to the last words of a dying woman and take them seriously."

"I agree, but you know, the EMT might have misunderstood her. It was a tense situation."

"You're right," Tony said. "Now I'm going to be running comparable phrases through my mind."

River grinned at him. "Maybe if you put our client's needs first, it will help redirect your slight obsession with characters from a children's fable."

"Okay, you win." Tony took a doughnut out of the box on the credenza where they kept the coffeemaker and brought it to River on a small paper plate. Then he went back to get his coffee and another doughnut.

River smiled to herself. Chocolate, of course. He also pulled out a plain doughnut and broke off a piece for Watson, who was now awake and watching his master with razor-sharp focus.

"Not too much, buddy," Tony said, carrying the piece over

to the excited dog. He knelt down and held it next to Watson's mouth. He took it gently from Tony's hand and then wolfed it down. Then he looked up with such obvious expectation that it made River laugh. "Not now, pal," Tony said. "Maybe later."

Once Tony was settled back at his desk, he nodded at her. "Whenever you're ready."

"Okay, next we have the Virtuous Volunteer. This was eight and a half years ago, in December. Shelly Evans was twenty-three when her body was found in a ravine near Kimmswick, Missouri, on a Sunday night a little after nine at night. A police officer who'd been called out to check on a domestic dispute stopped to investigate when he saw her abandoned car. It wasn't on a main road, it was found on one of these country roads, but still, he thought it was odd. Then he noticed her body in the ravine several yards away."

"Kimmswick's not too far from here, is it?" Tony asked.

"No. It's such a charming little town. Hard to think about anything awful happening there." Of course, it was hard to think about something awful happening anywhere, but Kimmswick was a favorite spot for many tourists as well as Missourians. Several different festivals were held there during the year, and it hosted a wonderful restaurant that was a favorite of River's. Her father had taken the family there many times, but since he'd left, she hadn't been back. Maybe someday soon. She looked back at her laptop. "It seems Shelly was very active in her church and volunteered with a food program in St. Louis, near where she lived in Kirkwood. A bloody rock was found next to Shelly's head. At first, the medical examiner said it could have been accidental . . . that she struck her head on the rock when she fell into the ravine. However, Shelly had MS and couldn't have made it from her car all the way to the edge of the ravine by herself, so it was ruled as *undetermined*. Although her purse was found in her car, her phone was gone. She'd tried to call her dad at one point, but by the time he answered, she'd hung up. Her car was searched, as was the area around it and where her body was found, but the phone wasn't located. It was never recovered."

"She was driving with MS?" Tony asked.

"Sure. Many people with MS drive. It's only when the disease is advanced that driving is restricted."

"And you know this how?"

River shrugged. "I had a friend in college whose mother had MS. She told me."

"Good memory."

"Hard to forget. At graduation, her mother had a hard time getting around. I'll never forget my friend's face. She was embarrassed." She shook her head, the memory still hard to bear. "Her mother knew it. The look on her face . . ." River cleared her throat. "Sorry. I told my friend what I thought about it. That ended our friendship, but I didn't care."

"Maybe you helped her," Tony said gently.

"I have no idea, but that's a nice thought." River forced herself to refocus on April's notes. "April received a lot of responses to this story, but it seems almost all of them were from people praising Shelly. It appears that she touched a lot of lives."

"No motive for the killing?"

"Doesn't seem to be. No one could figure out why she was killed. No one had motive."

"So, no tips at all?"

"Only one. A woman said she'd spotted Shelly's car on the side of the road around seven the night her body was found. She slowed down to see if someone was having car trouble, but when she realized no one was inside, she decided it had been abandoned and drove on. She didn't notice any other car nearby at that time."

"Shelly was probably already dead," Tony said.

"Yeah, most likely. The ME said she died instantly from her

head wound. Somehow, April was able to obtain information from the autopsy. Wonder where she got this?"

"Maybe Shelly's dad?"

"That would be my bet," River said. "We could think about contacting him, but even though it's been quite some time, I doubt he'd want to relive his daughter's death unless we were working her case."

"I agree," Tony said. "So, anything else interesting in the autopsy results?"

River read further through April's notes. "Not really. She wasn't sexually assaulted, thank God. There were other bruises, but that would be normal for someone tumbling down a ravine full of weeds and rocks. Stomach contents . . . nothing out of the ordinary. Toxicology came back clean except for the meds she took for her condition." She scrolled down and found another report from the police. "Her clothing was torn, dirty, bloody." She looked up at Tony. "April was convinced that this was murder because Shelly was found so far away from her car—and because her phone was gone. She says Shelly's father believed the same thing. If she'd tried to call him around the time she died, it means she obviously didn't forget it or leave it somewhere. He suggested that someone called Shelly and asked for help since she was always doing things for people. But without someone coming forward, there simply wasn't enough evidence for the police to do more than call it a suspicious death."

"Okay. Any solid reason for Shelly being at the location where she was found?"

"No," River said. "All they had was her father's hunch. She was supposed to be at church that night, in Kirkwood."

"What time did church start?"

"Again, you're reading April's mind. That's next. She checked and church started at seven."

"She obviously didn't call anyone to tell them she'd be late, or it would have been mentioned," Tony said.

"I'm sure you're right, but there's nothing here saying they heard from her. There's a number written here for the detective assigned to the case. Maybe we can see if he has any other information."

"Before we call, let's check to see if this case has been solved."

While Tony searched, River finished her doughnut. She got up, brewed another cup of black coffee, and snuck another piece of the plain doughnut to Watson, who wagged his tail so hard his bottom wiggled with happiness.

By the time she sat down, Tony was finished. "No, nothing about this case being solved. In fact, there was a story a little over a year ago in the St. Louis Post-Dispatch about the case. Sadly, Shelly's father, Brian Evans, passed away, never knowing for certain what happened to his daughter."

"That's awful."

"Yeah, it is," Tony agreed.

"I'm not seeing anything in April's notes that makes me think she was on to something that would have threatened the killer."

"This case doesn't make any sense," Tony said. "No motive. No sexual assault. What was Shelly doing on that road? How could she have made it to the ravine alone? And where was her phone?"

They looked at each other, but there simply wasn't an answer.

"Anything else?" Tony asked.

"No . . . wait a minute. That's odd. April drew a picture on the bottom of the page. A flower. Looks like a flowering dogwood."

"A flowering dogwood?" Tony frowned. "I thought you said this happened in December."

"It did. Dogwood trees and shrubs flower in April. The blooms are usually gone in May. April must have been doodling this for some reason." She noticed his expression. "We had flowering dogwood bushes in the backyard of the house I grew up in."

"Okay. So, is that it?"

River looked again. "Oh, here's something else about the flowers. Seems Shelly had a sprig of silk dogwood flowers in her hand when they found her. After that, April's notes end."

"That seems a little odd."

River shrugged. "Maybe, but it's hardly sinister. I don't see anything here that should have made April feel threatened in some way. If there was, wouldn't she have mentioned it in her notes?"

"I'd think so, but we can't be sure."

River looked at the next page. "There's only one more case here. Unless we can see something in it that makes us think it's what led to her abduction, we may be at a standstill. For Nathan's well-being, I hope that's not the case. Whoever killed Kevin could target him next. I don't want to see anything happen to him."

"I don't either," Tony said. "If it did, I think I'd blame myself for it."

"I'd blame both of us," River said, trying to swallow past the lump in her throat.

TWENTY-SIX

The last case is titled the case of the Disappeared Diabetic," River said, reading from her laptop.

"I'm really getting tired of these titles," Tony said, moaning dramatically. "We're never giving our cases titles."

"I think it could be interesting," River said, grinning. "Maybe we're working on the case of the Not-Present Podcaster."

"That's truly terrible. Now I know we'll never do that."

"You're just jealous that you didn't think of it sooner."

"Yeah, that's it," Tony said sarcastically.

"Anyway, back to April's notes. . . . Six years ago, a thirty-year-old man named Ted Piper from Imperial, Missouri . . ." She looked at Tony. "Another one from Missouri." Then she went back to her laptop. "Ted was walking along a road near his home." She paused and frowned. "This happened in December too. Anyway, he liked to walk every day for exercise. When he didn't return home, his mother went looking for him. She found his body a few yards from the road, his head bashed in with something. She found the fanny pack he always took with him that contained his insulin several feet from his body. He should have been wearing it." River stared at Tony.

Tony paused a moment before asking, "Did April make any notes about this case?"

"Yeah, quite a few."

"This sounds a lot like the previous case."

"Yeah, it does. Again, not many tips April took seriously. Of course, since Ted was walking in an isolated area, no one really saw him except for one man. This neighbor, a man named Charles Lee, said Ted walked past his house about an hour and a half before his mother found his body. Mr. Lee had just gotten home and was checking his mailbox. He said hello to Ted and asked him if it wasn't a little cold to be out walking. Ted just smiled and said he liked it that way. Mr. Lee said Ted seemed just fine. He went back into the house and didn't see Ted again. Had no idea anything was wrong until the police came by later, asking questions."

"So, whoever killed him wasn't seen by anyone else?"

"No, I guess not," River said slowly.

"Something bothering you?"

"April's drawn another picture here."

"Of?"

"A dogwood flower."

"You said this happened in Imperial?" Tony asked. "And Shelly was killed near Kimmswick?"

River nodded.

"I might be wrong, but I think the same police department oversees both towns."

River frowned. "And how would you know that? I'm the Missouri girl and I wasn't aware of it."

"I was researching something else and it came up. I remembered it for some reason." Tony started typing on his laptop. A few moments later, he said, "I was right." He picked up his phone. "I'm going to call them. All we can do is try."

"I'm not sure they'll tell you anything."

"These are cold cases. Since they're not active . . ." He held up his index finger, indicating that someone had answered the phone.

While Tony talked to whomever answered, River went back to April's notes. There was no indication why she'd drawn the flowers or that she'd followed up on anything concerning them. River looked through the pictures she had taken of the podcast pages before it disappeared. She couldn't help but notice that the hit-and-run case was a little similar to the two Tony was calling about. However, it didn't happen in December. In fact, it occurred in the summer. In June. She looked up the case online and saw that Detective Porter, the detective April had interviewed, had been quoted by a reporter about Cheryl's death. "This was a senseless act," he'd said. "If only someone had called us earlier, we could have prevented this. It makes all of us angry."

He sounded like someone who might be willing to help them. River looked up the substation's number where Detective Porter worked and called them. When she asked for him, she was told he'd retired. After explaining to the woman who'd answered the phone why she was calling, she took River's number and promised to call the detective.

"He was always bothered by this case," she said. "Told us that if anyone ever called about it or if we came up with a suspect, to let him know."

"Thank you, I really appreciate your help," River said.

"That was an awful thing. Still bothers me to think about it. We never could understand why so many people ignored that poor woman."

River thanked her again and disconnected the call just as Tony finished his.

"Did you get what you wanted?" she asked.

"Let's just say that the police were not forthcoming," he said. "I was informed that the case is closed, and they have no intention of talking about it."

"I guess we could try contacting the families," River said. "Of course, Shelly Evans's father is gone. We'd have to locate someone else."

"That wouldn't be hard. Just pull up the obituaries."

River told him about her call concerning Cheryl Armitage.

"Do you think he'll really reach out?"

"I don't see why not, although April hasn't drawn a dogwood flower by Cheryl's name. I also noticed that this happened in the summer and the others occurred in December. Could be coincidence—or it might just mean that we have serial killers on the brain."

"That's not impossible," Tony said. "I'll see if I can scare up some numbers for Ted's mother and Shelly's family. See if they know of any reason April would make a note about a dogwood flower."

"The dogwood symbolizes rebirth, resilience, and renewal," River said.

"My turn to ask once again how you know that."

River grinned at him. "I looked it up once."

Tony shook his head. "Isn't there some kind of religious meaning to it?"

"Yes. Some people believe the cross Jesus died on was made of dogwood. However, the dogwood isn't native to Israel, so that's not likely. I think the symbols can relate to faith though. But I wouldn't put too much stock into it."

"Well, it's possible someone did," Tony said."

"You really think we may have another serial killer on our hands?"

Tony shrugged. "Probably not. But I want to know why April drew a picture of the same flower in reference to both of these cases, don't you?"

"Maybe it was some kind of wish that both victims would be

reborn with God. A drawing of a flower is pretty flimsy." She sighed. "These deaths are so similar though. Both victims were found by the side of the road. Both had blunt force trauma to the head. No one saw anything. And . . ."

"They both had a physical condition. Shelly had MS and Ted was diabetic."

River shook her head. "I can't imagine that had anything to do with their murders. I mean, diabetes isn't something anyone would know about unless Ted told them. And Shelly probably wasn't showing clear signs of MS. I doubt most people would notice anything different about her. She may have been too weak to walk all the way to that ravine, but she was in the early stages." She met Tony's gaze. "You're thinking of that case we worked three or four years ago when we were still at the BAU."

"How could I not? The only time we ever profiled someone who killed people he decided were *damaged*."

River and Tony had seen some awful things when they worked for the FBI. This case was one of the worst. A man named Edwin Siebert killed people he thought were impaired—marred in some way. He believed he was ridding the world of human beings who were a drain on society.

"His abusive father was deaf," River said. "Siebert's hatred for him triggered his killing spree. Thankfully, the police were able to catch him. He'll never see the world outside of prison again. That was one time our profile was completely on target."

"One time?" Tony said. "We did pretty well. Of course, we can only profile with the evidence in front of us, but you and I had a pretty good track record."

"That's because we are the queen and king of profiling."

Tony laughed. "Okay, your highness, so what do we do next?"

"I think we need to work these three cases. Find out if there are any other connections besides the fact that they died near or on a road."

"Cheryl Armitage was drunk," Tony said. "Does she really tie into the other two cases?"

River thought for a moment. "Alcoholism is considered a disease. Could the killer have decided she was an alcoholic?"

"I don't know. I mean, being drunk once doesn't mean she had an ongoing problem. If she did, the killer would have to be someone who knew her."

Tony and River just looked at each other. Had they just uncovered another serial killer from April's cold cases? Could he be aware that they were investigating April's cases? Was this the person who killed Kevin Bittner? The possibility sent a chill up River's back.

TWENTY-SEVEN

While Tony tried to find Shelly Evans's family and a number for Ted Piper's mother, River's phone rang. Mrs. Weyland. "Hello?" she said after accepting the call.

"Hi, honey. I'm sorry to bother you at work, but I thought you'd want to know."

"Know what?"

The elderly caregiver hesitated a moment. "Your brother called. Instead of just comin' by, they asked if they could have dinner here tomorrow night. I told them it was okay with me, but I'd have to see how you felt about it."

"That's fine. Eating supper might actually help to ease some of the awkwardness," River said. "Are you sure this is all right with you? I can help with dinner."

"I don't mind cookin', honey. I just wish I could be certain how your mother is going to take this. She's . . . she's a little flustered today."

"What do you mean by *flustered*?"

"Confused. When I told her your father was comin' tomorrow she got quite upset. Angry. It was as if he'd just left. I finally got her calmed down, but now I'm a little worried."

174

River took a deep breath to calm herself. "You said that in the natural course of things, she won't get better, Mrs. Weyland. I agree that this may be the only chance she'll have to get things straightened out with my father. I think forgiveness could be very healing . . . for all of us."

"All right, honey. I'm gonna call 'em back and tell 'em to come. We're gonna need some things from the store. If you'll watch your mama in the mornin', I'll fetch what we need."

"Sounds good. Let's just pray that dinner will go well. All we can do is give it to God."

"You're right. Thanks. And sorry to bother you. I know you're probably busy. We'll see you tonight."

River said goodbye and hung up. She truly hoped her father and mother would finally find some peace, but the truth was, she really wasn't that concerned about how her father would react if her mother was antagonistic toward him. He should have been here. He was the one who should be taking care of his wife. Not River. And not Mrs. Weyland. River's only real concern was Rose. She planned to do everything she could to help her mother through this. She didn't want to see her upset or humiliated. Since it appeared that all the details were worked out, River decided not to call her brother. There wasn't really much point. When she saw Dan, she'd do her best to let him know she wasn't angry with him. Hopefully, they'd also find a way to move on and mend the past.

River forced her thoughts back to the case she and Tony were working. The woman she'd spoken to at the police department had said that the Cheryl Armitage case had always bothered Detective Porter. The chance that Cheryl's death was related to Shelly's and Ted's murders was a long shot. River certainly didn't want Detective Porter to get his hopes up, but if there was any chance that all three were killed by the same person, she and Tony had to follow up.

The phone rang and River answered.

A man with a gruff voice asked for her.

"This is she. It this Detective Porter?"

"Yes, but I'm really not Detective Porter anymore," he said. "Most people just call me Vincent. Maureen from the station said you have information about a case from a few years back."

"Yes, sir," River said. "I'm a private investigator in St. Louis. My partner and I were hired to find someone. A woman with a cold case podcast."

"April Bailey?" he said. "Yeah, she contacted me a while back. Wanted to see if she could help us find the person who ran down and killed a woman. I haven't heard from her for quite some time, though. I don't believe she was ever able to uncover anything we hadn't already investigated."

"Unfortunately, she's missing, sir."

"Vincent, please. And that's terrible. She was a sweet gal. If I can do anything to help you, I'm happy to do it."

"Thank you, Vincent," River said. "We're just going through her cold cases, trying to find out if anyone connected to one of them might have had something to do with her disappearance."

"You mean, maybe she got a little too close to the truth?"

"Yes. I was told this case she was working on is important to you. I know it's been a long time, but do you mind if I ask you a few questions?"

"I'm sorry, but I don't know you, ma'am. If you'd like to meet me for a cup of coffee, I'd be happy to talk to you in person. I worked for the police department for a long time. I can tell a lot about people when we're face-to-face. A lot less so on the phone."

Since Tony wouldn't let her out of his sight, River only had one option. "Would you be willing to come to our office?"

"I can do that. Give me your address."

Once River had given him their location, he told her he'd be there shortly. She hung up and waited for Tony to get off the phone. When he finally hung up, she told him that the retired detective was on his way to see them.

"I just got off the phone with Ted's mother. She invited me to visit her. She doesn't get out much. I think she's disabled. I'll tell her I can't come today. I'll wait until we can go together."

River sighed. "Tony, I'll be fine. I'll keep the office locked except when I'm with Detective Porter."

Tony hesitated a moment before saying, "I guess that would be all right. Mrs. Piper lives near Imperial, so I won't be gone long."

"Sounds good. I hope we learn something helpful from these people."

Tony stood up and grabbed his coat. "Call me if you need me." He smiled at her. "And by the way, I'm asking the security guard to check on you every thirty minutes."

She frowned at him. "I told you I'll be all right."

"I know. But I'm overprotective. Just deal with it."

River shook her head. "You're a dork."

"I know."

After he left, River made additional notes about April's various cases, trying to find something that made sense to her. Many times, writing things out helped her to think. She was so focused that she didn't notice anyone had opened the office door until she heard someone call her name. She realized she'd forgotten to lock the door. Standing in the office was an older man, tall with salt and pepper hair in what used to be called a butch cut. He had steel gray eyes that showed intelligence. He wasn't what she was expecting.

"You're Vincent?" she asked.

"Yes, ma'am."

"If I'm going to call you Vincent, you need to call me River," she said.

Vincent grinned. "You gotta deal. Mind if I sit?"

177

River nodded, and Vincent took a seat in one of the chairs in front of her desk.

"Coffee?" River asked.

"Thanks, but no. My blood pressure is a little high. Caffeine doesn't help." He leaned back in the chair. "So, Miss Bailey is missing? I hated to hear that. I couldn't help her, but I appreciated her commitment to finding out what happened to Cheryl Armitage. That was a terrible situation. I sure didn't like retiring before we found out who killed her."

"You think she was hit on purpose?" River asked.

"I don't know. It could have been an accident, but even if it were, the person who hit her should have fessed up. And she certainly shouldn't have been left alone in the road to die. If someone had called 911, she might have lived." He sighed. "I really don't know any more than I did back then. We looked everywhere for the car that hit her. Found some with damage, but none of them were the right one. Either the driver had an alibi, or the blood didn't match hers. Unfortunately, most of the cars around here with blood and hair come from cars that ran into deer. I even hit one that night, on the way to the scene. It's a sad fact in Missouri. A lot of wildlife and too many vehicles."

"So, you never got a tip that made you wonder?" River asked.

"Well, there was one. A woman phoned the station about six months ago—I was already retired—but they called me about it. Said she believed Cheryl's ex-husband was the one who killed her. He was dating this woman when the accident happened, and he came home with damage to his front end. She also said he got it fixed right away and then paid someone to give him an alibi."

"My partner and I were wondering about the ex-husband, but according to my notes, he had an alibi."

"Yeah, he did," Vincent said. "But he was the only one with any motive. And his alibi was only backed up by one person."

"Can you tell me how to find him?"

"I could, but you'd have to go to the cemetery. He died about ten months ago. Cancer."

Well, so much for that idea. "So do you believe he did it?"

"That's just the thing. I don't know. I'd love to see this case solved, but I could never prove that his alibi was false. Or that the second wife, the woman who called, wasn't saying what she did because she was angry with him. Seems their marriage was breaking up too. But even after Tom died, his boss stuck to his claim that he was working out of town at the time Cheryl was killed."

"Where did he work?" River asked.

"He worked for a building maintenance company. Cleaned offices at night."

"Kind of hard to be certain he was at work then, right?"

"True," Vincent said. "Most of the buildings he cleaned had security systems. It's not impossible to leave a building if the alarm is turned off and come back in later, but here's the reason we couldn't make a case. Why would he leave work, drive twenty miles away, run down his ex-wife who he had no way of knowing would be drunk and out on the road that night, and then hightail it back to work and enter a building, just hoping no one would see him? And then keep his messed-up truck with him until he drove home the next morning . . . in daylight when everyone could see the damage? It's not entirely impossible, but the idea has too many holes in it. We just couldn't prove anything."

"I understand."

"I wish I could help you," Vincent said, "but Tom couldn't have taken April. He was dead when she went missing. I'm not saying he didn't kill Cheryl, but unless you find new evidence, this case is pretty much a dead end."

"Just two more quick questions?"

"Sure," Vincent said. "Like I said, I'm retired. I have all the time in the world."

"I read that before she died, Cheryl whispered the phrase *three little piggies* to the EMT who was with her. Do you have any idea why she would say that?"

"No, we couldn't connect that to anything. In the end, we decided she was probably hallucinating. She had three times the legal limit of alcohol in her system."

"This may sound really odd, but does the dogwood flower have anything to do with this case? I ask because it might be connected to two other deaths, both victims found near the side of the road."

Vincent frowned. "No, I'm sorry. Nothing like that ever came up. No flowers were found on Ms. Armitage." He shrugged. "I'm afraid this is a case that will never be solved. I really wanted to close it before I die. It's a sad thing."

"Yes, it is. I appreciate your time."

Vincent stood. "Listen, if you run across anything that might shine a light on this case, will you contact me again?"

"I absolutely will. It may not seem like you've helped us, but you have. We obviously need to move on to something else. Thank you, Vincent."

"You're very welcome, River. And I hope you find April. I'd like to know about that too, if you don't mind."

"I'll make sure to call you if that happens. Thank you again." She held out her hand and he shook it.

After he left, she locked the door. Then she wrote down the details of their conversation. She was disappointed. Talking to Vincent hadn't helped at all. She wondered how Tony was doing. So far, they didn't seem to be making much progress.

The doorknob rattled. River looked up and saw the security guard. She got up and opened the door. "Just making sure you're okay," he said.

River smiled at him. "I'm fine. Sorry to put you out."

"This is probably the most interesting thing that's happened today," he said. "Mr. St. Clair must care a lot about you."

"Maybe a little too much."

"Not sure anyone can care about you too much." He nodded at her. "I'll be back in a while."

After he left, she locked the door again and went back to her notes. But the guard's words echoed in her mind. *Not sure anyone can care about you too much.* Was that true? Because she wasn't sure anyone could possibly care more about Tony than she did right now. Her feelings for him were so strong that sometimes she felt as if she could barely breathe.

TWENTY-EIGHT

She was so cold. Audrey had told her not to move until she came back for her, but that had been hours ago. She gazed around the room. Where was she? Even though she hadn't received the last shot, the effects of all the others were still messing with her mind. They'd gone out the back door and then walked to this place. Was it a storage shed? Audrey said she'd drive by and get her when she could. Should she leave? Try to find help? Or just wait the way Audrey had instructed? What if she'd been caught? If so, they'd soon be looking for her, too. She grabbed the edge of a nearby storage shelf and pulled herself up. Immediately, the room began to swim. She used her other hand to steady herself, praying that the world would stop spinning. Finally, when she felt steadier, she gazed around her. She could see the door they'd come through. She'd just decided to open it, so she could figure out where she was, when the doorknob began to turn. Panic set in and she tried to run, but she was too unsteady on her feet, and she fell to the hard floor. Pain exploded in her wrist, and she yelped. She attempted to pull herself along the floor using her other hand, but she couldn't move quickly enough to hide. When someone put their hands on her, she cried out.

"Hush, it's me. Be quiet or someone might hear you. My car's outside. We need to leave before they realize you're gone. I fixed your bed to make it look like you're in it, and I marked your chart as if I'd given you your meds. But the next shift nurse will be checking on you before long. We don't have much time."

Although she tried to understand what Audrey was trying to tell her, nothing made much sense except that she was out of the hospital, and they were leaving. That was all that mattered.

Audrey helped her up, and she leaned on the kind nurse as they walked out of the building and hurried to Audrey's car. When she got inside, the warm air surrounded her like a hug. She stared out the window. She'd dreamt about leaving before, only to be disappointed when she woke up and realized it was a dream. She began to cry and pray that this was real. That she really was on her way to freedom.

"Don't cry," Audrey said gently. "We'll make it. I can't take you to my place. They'll look there. We're going to a motel for a while. You need to get all that stuff out of your system. We also need to get you cleaned up. I brought some clothes that should fit you."

It was then that she looked down and realized she was only wearing a hospital gown and the coat Audrey had given her. Her feet were still in those weird yellow booties the hospital kept on her feet. She couldn't remember the last time she'd worn real shoes, and she wanted to. More than anything.

"I hope you didn't break your wrist," Audrey said. "We'll stop at a drug store and get you something to support it. I can't give you anything stronger than acetaminophen. I hope it will control your pain."

She smiled and laid her head back on the seat. "I don't care about that. I'm free. I'm finally free." After that, she allowed herself to drift off, feeling warm, relaxed, and happier than she'd been in a very long time.

TED'S MOTHER WAS A FRAIL WOMAN who looked beaten down by life. Although she was moving slowly around her kitchen, a wheelchair sat in the corner. Besides dealing with physical issues, it was obvious that her son's death had affected her greatly. Her small house showed neglect, as did she. It seemed as if she'd just stopped caring. Tony felt great empathy for her.

"Thank you for seeing me," Tony told her after sitting down at her kitchen table.

Mrs. Piper carried a half-full carafe of coffee over to the table, holding onto the chairs with her other hand. She shakily poured the hot liquid into a cup faded by age. Although Tony didn't want coffee, he thanked her. She put the carafe back on the old coffeemaker and then took the seat next to him.

"You're welcome," she said. "No one has asked about Ted for a while. I'm happy someone still cares about what happened to him."

"My partner and I are trying to locate a missing woman who investigated cold cases. Your son's case was one of them."

"You think this woman's disappearance has something to do with my Ted's death?"

"I don't know," Tony said. "Right now, we're looking at every case she was investigating to see if one of them might be connected." He took a sip of coffee, then said, "I know this may seem like an odd question, but did the police find any flowers at the scene?"

Mrs. Piper frowned at him. "What do you mean?"

"We've found a couple of other deaths where flowers were left behind," Tony said. When he originally decided to talk to Ted's mother, his main goal was to get information. But he and River were both learning that writing profiles inside the confines of the FBI was very different from looking into the eyes of those affected by the criminals they profiled. Mrs. Piper was in pain, and at that moment, Tony was second-guessing his decision to resurrect her anguish. The only reason he was here was because of some old dogwood flowers that may have nothing to do with April's disappearance or Ted's death. He was getting ready to apologize for taking her time and leave when she grabbed his arm. She peered into Tony's eyes, a tear running down her cheek.

"A lady called me once about those flowers," she said, her voice trembling. "It was a long time ago. I think her name was . . . April. I told her the police said they didn't have anything to do with my Ted. Now you're asking about them. Are you saying they meant something after all?"

"I can't be sure, Mrs. Piper," Tony said. "Like I said, my partner and I are just looking into what happened. I . . . I don't suppose you saw the flowers?"

Mrs. Piper nodded. "I went to the spot where he died. They were lying on the ground where Teddy was found. White flowers. Silk. I think they're called dogwood flowers."

A chill ran down Tony's spine and it wasn't because Mrs. Piper's house was cold. The deaths were connected. He and River may have just uncovered a serial killer.

TONY RUSHED BACK TO THE OFFICE and hurried up the stairs. When he unlocked the office door and stepped inside, River looked up at him and frowned.

"You look like the cat that swallowed the canary," she said.

"First of all, that phrase is supposed to denote guilt," he said. "I don't feel guilty. Secondly, the last time I heard someone say that, it was my grandmother.

"Okay, okay," she said, rolling her eyes. "So, why do you look the way you do?"

Tony sat down and quickly told her what he'd learned from Mrs. Piper.

"So, Shelly and Ted's deaths might actually be connected?" River said. "Why didn't the police suspect it?"

Tony sat down at his desk. "As far as Ted's mother knows, the flowers weren't even entered into the police report. The police decided they were already there and had nothing to do with Ted's death. Seems April contacted Mrs. Piper before she disappeared and asked about the flowers. She told her exactly what she told me. That she saw the flowers herself after Ted's body was removed."

"Okay. The police also didn't seem to think it was important that Shelly had flowers in her hand when they found her body," River said.

Tony could hear the frustration in her voice, and he shared it. "After I talked to Mrs. Piper, I found a number for Shelly's aunt and called her. She said that Shelly's father told the police that his daughter loved flowers and probably just had them with her when she fell. I know that doesn't make a lot of sense, but I guess he was in a lot of shock when Shelly died. She was his only child, and they were very close. Seems like the police never followed up on the flowers."

"They need to reopen these cases," River said.

"The way they treated me when I talked to them, we're going to need some help," Tony said with a sigh.

Before he could say anything else, their office door opened, and Arnie walked in.

"Just the man we need to talk to," Tony said, surprised to see him. "What are you doing here?"

"I'm here for a couple of reasons." Arnie sat down in the chair near Tony's desk. "First of all, that reporter? Brent Wilkins? He was taken in for questioning a little while ago in connection to the deaths of those young people you were concerned about. He hasn't confessed, but officers found some interesting things in his apartment. Could be souvenirs from the crime scenes. From what I was told, he seems pretty shaken up—and very guilty."

Tony looked at River and smiled. "Great job," he said. "I know you went on instinct, but you were right. I'm proud of you."

"Thanks, but we both profiled him. And April provided the real clues." She frowned at Arnie. "Any disabilities? We profiled him as someone who might feel uncomfortable around people."

"The officers said he had trouble talking to them. He's a stutterer. Seems he writes his articles from his apartment. Doesn't get out much. I'm not saying he's their man, but if I had to bet my pension on it, I'd say he did it."

Tony shook his head. "That's amazing."

"Yes, it is. Thank you both for your help. Now," Arnie continued, "I know you said you'd come to get the thing we talked about, but I decided to bring it to you." He frowned at River. "You sure about this?" He took a small metal box out of his coat pocket and put it on Tony's desk.

"I am," she said. "It's the only way."

"Before we get into that," Tony said, "we have something else to discuss with you. In going through April's cases, we may have uncovered a serial killer."

Arnie's eyebrows shot up. "Another one? Let me get this straight. April Bailey's information has led to solving several cold cases—and now may uncover another serial killer? If this young woman is found alive, I want to talk to her. She needs to come to work for me."

River grinned. "I was thinking she should come to work for *us*."

Arnie grunted. "You know as well as I do that there are more serial killers out there than the public knows about. Too many of them are getting away with it. A recent study said that there are over two thousand serial killers active right now. Killers who haven't been caught—and might not be. So any time we take one down, I'm relieved. Even if it's only a drop in the bucket." He sat down next to Tony's desk. "So, tell me about this one."

As Tony began to go over the flowers found at both murders, Arnie's face turned pale. "Are you okay?" he asked his friend.

"Not really. Recently, one of my detectives pointed out something about silk dogwood flowers discovered near a couple of bodies. One was in an apartment. We assumed they were some kind of decoration. There were a lot of broken items in the room, including a vase that was full of fresh flowers. The detectives in charge assumed the dogwood flowers were added to the vase to make the arrangement look larger."

"The two deaths April was investigating happened outside," Tony said. "Doesn't mean they're not connected, but as you know, serial killers are usually driven to follow established patterns. Even to the point of obsession."

"But what if our killer's signature is leaving the flowers at a crime scene—not *where* he leaves the bodies?" River interjected.

Tony nodded. "We've seen that before." He frowned at Arnie. "You mentioned a couple of bodies?"

"One was recent," Arnie said. "Very recent. A body found not far from here. She was in an alley, behind a small mall. Head bashed in. Our Crime Analysis Unit processed the items discovered at the scene. One thing they found was a sprig of white silk flowers. I might be wrong, but I have a strong feeling they were probably dogwood. Can you compile your information and email it here?" He picked up a pad of paper from Tony's desk. "She's the lead detective on the case. Before you send it, I'll let her know it's coming."

"Sure," Tony said. "By the way, were either of these victims disabled or sick?"

Arnie's eyebrows knit together. "I don't think so. I don't remember anything like that. Why?"

"Shelly Evans had MS, and Ted Piper was diabetic. Could be a coincidence, but we wondered about it."

"I'll check, but I don't think so. Were these physical problems readily apparent?"

"You mean would the killer have noticed it by just observing them?" Tony asked. "No, I don't believe so."

"Then I'd mark that down to coincidence, but I'll still run it by my detective. Sometimes catching these guys is like putting together a puzzle. You're never sure what piece goes where."

"You're right," Tony agreed. "Will you keep us in the loop? This might be the person who's been threatening us and Nathan—and who may have killed Kevin Bittner."

"Sure, not a problem." Arnie looked back and forth between them. "I'm still hoping for a confession from your Casanova guy. I'll keep you updated." He smiled at them. "So do you two plan to solve all of April's cases?"

Tony shrugged. "That would be nice, but it's probably unrealistic. Right now, we're trying to focus on our client, Nathan Hearne. He wants to know what happened to April. If this guy is responsible for these other murders, he may be the one trying to keep us from looking too closely at her cases. Which is good news and bad news."

"What do you mean?" Arnie asked.

"The good news is that we can give you a profile that should help you find him. The bad news is that if he's the one who took April, we can be almost certain that she's dead."

TWENTY-NINE

River had to agree with Tony, but she wished it could be different for Nathan's sake.

"Before I leave," Arnie said, "I want to talk to you about this." He tapped the box.

"I'm not crazy about this plan either," Tony said. "But we agreed that this was our best option. We have to make certain this ends now. Without any evidence, I can't come up with a better plan. This may be our only way. At least now we have control, and we're better off than we were just waiting around for something terrible to happen."

"I hate to agree, but I do. I just wanted to check with you one more time."

"I'm convinced it will work," River said. "I'm confident everything will work out just the way we planned it."

"All right," Arnie said. "But be careful and stick to our arrangement."

"Trust me, we will," Tony said.

After promising Arnie they'd send him a profile and that they'd also email him everything they had on Shelly and Ted, Arnie left to go back to the station.

He'd only been gone a few minutes when someone else opened the door. A young woman stuck her head inside and asked, "Is River Ryland here?"

"I'm River."

The woman came inside holding a vase full of white lilies and baby's breath. She set it down on River's desk and smiled. "Have a good day," she said. Then she left.

"What in the world?" River said. She stood up and removed the card from the flower arrangement. When she read it, she looked over at Tony. "Can you guess who this is from?"

"Not a clue. It wasn't me." River walked over and handed him the card. Tony's face flushed and he looked angry. "Sorry for your upcoming loss?" he read. "This makes me furious."

"I know, but he's just reminding us he's around." River smiled at him. "I'm not afraid of him anymore, Tony. God is teaching me that no matter what, I can rest in Him. I've been memorizing Psalm 91. It ends with this: 'Because he has set his love upon Me, therefore I will deliver him; I will set him on high, because he has known My name. He shall call upon Me, and I will answer him; I will be with him in trouble; I will deliver him and honor him. With lone life I will satisfy him, and show him My salvation.'" She put her hand on Tony's arm. "This guy may think my life is in his hands, but it isn't. I believe God will deliver me. There are things I want to do. I need to be here for my mother . . . and you. I'm not worried. The only person who should be afraid is the Strangler's accomplice. He's almost done."

Tony nodded. "I'm so proud of you," he said, his voice husky. "You've changed so much. Now you're the one reminding me that I need to trust God."

"You showed me how."

Tony smiled at her. "Should I call the flower shop? See what they can tell us?"

"No. We can do it later if we need to. Besides, you know as well as I do that he paid cash, and he went to a shop without cameras. He's too smart to have done anything else."

"All right. We'll let the police follow up if they need to."

"Let's get back to work," River said, walking back to her desk.

"I'll start working on that profile," Tony said. "I think we agree that this is an organized killer. White, probably in his late twenties or early thirties since he has the strength to overpower all of his victims. I'm going to say he probably dresses well and has a good job. He's reasonably attractive since he was able to get close to all the victims. He doesn't feel ashamed of his looks. He kills mostly women but will kill a man if he feels drawn to do it. I think Ted was convenient. He was walking along a rather isolated road, and the killer saw an opportunity."

River looked up from what she was doing. Her training was always there, always working. Always whispering in her ear. There was really no way to turn it off. "So, his compulsion isn't sexually based, which is unusual. He's obsessed with something else. He entered an apartment to kill." She met Tony's gaze. "That's the murder the police need to focus on. The one that will lead police to the killer. I think that victim was someone he knew. He departed from his usual MO to murder her."

"I agree," Tony said. "He's clearly a psychopath. Has no compassion. Hasn't shown any remorse toward his victims."

"His comfort zone is rather extensive," River added. "My guess is that he has some kind of job that causes him to travel in Missouri, but not too far from St. Louis. I'd say he used his job to get into the apartment to kill the woman Arnie told us about, but I think he's too sophisticated to wear a uniform. I think he'd feel it's below him."

Tony's eyes widened. "Kenneth Bianchi and Angelo Buono. They posed as off-duty police officers. That would fit this guy's MO."

"It would also explain how he could get close to people," River said. "And why Shelly pulled off to the side of the road."

She and Tony stared at each other for a few seconds before River said, "I'm sure Arnie knows this is just guesswork, but I think it could be pretty accurate. But what about the flowers? We don't see them as a sign of remorse?"

"No, not in this situation. Do you?"

River shook her head. "I don't think so. The only person holding the flowers was Shelly. Ted was lying on top of them, and they were on the floor of the other woman's apartment. Lying in an alley next to another body. I think they mean something different."

"Then could Shelly be the murder that means the most?"

River sighed and leaned back in her chair. "I'm not certain, but I think the police should look at Shelly and the woman in the apartment first." She turned her head to look at Tony. "Why was the apartment such a mess? Did he tear it up out of anger, or did she fight back?"

"Hard to say, but my guess would be that she fought back. I think he enjoys the killing. If he goes to all the trouble to get close to them, I'm thinking he doesn't want to fight them. He just wants them to die. I doubt that he'll try killing inside anymore. It doesn't fit with his personality."

"Except that there might be other victims we don't know about." River straightened up. "This is what makes profiling so complicated. We can only work with what we have. So now, back to the flowers. What do they mean?"

"Okay, so we don't believe they're given out of remorse since we don't see any of the other usual signs. They must have something to do with what incited his urge to kill. Maybe a mother figure?"

"Maybe his mother was religious?"

Tony crossed his hands behind his head. "I don't know. That doesn't feel right. Why not leave a Bible verse or a crucifix? Maybe the mother loved dogwood flowers?"

"Yeah, maybe," River said. "It means something, but we don't have enough information to be certain why it's important to him. All we know is that he always leaves a sprig of silk dogwood flowers behind when he kills." She frowned and tapped her fingers on her desk, trying to pull information from her years of training. "Okay, let's brainstorm for a moment. Dogwood trees bloom in the spring and summer. They take five to seven years to bloom. There are several colors, including red, pink, and what our guy chose—white. Like I said earlier, the flower symbolizes quite a few things. Life, rebirth, joy, beauty, purity, innocence, resilience, strength, beauty, faithfulness, and hope." She frowned. "They seem to be his signature. Or part of it anyway. But what's his trigger?"

"I don't know. So far, almost everyone we know about was killed in the winter." Tony shook his head. "Kind of reminds me of our snowman killer."

"I can't believe we could encounter two killers in a row who only kill in winter," River said.

"I don't think we can assume anything about that since we don't know how many victims there actually are. It's entirely possible he doesn't stick to winter. In fact, maybe he only uses the silk flowers in winter. He might use the real thing in the spring and early summer."

"That's true," River said slowly. "So, let's take out the winter theme since we can't be certain. Of all the symbolism associated with the dogwood, I think rebirth and purity are the most powerful. So, is he trying to make certain people are reborn? Or does this relate to his childhood in some way? We know that most serial killers had messed up childhoods."

"I agree that he's trying to say something with the dogwood." Tony sighed. "Didn't we write a profile a few years ago where the killer left flowers behind? What was that?"

River thought for a moment. "You're right," she said as soon as she remembered what Tony referred to. "It was the guy who left lilies." Her gaze drifted to the arrangement of lilies on her desk. She got up, got a napkin from the credenza, and moved the flowers over to a spot on the floor next to the printer. She was pretty sure the only fingerprints that would be found on the vase belonged to the people who worked for the flower shop. "Sorry," she told Tony, "but I don't want to look at them."

"I understand," he said. "And I agree."

"Okay, back to the guy who left lilies. We thought they symbolized death, but we found out later that his abusive mother's name was Lily."

Tony burst out laughing. "I'm sorry. I know this isn't funny, but are you saying that this killer's mother's name is Dogwood?"

"No. . . . You're ridiculous, you know that?"

"Well, at least I'm not saying some woman's name is Dogwood."

"Anyway . . ." River tried to ignore him and concentrate on the flowers. "I think all we can say at this point is that the dogwood tree has something to do with his past and leave it at that."

"There are so many possibilities. Maybe his parents made whips out of the tree branches. Maybe his mother grew dogwood trees and spent more time with them than she did with him." He shrugged. "We'll just tell Arnie to look for a connection. If there was just one other sign that this killer feels remorse, I'd go with that. But he leaves the body on display, which means he's proud of what he's done. The eyes are open. The hands not crossed. I just can't make that jump."

"I agree," River said. "So, you'll write that up and send it to Arnie while I send our information on Ted and Shelly to the detective?"

Tony nodded. "I'm working on it now."

River started compiling photos of April's podcast episodes with her notes about Ted and Shelly. Then she sent everything to the detective in charge while Tony concentrated on the profile for Arnie. River didn't like putting together a profile so quickly. It made her feel as if they were missing something, but Arnie needed it now, so there wasn't much they could do about it. She kept running the flower connection through her mind. She knew she should let go of it, but it wasn't easy. Was the killer getting ready to strike again? It would take some effort, but she had to put that case on the back burner and concentrate on finding out what happened to April. Was it the same person who killed Kevin and threatened Nathan? Or were they dealing with someone else? They had to discover the truth quickly. Before someone else paid with their lives.

THIRTY

The motel room was pretty basic, but at least it seemed clean. Audrey had wrapped her wrist, so it was feeling better. The pills she took weren't strong, but they helped. She'd slept for quite a while. When she woke up, Audrey smiled at her.

"I picked up some food while you were sleeping. Are you hungry?"

She nodded. She still felt a little groggy, but she knew she needed to eat. Audrey put some food on a paper plate and stuck it into the microwave in the small kitchen. Then she opened the refrigerator and took out a bottle of water, which she put on the nightstand next to the bed.

"Drink something," Audrey said.

She sat up in the bed and swung her legs over the side. Then she reached over, took the cap off the bottle, and put it to her lips, which were dry and cracked. The cold water tasted so good. The water at the hospital was always lukewarm. She hated lukewarm water. She drank almost the entire bottle before Audrey gently took it from her.

"Slow down, honey. I don't want you to make yourself sick." She put the bottle down and went over to the microwave when it dinged. "I warmed this up for you. Just a hamburger and fries, but I think you'll like it. It's pretty good."

"Could anyone know we're here?" she asked.

"I don't think so." Audrey sighed. "We'll only be able to stay here for a short time."

She unwrapped the cheeseburger and took a small bite. This was the first cheeseburger she'd had in a long, long time. It was so good. For some reason she wanted to cry. It wasn't because of the burger, it was because her world was beginning to feel normal again. As if someone had opened the door to her cage and allowed her to finally come out. The truth was, she really had been a prisoner. Trapped and unable to escape. Until today. She'd just taken a second bite when there was a loud knock on the door. She dropped the burger onto her lap, and it fell to the floor. Audrey got up and went to the window, pulling the curtain back a bit. She looked out and then turned around, a look of horror on her face.

"I don't recognize these men," she whispered. "Don't say anything. We have to be quiet. Don't let them know we're here."

She started to cry. Surely this couldn't be happening. She noticed a notepad and a pen on the nightstand. She grabbed it and started writing out a message. Before she could finish it, the pen ran out of ink. She quickly looked for another one, but there weren't any. She tore the top piece of paper off and put it under her pillow, out of sight. Suddenly, the knocking stopped. Audrey looked out the window again.

"They're gone," she said. "We need to leave, right now." Audrey grabbed her tote bag and put the food in it. Then she grabbed some bottles of water and shoved them in as well. "Get up," she said, her voice high and shaky. "Can you walk?"

Before she could say yes, someone began yelling outside the door. Audrey turned toward her and smiled sadly. "They must have followed us. I'm sorry. Whatever happens, I want you to promise me that you won't give up. I sent a letter to Nathan letting him know you're alive. I couldn't risk telling him where you were. If the authorities started snooping around before I could get you to safety, we would both be in danger. But you need to know that someone is looking for you, okay?"

As the tears ran down her face, she nodded. "Thank you. Thank you so much," she said. Her voice was hoarse from not talking for so long. Could Audrey understand her?

Someone hit the door hard, and it broke open. Two men walked into the room and smiled at her. She tried to scream but she couldn't. One of them walked over to her, reached into his pocket, and took out a syringe.

She yelled, "No!" as loudly as she could, but it was nothing more than a quiet croak. Even if there were people outside, they couldn't possibly have heard her.

She felt the needle in her neck and almost immediately the room began to grow dark. She looked for Audrey, but the other man had her and was leading her from the room.

Then the familiar darkness overcame her.

WHILE TONY WAS PICKING UP LUNCH, River decided to do some research on Jeffrey Bailey. He was clearly a devoted father, but they didn't know much else about him. Besides checking out his job as an investment banker, she also pulled up articles about April's mother. What she discovered surprised her. By the time Tony got back, she was waiting for him.

"Hey, I found something. Maybe it doesn't mean anything, but we need to talk about it."

"Sure, but let me put this down first," he replied. Tony put one sack on his desk and handed the second one to River. "What do you want to drink?"

"Water's fine."

Tony grabbed two bottles of water from the mini-fridge and handed one to River. Then he sat down. As River was reaching into her bag, she looked down to see Watson staring up at her. He looked like he was smiling.

"Tell him to lay down," Tony said firmly.

"Oh, Tony. I can't do that. Can't he have a couple of french fries?"

Tony shook his head. "You're spoiling him, but I guess it's okay."

"Good. Thanks." She took out one of her fries and handed it to the happy little dog. His tail thumped loudly against the floor.

River reached into her bag and pulled out her BBQ sandwich. It smelled so good. She smiled at Tony. "Once the Strangler's partner is behind bars, I think I'm going to miss this. You picking up my lunch and bringing it to me."

"I doubt that," Tony said. "My guess is that you'll feel much better not having me hanging around all the time."

"No," River said. "I'll be happy to get out more, but I enjoy spending time with you."

Tony smiled at her. "I like spending time with you too. Now, what is it you couldn't wait to tell me?"

River had to stop and think for a moment. What was it? "Oh, yeah. I was doing some research on Jeffrey Bailey. We both know that most murders are committed by friends or family members of the victims."

After eating a couple of fries, Tony nodded. "Sure. Didn't get that kind of vibe from Jeffrey though, did you?"

"When did we start going by vibes?"

"Okay, okay," Tony said. "I stand corrected."

"What with Kevin's murder, worrying about Nathan, and my dad coming to visit tomorrow, it's like my brain has been going several different directions at once. We should have talked about him sooner."

"He didn't have to approach us," Tony said. "If he had anything to do with April's disappearance, why would he come here?"

"To make us suspicious of Nathan?"

Tony frowned. "What did you find that brought this up?"

"Did you know that Jeffrey isn't April's biological father? He adopted her after he married her mother. She was seven."

"That doesn't mean he doesn't love her."

"Of course, you're right," River said. "But let's look at this logically, without emotion."

Tony laughed. "Isn't that what we always do?"

River felt Watson nudge her leg. She slipped him another fry.

"Not in this case, and I wonder if we should have. I feel like we've been looking at all these different cases, wondering if it could be the one that leads us to April. It's like we're trying to juggle a bunch of balls—keep them all in the air. But we may have missed what was right in front of us. I mean, Jeffrey isn't her biological father. Her mother was murdered, and now April's disappeared. April has a trust fund, which I think was left to her by her mother. My research revealed that Katherine Bailey came from a wealthy family. Jeffrey didn't. Now he's the trustee of all this money. With April gone . . ."

"If she's declared deceased, the money will probably be his," Tony said. "In fact, he'll most likely inherit everything."

"You're right." River shook her head. "We've been so busy going through these cases and looking at serial killers . . ."

"Hey, hold on a minute. We spent years in the FBI writing profiles. Trying to think like psychopaths. Out-of-the-box thinking has become our go to. It might take a while for us to learn how to pay attention to the obvious."

"Yeah, maybe so." River leaned forward in her chair. "So, what do we do now? How do we investigate Jeffrey Bailey?"

Tony shrugged. "I don't know, but if her stepfather is involved, does that mean it's more likely she's alive? I mean, because he cares about her?"

"Maybe, although her mother dying makes me uncomfortable."

Tony frowned. "Supposedly, he was cleared."

"Maybe he hired someone to do it. He had access to his wife's money."

"True, but I'm sure the police investigated this possibility," Tony said. "I don't think we can assume Jeffrey killed his wife. And because he has money, isn't it possible that he found a way to get April out of the picture instead of killing her?"

"I understand what you mean, but if he has her hidden away somewhere, just how long can that go on?"

Tony grunted. "You mean how long until he finally gives up and decides it's too risky to keep her alive?"

THIRTY-ONE

Tony and River were still discussing how to proceed with Jeffrey Bailey when Tony's phone rang. While he took the call, River gave Watson one last fry. He seemed to understand that his special feast had come to an end and went back to his bed.

River began writing in a new section of her notebook. She started by making notes about Jeffrey, but she couldn't figure out a way to continue. She would love to get a warrant for Jeffrey's bank accounts, but there wasn't any way for her and Tony to do that. When they worked for the FBI, they never had to think about things like that. At this point, she realized that all she and Tony could do was to turn their suspicions over to Detective Armbruster. She had to wonder if they were already investigating Jeffrey. She looked up Armbruster's number and called him. He picked up right away. First, she asked about Nathan.

"He's doing pretty well," the detective said. "We're talking about letting him go home but keeping an officer with him. Security has been beefed up even more at the apartment complex, and we feel it would not only be safe for him, but that he would be more relaxed."

April's first reaction was negative. Keeping Nathan in another location seemed the most secure decision. But she knew if she were in his shoes, she'd want to go home too. She felt certain the detective wouldn't let him leave unless he was convinced Nathan wouldn't be in danger.

"I need to talk to you about something else," River said. "I feel a little silly even bringing this up. I know you're investigating Kevin's murder, and that you're also looking into April Bailey's podcasts in case there's a connection. We gave you everything we have, and Tony has been emailing updates about her cases, some of which I'm sure you've already found on your own."

"That's true, and your updates have been helpful, but right now, we have to concentrate on Kevin's murder. We're trying to come up with possible suspects. People Kevin knew. April Bailey's cold cases haven't been our main focus."

"So, you don't think her podcasts might be connected to Kevin's death?" River asked. "His connection to Nathan Hearn is obvious. Kevin was killed because he saw the man who threatened Nathan."

"We realize that, but that could be for a myriad of other reasons."

River was confused. How could he not see that Kevin was killed because Nathan came to see them about April? She said as much to Detective Armbruster.

"I'm sorry," he said. "We're just not sure Kevin Bittner's death is connected to the podcasts of a young woman who fancied herself an amateur detective."

Now River understood. "Have you looked at her site? Read her notes?"

"No. Of course, we can't do that now. But my partner is going through everything you sent us. So far, she hasn't seen anything that has overly concerned her. She did mention that some of the cases have already been solved by real law enforcement officers."

River was trying not to lose her temper. Was this guy more concerned about his ego or solving the case?"

"Okay, look. Tony and I were just wondering if you were looking into Jeffrey Bailey."

"Yes."

He didn't seem to want to expand on his one-word response. She looked over at Tony, who was off the phone and was watching her. She rolled her eyes.

"We just wanted to point out that Jeffrey Bailey isn't April's biological father, and that her mother was murdered when she was young. There's a trust fund that Jeffrey oversees. April hasn't taken any of the money yet. If she doesn't show up for five years and is declared dead, most likely the money will go to him. We think you should check that out."

"*You* think we should check it out?" The detective sighed. "Look, Miss Ryland, we do know how to investigate a crime. As I told you, we are looking into everything that might be connected to Mr. Bittner's murder. And yes, we are also looking into Mr. Bailey. However, he has a solid alibi for the time of Kevin's murder. And he wasn't anywhere near the guard house the night the letter was dropped off to Mr. Hearne. Also, he was cleared of his wife's murder years ago."

"Thank you for sharing that, but . . ."

"Yes?"

River fought back a sudden rush of anger. This guy was treating her like some kind of naïve idiot who had no idea what she was talking about.

"For your information, my partner and I were trained by the FBI and worked for the BAU. We both served with distinction for several years. We do know what we're doing. I'm telling you that Jeffrey Bailey may be involved in this."

Armbruster snorted. "I'm trying to make it clear to you that we have things well in hand. If we need your help, we'll let you know. I'm sure Nathan will contact you if we move him back to his own apartment."

Before River had a chance to respond, the line went dead. She was boiling when she slapped her phone down on her desk.

"Whoa. What's got you so upset?" Tony asked.

River told him about her conversation with the detective.

"I can see his point of view," Tony said. "I mean, he doesn't really know us. I don't get the feeling that he's stupid. I'm pretty sure he'll look into Jeffrey with an open mind. He has no reason to cover for him."

"He says he did," River said, unable to keep the irritation out of her voice. "But he needs to dig deeper . . ." She took a deep breath. "Couldn't you tell Arnie . . ."

"No." Tony looked at her through narrowed eyes. "You can't ask me to *tattle* on Detective Armbruster like he's some kind of kid and I'm his babysitter. We just started wondering about Jeffrey Bailey, and it sounds like they already looked into him. That means they've been one step ahead of us. I know your ego may have been injured by this guy, but no one can take away your years of service and your incredible ability to see things most people never do. Just chill out and let's keep working the case."

"Did you just tell me to *chill out*?"

Tony grinned at her. "Yeah, but now I'm regretting it a bit. You're still armed, right?"

River's anger dissipated and she laughed. "Always."

"Look, I know you're probably concerned about Nathan going home, but if the complex has beefed up security and he won't be alone, I'm sure it will be fine."

"If you say so. I just want him to be safe," River said.

"Well, maybe you'll feel better when I tell you what that call was about."

"Go for it."

"I just heard back from the police in Walker, Michigan," Tony said. "You know, about the missing mother, Emily Smallwood?"

"Sure."

"Well, April solved another one." Tony shook his head. "I can't say this makes me completely happy, but it turns out that Emily's son, Brandon, hired a couple of his friends to kill his abusive mother. The friends cracked under questioning. Brandon had promised them money after he inherited Emily's estate. Brandon gave them some of it, but not all of it. He knew they would keep his secret because they didn't want to go to prison. The police were able to convince them that Brandon was blaming them for the whole thing, so they shot their mouths off."

"But Brandon hadn't said anything, right?"

"Right."

"I realize Brandon may have told himself he was trying to protect his sister," River said, "but as we both know, there are much better ways. He could have contacted his father or family services for help."

"You're right. Anyway, the friends told the police where Emily is buried." Tony shook his head. "This case makes me sad."

"Me too," River said. "But you know what? April seems to be closing more cases than a lot of police departments. I keep saying this, but she really impresses me."

"I hear you." Tony looked at the clock. "I think it's time to get out of here. You have to prepare for tomorrow. What time do you want me there?"

"Supper is at six. Why don't you get there at five? I may need you to talk me off the ledge."

Tony chuckled. "Well, since your mother's house is only one story, I think you'd survive the fall."

"You know what I mean."

"Yeah, I get it," Tony said, grinning. "What can I bring?"

"I'd say wine if any of us drank." River sighed. "Let me check with Mrs. Weyland. I'm not sure what's on the menu."

"Sounds good. Just call me later."

While Tony gathered Watson's things, she picked Watson up and held him in her arms.

"He can walk, you know," Tony said.

"It's a long way to the car and it's freezing outside. I don't want his paws to get cold."

Tony shook his head. "You just want to carry him, don't you?"

"Oh, hush. Let's get going."

As they walked toward the door, she realized she hadn't grabbed her laptop or her notebook. She wouldn't be working much over the weekend, and all of April's information was with the police. Rather than put Watson down, she decided to leave her stuff behind. Monday would be here soon enough.

As she got her coat and waited for Tony, she tried to ignore the knot in her stomach. Tomorrow she would face her father for the first time in decades. She was an adult now. A former behavioral analyst for the FBI. So why did she feel like that same little girl who'd watched her father walk out of her life so many years ago?

THIRTY-TWO

After dropping River off at her house and watching her go inside, Tony drove home. He pulled up in front of his apartment complex and got out of his SUV. Although there wasn't a guard on duty, there was an entrance door that needed a code to open. The apartment doors faced inside, which also added security. Tony got Watson and his things out of the car, then headed to the entrance. Although he didn't believe anyone was following him, he looked around, making certain no one was hanging around who shouldn't be. He entered the code and went into the building. Once inside, he walked down the hall to his own apartment and let himself in. He had his own security system, even though he wasn't sure it was necessary. River had insisted on it when they'd first realized the Strangler's partner was stalking them. She'd told Tony that if she needed one, he did too. Rather than argue with her, he'd given in so she wouldn't worry. He punched in his code, then put his stuff down and got Watson settled. He walked into the bedroom and changed his clothes. After that he headed into the kitchen and took a pizza out of the fridge. He'd just put the pizza on a plate and stuck it in the microwave when he heard a strange noise. He was on his way to check it out when a huge flash and the sound of an explosion knocked him to the floor.

SHE WAS BACK. She couldn't believe it. How could they have found her? She tried to move her arms, but they were strapped down. She cried out for help, but no one answered. Where was Audrey? Was she all right? She started to cry. Then the door opened, and he came inside. How could he just show up? How could he face her? When he stepped up next to the bed, she wanted to hit him, but she couldn't move.

"You shouldn't have done that," he said in a low voice. "Don't ever try it again. If you do, I may not be able to keep you alive. Promise me you'll settle down and quit causing trouble."

"I can't do that. I won't promise you anything of the sort. I'll get away from here someday, and then I'll tell the world the truth about you."

"You know I can't let you do that," he said. "You've got to accept this for now if you want to live."

"You mean if I don't want you to kill me?" she asked. As he started to walk away, she called after him. "Where is Audrey? Is she okay?"

He never looked back or responded to her question. As the door closed behind him, she felt the tears roll down her cheeks, but she couldn't wipe them away.

RIVER WAS DOING THE DISHES when her phone rang. Tony. She realized she'd forgotten to ask Mrs. Weyland what he could bring for supper tomorrow night. She answered by saying, "I'm sorry. I totally forgot to find out what . . ." As soon as she heard Tony's voice, she knew something was wrong.

"First of all, I'm okay," he said, his voice hoarse. After coughing several times, he said, "Look, there's been a fire at my place. I'm going to check into a hotel near you. I felt like I had to call you tonight in case you heard about it some other way. There was a news crew filming . . ."

River waited until he finished another round of coughing. "On the news? How big is this fire?"

"Pretty big. Most of the damage was to my apartment, but some of the nearby apartments were affected too."

"How in the world . . ."

"Look, River. Can I talk to you about this later? I'm really tired, and I need to find a hotel that will take Watson and doesn't mind how much I stink right now."

"Hush up," River said. She was trying to sound forceful, but her voice shook. "You're not going to a hotel. You'll come here. Both of you. Now. You'll stay with us. We've got a washer and dryer for your clothes."

"I appreciate that, but you've got your father coming tomorrow. I don't want to cause a problem."

"Tony, I care a lot more for you than I care about my father. You get yourself over here, and I mean it. Our couch makes into a bed, and there's even a bed somewhere downstairs in the basement if you decide you'd feel better down there."

"Okay, okay," he said. He sounded so tired.

"Are you sure you're all right? And what about Watson?"

"Thank God he was with me. Sometimes he goes to bed before I do. If he'd been in the bedroom . . ."

This time, the sound River heard wasn't from his coughing. She couldn't help but cry along with him. "I'll be watching for you. How long will it take you to get here?"

"Not long. I already loaded the car. As soon as the paramedics say I can leave, I'll be on my way."

"The paramedics? Oh, Tony, are you sure you're all right?"

"Yeah, just some smoke inhalation."

"Did they treat you? What do we need to do?"

"Listen, River. I'll give you all the details when I get there. If you don't let me off the phone, it will be next week before I leave."

In spite of herself, she laughed. "Okay. Just get here as soon as you can."

"I will."

When she heard the phone disconnect, she put her phone down and began to cry. Then she prayed, thanking God that Tony and Watson were all right.

"Honey, are you okay?"

River looked up and saw her mother standing there. She tried to tell her about the call, but she couldn't get the words out. Rose came over and put her arms around her. She let her cry while she stroked her daughter's hair. When River could finally talk, she told her mother about the fire.

"I told him he could stay with us, Mom. Is that okay?"

"Of course. I wouldn't want him going anywhere else. We'll put him on the couch tonight. I think we can fix up that extra room downstairs sometime in the next few days if he would prefer to stay down there."

"That's exactly what I told him," River said. "Thanks, Mom. I really appreciate it."

"I love Tony," Rose said. "I only have one question." She dropped her arms and took a step back. "Just when are you going to tell him that you love him too?"

River could only smile at her mother. "Is it that obvious?"

"I may have Alzheimer's, but I'm not blind. You tell him how much he means to you, River. I want as many of my faculties working as possible when you get married, you hear me?"

"Oh, Mom," River said, not caring about the tears running down her cheeks. This was the mother she'd always wanted. "I'll tell him soon," she said. "And after I do, you'll be the first person I share it with."

It was her mother's turn to cry. She sat down at the small desk in the kitchen that River used when she paid the bills.

"I can't tell you how much that means to me," Rose said. "I

have something I need to say. First of all, I'm sorry I wasn't there for you after Joel left. I was just so . . . shattered. I thought I was a good wife. A good mother. I'd believed our marriage was ordained by God. When he walked out, I wasn't certain who I was angrier with, God or your father. I felt so betrayed. Eventually, I blamed myself. I mean, there must have been something wrong with me, right? I was convinced your father was a godly man, so I must have been the problem."

"Oh, Mom. That's not true. You were a great wife. What he did wasn't your fault. It was his. And hers. I hate that you believed that for even a moment."

"Thank you, honey. Agatha has helped me so much. She reads the Bible to me and shows me Scriptures that prove how much God loves me."

For a moment, River was confused about who her mother was talking about. Then she remembered that Mrs. Weyland's first name was Agatha. She never called her anything except Mrs. Weyland. For some reason it seemed wrong to call her anything else. "I'm so glad," River said. "I'm sorry I haven't been more supportive, Mom. I'm going to try harder."

"More supportive? Oh, my dear girl. You left your home and moved here to take care of me. What more could anyone do? I want you to know how much that means to me." She paused for a moment and stared down at her hands, which were clasped tightly in her lap. "River, tonight, I feel like myself," she said softly, her voice breaking as she spoke. "I want to talk to you about something, and I don't want you to interrupt me, okay?"

"All right, Mom."

"I know you're praying for me. You and Tony and Agatha. You believe that God heals, and now, so do I. I keep hanging onto that Scripture that says we have the mind of Christ. But . . . Look, honey, if things don't go the way we want . . ." She held her hand up when River started to say something.

She wanted her mother to stay positive. To believe she could fight this giant, but River suddenly realized that Rose needed to say what was on her heart, so she forced herself to stay silent. She simply nodded at her mother to continue.

"I want to add you to the title of my house, and on my checking and savings accounts. The house is paid for. It will just transfer to you. I want so badly to stay in my home." Her voice cracked and she fought to continue to talk. "But if I can't, I never want you to feel guilty about moving me to a facility that can care for me. I want you to live your life, River. I don't want you to be tied down to someone who doesn't even know who you are. You are never, ever to feel guilty about doing what needs to be done."

"I understand, Mom," River said, "but I'd hire round-the-clock help before I made a decision like that."

Rose smiled. "I appreciate that, but . . ." Rose sighed. "I'm a proud woman, River. You know that. I don't want to lose my dignity. Please, move me someplace if that ever begins to happen. Please. I don't want anyone to see me if I'm . . . Well, if I'm not me. Promise me, okay?"

River was aware that if the disease progressed as it had for so many, putting her mother in a memory care center might happen at some point, but right now she couldn't think about that. River was determined to keep her mother at home, but for Rose's own piece of mind, she said, "All right, Mom. I promise. But my intention is to keep you at home as long as possible. And I'll safeguard your dignity. You have my word."

Her mother stood up. "Thank you, honey. Now you get things ready for Tony. I want him to feel comfortable here." She started to leave the kitchen but turned back and looked at her daughter. "I love you, River. I always have. I need you to know that. Never forget it, okay?"

"I won't, Mom."

When Rose left, River grabbed a paper towel and dried her face. At that moment, she felt the kind of love for her mother that a daughter should feel. It was wonderful and awful all at the same time. Now that she and Rose had grown closer, the fear of losing her was so strong her body trembled, and she couldn't seem to make it stop.

THIRTY-THREE

Tony put his suitcases in the rear of the SUV. In the back seat were duffel bags full of the other possessions he was able to save. Files, records, photos, and a few knickknacks that meant something to him. The apartment owner was on site, making sure the building was secure. Tony still had things in his apartment that he didn't want to lose, but as long as looters couldn't get inside, he felt assured for now. The owner had advised him that he would need to put any furniture he wanted to save in storage while repairs were being made. Thankfully, he had good renter's insurance. On Monday he'd call his agent.

He climbed into the driver's seat. Watson was in his crate, which was balanced on the passenger seat. The way he looked at Tony made him emotional. The little dog looked sad and confused. When the explosion happened, Watson was on the couch. Tony immediately dove for him, covering Watson with his body. Thankfully, the flash from the fire didn't burn his back, even though he felt the heat. He'd quickly found Watson's crate, put him in it, and gotten him outside. He knew smoke could really hurt an animal. A kind neighbor who was already outside stayed with Watson while Tony ran back in to quickly grab what he could. After the fire department put out the fire, he was allowed to go back and pack anything else that wasn't ruined. His bedroom was a total loss. All of the furniture. All the clothes in his closet. It was such a blessing that he'd just done a load of laundry and that there were clean clothes in the dryer. If it hadn't been for that, he would have had to go to the local department store in his dirty sweat pants and FBI T-shirt to buy something to wear.

He'd changed into a pair of clean jeans and a sweatshirt. His jacket was okay. It had been in the front closet. It had a faint smell of smoke, but it wasn't too bad. All in all, Tony felt blessed. He looked over at Watson, who was watching him closely.

"Thank you for taking care of us, God," he said. "Thank you that Watson is safe. If he had gone into the bedroom . . ." He broke down and cried from the wave of gratitude that washed over him. God was good.

He'd asked the fire chief who was at the scene what had caused the explosion. Tony hadn't been able to inspect his bedroom because of the fire.

"Until our investigator looks things over," the chief had said, "I'd only be guessing. It will have to wait."

"There wasn't anything in my bedroom that could have exploded like that," he told the chief. "I may have heard glass breaking before I saw the flash and heard the blast."

"We may need to talk to you," the chief said. "How can we reach you?"

Tony pulled his wallet out of his back pocket. Thankfully, he'd put it in his desk drawer when he got home. He handed the chief one of his cards.

"You're a private investigator?" he asked.

"Yeah, now. I used to work for the FBI—in the BAU. Left about a year ago. Then a few months back my partner and I moved here. Her mother is ill, and she needed to care for her."

Tony wasn't certain why he was telling the chief, whose last name was Magruder according to the name on his badge, his whole life story. For some reason, the chief's demeanor made him a little nervous. Surely, he didn't think Tony was responsible for the fire. Of course, it did seem as if the initial detonation happened in his bedroom. Did that seem suspicious? He wanted to ask Chief Magruder if he was a suspect, but he was suddenly afraid it might make him look guilty. Tony wasn't used to being on this side of a possible crime. He didn't like it.

He'd quickly thanked the chief for everything he and his crew had done to put out the fire and then went to his car. Before driving away, he surveyed the building and thanked God, once again, that it wasn't worse. He started his car and headed for River's house. He was so grateful she'd told him to come there instead of a hotel. He felt the need to talk to someone, and there was no one he wanted to talk to more than River. He needed her.

RIVER SAT IN THE LIVING ROOM, waiting for Tony's SUV to pull into the driveway. It felt as if she'd been waiting for hours. Finally, she heard him and ran to the door. She was halfway to his car before she realized how cold it was. She'd left her coat inside, but she didn't care. She was just so grateful he was alive.

"Oh, Tony," River said, as he got out of his car. "I'm so glad you're okay. If anything had happened to you . . ." She wrapped her arms around him, sobbing into his chest.

He stroked her hair softly. "It's okay. God took care of us, River. I may smell like smoke for a while though."

She couldn't help but laugh. "That's okay. I think we can deal with that."

He put his hand under her chin. "Good. I'm so grateful that Watson is unharmed. Usually, he would have gone into the bedroom before me, but tonight for some reason he didn't. Had to be God watching out for him."

"I believe that. But before you both get frostbite, let's get you inside."

"Sounds good," Tony said. "To be honest, I'm exhausted." He grabbed his bags from the back of the SUV while River went around to the other side and fetched Watson. Tony followed her to the front door, which she held open.

Once they were inside, River set Watson's crate down and turned to look at Tony. What she saw startled her.

"Oh, Tony, your eyes are so red."

He nodded and then started coughing. "It's from the fire," he choked out.

"Hey, I'll get you something to drink. Let's get you some water first. After that, I'll make you a cup of hot chocolate to warm you up."

"I'd love that."

"We're going to put you on the couch tonight," River said. "Like I told you, it folds out into a bed, so I think you'll be comfortable. If you want more privacy, there's a nice twin bed in the basement that belonged to Dan. There's also an extra room down there. We have some boxes stored in it, but they can be moved out and put into another part of the basement. At some point I think you'd be very comfortable there, and it would give you some privacy."

"Right now, all I want is something to drink and someone to talk to." He smiled when Watson made a soft sound that sounded exactly like "woof." "And Watson needs to get out of that crate and see his friend. He's had a tough night."

River knelt down and opened the crate. Watson came out with his tail wagging and put his front paws on River's leg. She leaned down so he could reach her cheek.

"Doggy kisses?" Tony said with a smile. "He's going to be fine."

"Does he need to be fed?"

"No. I fed him earlier. I was able to grab his food and supplements before I left, but I forgot his dishes. We might need to borrow something in the morning."

"I think we can find a couple of bowls that will work." She rubbed the little dog's head. She couldn't imagine anything happening to him. "I'm so glad . . ." A sob was caught in her throat, and she struggled to control her emotions. She didn't want Tony worrying about her, which was what he'd do if she didn't quit crying. Finally, she was able to say, "I know I keep saying this, but I'm just so glad you're both okay." She stood. "Why don't you put your stuff next to the couch and sit down. I'll get some bowls out for Watson and make sure he has water. I'll also get you a glass of water, and then I'll get that cup of hot chocolate."

"Sounds wonderful," Tony said. "My mother used to make us hot chocolate when we were upset. It sounds perfect right now."

River smiled at him. "I loved it when your mom made it for me while we were in Burlington. I'm not sure mine is as good as hers though."

"I'm sure it will be fine." He frowned. "Have your mother and Mrs. Weyland gone to bed? I don't want to wake them up."

"Yes, it's late. They go to bed pretty early."

"Good. I'll try to be quiet so I don't disturb them."

River could hear the weariness in his voice. She quickly grabbed the tote bag with a picture of a dog on it. This was what Tony always used for Watson's things. She smiled as the little dog followed her into the kitchen. She found a couple of bowls, filled one with water, and then looked through the bag. Sure enough, his treats were in there. She opened the bag and said, "Don't tell on me, okay? I think you deserve a treat." She grabbed two small treats and dropped them into the other bowl. Watson's tail always pointed up when he was happy, and when it suddenly shot up, River laughed.

"I know what you're doing in there," Tony said from the living room. "Don't spoil him."

"Oh, hush. My house, my rules."

"Well, I see we're going to have to talk about how to be a responsible parent."

"Don't listen to that bad man," she told Watson. "He doesn't understand." She quickly poured a glass of water and took it to Tony, who accepted it gratefully.

"I'll be back with your hot chocolate in just a minute."

Tony grinned at her. "I don't suppose you have any of Mrs. Weyland's delicious cookies, do you?"

River laughed. "As a matter of fact, I think she just made some today. I think I can scare some up. Do you want a sandwich or anything?"

"No, thanks. I'm only craving a sugar rush right now. Hot chocolate and cookies should do the trick."

River went into the kitchen and began heating cups of milk and putting cookies on a plate. But before she finished, she stopped, leaned against the counter, and thanked God for saving the man she loved and the little dog they both adored.

THIRTY-FOUR

By the time River brought the two mugs of hot chocolate into the living room, she'd finally composed herself. She didn't want to cry in front of Tony again. She needed to help him get through this, not think about herself. She understood her earlier reaction. She'd faced the possibility of losing him once before, and tonight it was as if a nightmare had awakened from somewhere inside her. She'd suffered from PTSD after their confrontation with the Strangler, but she thought she'd moved past it. Now, here it was again, rearing its ugly head. She felt disappointed in herself. Shouldn't she be completely healed by now?

"Here we go," she said, trying to sound light-hearted even though she didn't feel that way.

Tony held his hand out for his cup. "Thanks." He took a sip. "Hot," he said.

"That's probably why it's called *hot* chocolate," River said, rolling her eyes at him.

"Oh, is that why?" Tony shook his head and smiled at her. When he set the cup down, he looked at River, his expression tight. "The fire chief on the scene tonight wanted my contact information. I got the feeling he thinks I caused the fire."

"What? That can't be right, Tony. Surely you misunderstood."

"Maybe, but I don't think so." He took another sip of his cocoa, then he said, "Before the explosion, I thought I heard something. Like glass breaking."

"You know hot temperatures can shatter glass," she said slowly. She met his gaze. "But are you saying you think someone threw something through your window? Something that started the fire?"

"What else could it be? I mean, there wasn't anything flammable in my room. An electrical short wouldn't explode like that. It would burn, but it would be a more controlled fire. This was . . . different."

"I guess there's no way to know for certain until the fire investigator looks things over," River said. "You don't want to jump to conclusions."

"What if it has something to do with the person who killed the security guard? Or maybe it's the Strangler's partner."

"I wouldn't think so. You know serial killers that don't deal with fire rarely change course. Fire is a very specialized signature."

Tony nodded. "Yet most serial killers set fires when they were young."

"True, but this guy has moved way beyond that," River said. "I don't buy it."

"So, could it have been whoever killed Kevin and threatened Nathan?"

"Maybe, but it could also be someone else," River said. "Teenagers trying to set a fire for kicks? They might not even know who you are."

"But most firebugs set something on fire—like trash cans or trees. They don't throw something flammable through an apartment window. They aren't trying to kill. I could have easily been in my bedroom. This was done at night."

"No, you're right," River said.

"If there was an arsonist working in the area, the police and the fire department would know about it. Even if he'd escalated, they'd be able to connect the dots. Hey, maybe that's why the chief said they might want to talk to me. Perhaps they're trying to link this guy with other cases." Tony hesitated for a moment. "But River, that wasn't how it felt. Or looked. His body language was guarded. He wasn't making eye contact. And he seemed uptight."

"He'd just been dealing with a fire, Tony," River said. "Besides, you know they always interview people. It's standard procedure." She wanted to reassure him, but the truth was, Tony was good at reading people. If he felt the chief was treating him like a suspect, he probably was.

"Hey, are you all right?" Tony was studying her closely.

She wanted to tell him she was fine, but her emotions were so strong, holding them back was almost impossible. She couldn't do it. "I . . . I guess what happened scared me. You know, realizing that you might have been hurt—or worse."

"But I'm fine."

"I know that," River said, looking down at the cup in her hands. "I think I flashed back to that night on the riverbank." She looked up at him, unable to keep the tears from her eyes. "Why do I still suffer from what happened? Aren't I supposed to be healed by now?"

"Oh, River," he said. "You're not *supposed* to be anything by now." He reached over and took the cup of hot chocolate from her hands. She'd been holding onto it so tightly her fingers hurt. "We've talked about this before. About how wounds can leave scars."

"Yeah, I know. You told me Jesus has scars too, and that He understands."

Tony sighed. "Look, eventually you won't remember what happened as clearly as you used to. It will fade. You'll learn not to

allow it into your head. But for now, you're in a healing process."
He took her hands and squeezed them softly. "What happened to
you—to us—was awful. We both have to deal with it. You think
I don't have flashbacks? Times when I hurt? Of course I do." He
smiled at her. "Give yourself some compassion and don't try to
hide your scars. And I'm here whenever you need to talk to me."

"Thanks, Tony. Maybe Jesus kept his scars because they reminded Him of His victory. Maybe someday, mine will do the
same."

Tony let go of her hands. "Exactly. Hey, let's talk about this a
little more tomorrow, okay?" He looked exhausted.

"Sure. You change your clothes, and I'll make up the couch for
you." She frowned at him. "Do you have anything to sleep in? I
think Mrs. Weyland has some extra nightgowns."

"Funny. And no thank you. I had some sweats and T-shirts in
the dryer." He shook his head. "Boy, I'm really, really glad I did
that load of laundry. I don't think I'd look good in one of Mrs.
Weyland's nightgowns."

River laughed. "That's an image I don't want in my head."

"Me neither. You know, even though I was able to save a few
things, I'm still going to need to buy some new clothes."

"We'll have to go shopping. Maybe I can help you choose a
new wardrobe."

"Just calling my clothes a *wardrobe* tells me I need to turn
down your magnanimous offer."

"Okay, okay," River said. "Go change. I'll have your bed ready
by the time you get back."

"Thanks, but I can do it. I'm tired, not feeble."

River pointed her finger at him. "Maybe not, but you are an
idiot. Go. Now."

Tony grinned. "Yes, ma'am. On my way."

Once Tony was headed toward the bathroom, River went to the
linen closet and fetched clean sheets, a blanket, and a couple of

pillows. She carried everything into the living room, moved the coffee table back, removed the couch cushions, and then pulled out the bed. She'd just finished getting it ready when her phone rang. It startled her. Who could be calling this late? She picked up the phone and saw it was a local number. She almost let it go to voice mail but decided at the last moment to answer it.

"Hello?"

"River, this is Arnie. I just heard about the fire and realized it happened at Tony's address. I tried to call him, but it just went to voice mail. Is he okay?"

"Yeah, he's fine. Lost a lot of his stuff, but it could have been worse. He's staying here until his apartment is fixed. Do you want to talk to him?"

"Yeah, well, I guess I want to talk to both of you."

River turned to see Tony walking into the living room. He gave her a questioning look.

"It's Arnie," she said. "He wants to talk to us." She turned on her speaker.

"Okay." Tony walked up next to her. "I'm here, Arnie."

"Look, the main reason I called was to see how you were. I called you first, but your phone kept going to voicemail."

"Sorry. I need to charge it. I usually do it before I go to bed, but I was a little busy earlier tonight. How did you hear about the fire? You're not running the STLFD now too, are you?"

"No, but the chief is a friend of mine. I called him to get more information after I saw the report on the news." He hesitated a moment before saying, "Look, this isn't to be repeated, Tony. An investigator needs to confirm it, but Garrett—the chief—thinks someone threw a Molotov cocktail through your window."

"Can't say I'm surprised," Tony said. "I kind of expected something like that."

"Don't jump to conclusions," Arnie said. "It's possible you might not be a target."

"But it's also possible he was," River said. She'd tried to convince Tony that the fire could have been a random incident, yet even as she tried to reassure him, her gut told her something different.

"Of course, anything is possible, but let's hope that's not the case."

"The chief made me feel as if he suspected me of something," Tony said.

"No, he doesn't, but he'll want to talk to you to see if you know anyone who could have started that fire."

"Okay, I understand," Tony said.

Arnie cleared his throat. "Look, there's another reason I called. I know it's late, but I felt this might be important."

Tony sat down on the side of the sofa bed. River knew he was tired and needed to rest.

"What is it?" she asked.

"This has to do with that cold case you're investigating. The police in Terre Haute, Indiana, contacted me."

"I don't understand," River said. "How does our case have anything to do with Terre Haute?"

"Seems like a clerk at a local motel thought something odd was going on there. They called the police who went inside one of the rooms and found a note stuffed underneath one of the pillows on the bed. The note read *I'm alive, and I need help. April Bailey. My father . . .* It stopped there. Looked like she was interrupted before she could finish."

THIRTY-FIVE

He saw the story about the fire on the late news. He immediately recognized the apartment complex. He'd driven past there more than once, even though Tony St. Clair wasn't his target. Still, it enraged him. One thing he was sure of—Tony St. Clair wasn't stupid or careless. That made him wonder if someone had caused the fire on purpose. No one else had the right to interfere with his plans. He didn't need River to take off, go to a place where he couldn't reach her. Would this spook them? Then he realized that this could actually work in his favor. If someone else had tried to hurt Tony, they would both be distracted. This could make it much easier for him. He leaned back in his chair and smiled. River Ryland's breaths were running out. Soon, she would stop breathing forever.

WHEN ARNIE WAS FINISHED, River hung up her phone. Then she turned toward Tony. He didn't look good.

"Do you want to talk about what Arnie said, or do you want to wait until tomorrow?" River asked.

"Look, I know it's really important, but if you don't mind, let's discuss it in the morning. I'm sorry. I think what happened drained me. I'm sure I'll be fine in the morning. I just need some sleep."

"Of course," River said. "Sleep as late as you want. We'll keep it down in the morning. When you wake up, I'll make you a great breakfast."

He smiled at her. "Pancakes?"

"If you want."

Tony lay down on the bed and was pulling the blanket up over him when, from behind River, came an ungodly shriek. She turned to see her mother pointing at her, her expression twisted into a mask of rage.

"You get out of here and leave my husband alone," she screamed. "Get out of my house!"

River got to her feet and hurried over to Rose. "Mom," she said, trying to calm her down. "It's me, Mom."

Rose raised her hand and slapped River across the face. "You can't have my husband. I need him. We need him. He has children, but you don't care, do you? You're selfish and evil. Get out of my house or you'll be sorry." Rose walked up to Tony, who was now sitting up on the bed looking confused. "You promised to be faithful. You're supposed to love me . . ." Rose collapsed to the floor, crying hysterically. Mrs. Weyland came running down the hall, her flannel nightgown flying behind her like a cape. She looked like a chubby gray-haired superhero. Which in River's mind, she was. She got down on the floor next to Rose and put her arms around her.

"Rose, it's okay. She's gone. She left. It's just us. River, me, and Tony. CeCe is gone and she's not coming back, I promise, honey."

"She tried to steal my family," Rose said, putting her head on the caregiver's shoulder. "I can't lose them. They're everything to me. You . . . you understand, don't you, Aggie? I know you understand."

"Yes, Rose, sweetie. I understand. Let's get you back to bed, okay?"

Mrs. Weyland grabbed the edge of the couch in an attempt to get up. River took her arm and pulled her to her feet. Then she put her arms around her mother and helped her up too.

"It's okay, Mom. It's River. I'm here. You're not going to lose me."

Her cheek stung from her mother's slap, but her heart hurt more. She saw her mother's pain and realized how hard it must have been for her to keep her true feelings from her children after their father left. She may have seemed distant, but it was because she was in pain, struggling to keep herself from falling apart. The hurtful things she'd said came from the pain she carried inside. What was it that River had heard somewhere? That hurting people hurt people?

Once she was standing, Rose looked around the room, blinking. Then she gazed at River, looking confused. "What am I doing still in my nightgown?" she asked, sounding bewildered. "Are you and Dan ready for school? I don't want you missing the bus again. I have to get to work."

River looked at Mrs. Weyland and nodded. She knew what to do. "Hey, it's okay, Mom," she said. "We're off today. It's a holiday, remember? And you don't have to go to work today. Why don't you lie down and rest for a while. We're fine."

Rose hesitated for a moment, but she let River take her arm and lead her down the hallway to her room. Mrs. Weyland followed behind them but stayed out of sight. Rose got back into bed and River covered her with the bedspread.

"Are you sure it's okay if I take a nap?" Rose asked. "Can you kids take care of yourselves for a little while? I really am a little tired."

"We'll be fine, Mom. You rest." River struggled to keep the emotion out of her voice. She didn't want to worry her mother.

"Okay, honey," Rose said. "I'll be up in a little bit."

"Okay, Mom." River walked over to the door and slowly closed it. Mrs. Weyland waited in the hallway.

"You were wonderful with her, honey," she said to River. "Perfect."

"It was hard. So hard." River took a deep breath. "What if she acts that way tomorrow night when my dad is here? I'm really starting to wonder if we're doing the right thing."

"River, I don't think we can worry about that. But even if that happened, would it really be that bad for your father to see the fallout his actions caused?" She shook her head. "Look, no one believes more in forgiveness and a new life in Christ than I do, but I'm thinkin' that you, your mom, and your brother have been carryin' the pain of your daddy's decisions for too many years. If he was forced to see the consequences, I don't think that's the worst thing in the world."

"I understand, and I've thought the same thing. But I don't want my mother to . . . to embarrass herself in front of my father. She would be mortified if that happened."

"I understand, I really do," the elderly woman said. "I can't promise what will happen. I wish I could guarantee you that everything will be okay. But like we both agreed, this might be her best and last chance to face your daddy. Find some healing. You can see from what just happened that she needs it."

River folded her arms and leaned against the wall. What should she do? Finally, she said, "Look, let's do this. We'll let my dad and Dan come for dinner. But if Mom starts acting up, we'll get her out of the room as quickly as possible. Will you help me?"

"Of course I will. Whatever you need." Mrs. Weyland opened her arms and River fell into them. Thinking that she could have lost Tony tonight and then watching her mother fall apart had overwhelmed her. Mrs. Weyland's hug was exactly what she needed. When she was ready, she gently disengaged herself from the elderly caregiver's embrace.

"Thank you," she said, her voice quivering.

"You're welcome, honey. This has been a tough night. Tony was in danger, and you saw your mama at her worst." She sighed deeply. "You know, I believe you're beginning to understand your mama, and now that you do, you're grieving for the mother you think you're losing."

"You're right," River said slowly. "I accepted that Rose Ryland has Alzheimer's, but now, I'm realizing that my mother is ill. *My mother*. I hate seeing what this disease is doing to her. And . . . and I don't want her to be humiliated in front of my father. She deserves better. I want him to . . ." She gulped. "I want him to look at her . . . and at me . . . and realize what he threw away. Does that make any sense?"

Mrs. Weyland smiled. "Yeah, it does. Now that you're bein' completely honest with yourself, I think you're really ready to face your daddy."

River returned the smile. "Maybe you're right."

Mrs. Weyland headed to her room while River went back into the living room. Tony was out and snoring softly, Watson snuggled up next to him. She really wanted to talk to him about Arnie's call. Was this real? Was April really alive? If she was, she was in trouble, and they needed to find her fast.

After checking on Tony one more time, she went back to her room, where she spent some time in prayer. She prayed for April and for Tony. Then she prayed that tomorrow would go well for everyone. But most of all, she thanked God for taking care of Tony and Watson. What if Tony had died tonight? What would she have done? How could she go on without him? She knew that sometime soon she'd have to talk to him. Tell him how she felt. She could only pray that he felt the same. She really couldn't imagine her life without Tony St. Clair.

THIRTY-SIX

River woke up early and walked quietly into the living room to check on Tony. He was sound asleep. She went into the kitchen and started the coffeemaker then went back to bed. Today her father and brother would be here. She lay in her bed and stared up at the ceiling for a few minutes, worrying. She finally reminded herself that worrying wasn't going to help anything, so she closed her eyes and asked God to take over. To let His will be done. When she opened her eyes, she felt better.

Her mind went back to the note from the motel room. Could they be certain it really was April? Could someone be playing an awful joke? With all of April's followers, it was possible. How devastating would that be for Nathan and April's father to be given false hope?

Although she tried to go back to sleep, her mind was unquiet and so was she. Finally, she sat up and grabbed her phone. Besides discovering a possible serial killer, she was thinking about a couple of the other cases that bothered her. The body found near the railroad tracks so many years ago—and the woman who was hitchhiking. At least she'd been identified so her family could grieve. But the dead man never had been, and it looked as if he never would be. He had to be someone's son, grandson, or brother. Surely, he'd had friends. Someone out there had to be missing him. It made her sad to think of him buried without anyone to mourn him. In all these years had anyone ever visited his grave?

She began to search for online articles about Cheryl Armitage's death. There were photos and an article from the local newspaper about the case. Cheryl Armitage looked like a nice woman, but there was sadness in her eyes. Some people didn't believe eyes showed emotion, but she knew they most certainly did. River had seen it many times. This woman had been hurt. That was probably why she was in the bar that night. Many people with pain in their lives use alcohol to self-medicate, but it only brings more sorrow. Poor Cheryl had paid the ultimate price for her choice.

After looking through the photos, she noticed another link under Cheryl's name and clicked on it. It pulled up an interview with a local news channel. The reporter shared the story of the hit-and-run, and then she went to an interview with Detective Porter. She thought he was a little brusque with the reporter, who was a rather young woman. Maybe he was just busy, but River felt as if he should have been more gracious. He assured her that the police were doing an extensive search for someone in the area who could have killed Cheryl. River wondered if the hit-and-run driver was from out of town. It might explain why the police were never able to close the case.

River glanced over at the clock. Should she let Tony sleep or wake him up? She'd promised him breakfast, and she was certain her mother would be up soon. After arguing with herself for a few minutes, she finally decided to head to the kitchen and get breakfast started. She hoped Mrs. Weyland would allow her to make a meal for her. She'd been cooking for River and her mother for months now. She got up and dressed quickly. Then walked quietly into the living room. Her concerns about disturbing Tony turned out to be useless. He was already awake and sitting on the edge of his bed.

"Boy, when someone promises you pancakes, you take that seriously, don't you?"

Tony laughed. "You know pancakes are one of my weaknesses."

"Your kryptonite?"

"Not sure I'm in the same league as Superman," he said with a grin, "but I think you've got the idea."

"Why don't you take a shower and get dressed while I get busy in the kitchen?"

"You don't find the scent of smoke and burned belongings agreeable?" he asked.

"Yes, I hear it's the hottest new men's cologne in the country. However, I'm more partial to soap and water."

Tony stood to his feet, his curly hair hanging down in his eyes. He swept it off his forehead and smiled at her. She couldn't help but think about how handsome he looked when he was unkempt and at his most casual. Surprised by her thought, she forced herself to focus on something else.

"There are towels and washcloths on the shelf in the bathroom," she said a little too quickly. She turned to leave, afraid for him to see her face since she was fairly certain she was blushing.

Before she reached the kitchen, she heard noises and smelled food cooking. When she entered the room, sure enough Mrs. Weyland was already there, and she was standing over the stove.

"I was going to make breakfast," River said. "I thought you might enjoy someone cooking a meal for you for once."

Mrs. Weyland turned around and smiled at her. "Oh, honey. That's so sweet. I was thinkin' about you and Tony and everything you've been through. I decided you needed a special breakfast." She put one hand on her hip and frowned. "I don't wanna take over if you really want to do this. For Tony, I mean."

Once again, she felt her face grow hot. "I said I wanted to cook for you, not for Tony."

Mrs. Weyland didn't say a word. She just smiled at her.

"Okay, okay. But it was for you too, I promise."

"I appreciate that, River. But why don't you make a meal for me another time? You just rest this mornin', And I don't plan to say anything to Tony about your feelin's for him."

River wanted to argue with Mrs. Weyland, but the older woman was too sharp. There was no way she would ever be able to convince her of something she'd clearly seen.

"I can't hide anything from you or my mother, can I?"

Mrs. Weyland laughed. "It doesn't take the sharpest person to see that you two are crazy about each other." She gazed at River for a moment and then said, "My husband and I had something really special, and I see the same thing when I see you and Tony together."

River sat down at the kitchen table and Mrs. Weyland poured her a cup of coffee. "You know, there aren't many couples who so easily put each other first." Her eyes got misty. "It isn't something they have to try to do. It's . . . it's like breathin' in and out. One breath. One heartbeat. And that's what you two have."

"It was like that for you and your husband?"

The older woman nodded. "From the first moment we met until I watched him take his last breath." She smiled sadly. "That's why I wanted to come here. I needed to take care of someone. Needed to pass on the love we lived for over forty years. I'll never be able to thank you enough for allowing me to take care of your mama."

River didn't know what to say. Mrs. Weyland was thanking *her* for everything she'd done for her and her mother? "I think we're the ones who are blessed," she said softly.

Mrs. Weyland turned back to the stove, and a peaceful quiet fell over the kitchen. River turned over Mrs. Weyland's words in her heart.

You know, there aren't many couples who so easily put each other first. It isn't something they have to try to do. It's . . . it's like breathin' in and out. One breath. One heartbeat.

She realized it was true. From the moment they'd met, she'd cared more about Tony than she did herself. Even before she'd let God into her heart, she'd loved Tony St. Clair with everything within her.

THIRTY-SEVEN

H e glared at Jeffrey over the tabletop. "I won't put up with it," he said in a low voice that almost sounded like a growl.

A feeling of panic rose inside Jeffrey. He knew how dangerous this man really was. "It wasn't my fault," he said. "It was that nurse. She was the one who—"

"No, it wasn't her fault. It's yours. I should never have let you talk me into this. I told you from the beginning that I wanted her gone." He struck his fist on the table and several people turned to look at them. "First you send that stupid picture. Then you threaten the kid."

"He told me he'd gone to see those PIs," Jeffrey insisted. "I wanted to stop him."

"It was stupid and amateurish. I had to clean up your mess by killing that guard. It's only gotten worse. This thing is out of control."

They'd decided to meet at a nearby coffee shop. Jeffrey looked around. The people who had glanced their way a few seconds ago appeared to have gone back to their own business. He hoped none of them were listening.

"She's my daughter," Jeffrey said, keeping his voice low. "I can't . . . I just can't let you kill her."

"You mean the way you killed her mother?"

"I didn't do that. You did."

He laughed quietly. It was ugly and full of venom. This was a truly evil man. Why had Jeffrey ever gotten involved with him? It was the stupidest thing he'd ever done.

"You wanted the money more than you wanted your wife. I gave you the perfect way out. You had an ironclad alibi because of me."

Jeffrey sighed. "It was wrong. *I* was wrong, and I'm sorry about it."

"Look here you little worm, I don't care about your regrets. You got the money. After the cops stopped sniffing around, you paid me. Since then, you've been raiding your daughter's—correction—your stepdaughter's trust fund like a bandit. You've padded your pockets and now you can't allow anyone to find out. If they do, you'll go to prison. You may know my secret, but I know yours too. We have a partnership. You try to break it, and you'll regret it, I promise you."

"What happened to the nurse?" Jeffrey couldn't help but ask, but he was afraid to hear the answer.

"You don't need to worry about her. She's not a problem any-more."

"You . . . you didn't kill her, surely. Dr. Marnet wouldn't put up with that."

"Dr. Marnet will do whatever you tell him to. He doesn't dare let anyone know what he's been doing. Just keep paying him. He'll keep his mouth shut."

"That money isn't going to last forever," Jeffrey said. "What happens when it runs out?"

He laughed in a low voice. "You better make certain that doesn't happen. If it does, you're going to be in a lot of trouble,

Jeff. You're used to living well. Trust me, you definitely wouldn't like prison."

He took a sip of his coffee, but Jeffrey felt too sick to his stomach to eat or drink anything. He wanted to tell this terrible man that the same fate awaited him, but he was too afraid to do that. How had he gotten himself into this predicament? He'd lost control of his life, and he didn't know how to get it back. He'd sent another warning to those PIs last night. He prayed the man sitting across from him would never find out. He was afraid for his life if that would happen. This man would kill anyone who stood in his way. If he decided to kill April. . . . Well, he couldn't think about that right now. He had to just take it day by day. But one thing he knew for certain. April couldn't escape again. No matter what.

TONY LEFT AFTER BREAKFAST to run to a local department store to buy clothes. River spent the morning mentally reviewing the case. The note that was found in Terre Haute was intriguing, but right now, there wasn't anything to prove it really came from April. The police were investigating and had told Arnie they'd stay in touch. She and Tony both felt the answer to April's disappearance had something to do with one of her cases, but so far, River just couldn't see it. When she heard the front door close, she glanced at the clock on her desk. It was almost noon. Where had the morning gone? Her father would be here in a few hours. Her stomach clenched. She thought she was prepared, but it seemed her body wasn't in agreement with her mind. She got up from her chair and headed to the kitchen. Tony was standing in the doorway talking to Mrs. Weyland, who was getting something out of the refrigerator. River's mother sat at the table eating a sandwich, and Watson was sitting on the floor next to her, obviously hoping Rose would drop something he could snatch up.

"There you are," Mrs. Weyland said when she saw River. "Want some lunch?"

"Maybe a little something." She looked at Tony. "How about you?" she asked. "Are you hungry?"

"No, thanks. Not now." He turned abruptly and left the room, grabbing some bags on the floor next to him. Watson looked a little confused but ran after him. River was surprised. Was he upset about something? She started to follow him, but before she could, Mrs. Weyland stopped her.

"Honey, before you try talkin' to him, let me say something." Mrs. Weyland sat down at the table and motioned to River to do the same. River slipped into the chair next to her.

"Tony has lost his home and a lot of his possessions," Mrs. Weyland said. "Right now, he's probably a little angry about the whole thing. He likes feeling independent. Now he doesn't know what he's gonna do. He's feelin' a little lost. I realize we're all supposed to be enlightened and everything, but a lot of men like to feel they're in control. Feelin' like they have to rely on someone else is hard for them, even if they know we care about them."

"Surely it's not because I'm a woman," River said.

"Well, God set things up in a way that may not make some people comfortable nowadays, but God's pretty okay with it. Men are supposed to see women as the weaker vessel. He wasn't callin' us weak, mind you. Most women I know are beyond strong. I think He meant that men are supposed to love and protect their wives. You two aren't married, but I think Tony has a real desire to take care of you. Protect you. He got shot tryin' to do just that. But now, he needs help himself." She smiled at River. "Give him a little space. Tony's a good man. A smart man. He'll figure it out."

"She's right, sweetheart," Rose said. "Tony just needs a little time."

River realized Mrs. Weyland and her mother were right. Tony had spent months trying to protect her from the Strangler's apprentice. Feeling as if their roles were suddenly reversed was an adjustment. But she knew him well enough to be certain Mrs. Weyland was right about something else too. He would definitely figure it out. He was smart, and he knew how to hear from God. She smiled at her mother, grateful she seemed okay today after last night's incident.

"Thanks," she said. "You're both right. But we need to give him a place to live until his apartment is renovated. I hope he won't try to leave. I want him to feel comfortable here—with us."

"He does."

River jumped at the sound of Tony's voice and turned to find him standing behind her.

"I'm sorry," he said sheepishly. "I'm upset about the fire, especially since it seems someone started it on purpose. At first, all I thought about was how grateful I was that Watson and I survived. But today at the store, I began to realize just how many things I was going to have to replace. All the things I lost. Then I started to worry about where I was going to live. Should I move somewhere else, or should I wait until my apartment is restored and go back? It upset me. I'm sorry I was rude to you, River. I hope you'll forgive me. I truly appreciate everything you're doing to help me."

"Of course, Tony. And I understand. It's okay to get upset. You've been through a lot." She walked over and took his hand. "I think sometimes, as Christians, we think it's wrong to have a human reaction. It isn't. God understands. You've told me that many times. So you can be mad. To be honest, I'm mad too. I hope they find the guy who did this and send him to jail for a long, long time."

"Yeah, me too." Tony squeezed her hand. "I would love some lunch. After that, I think I need to get out of your way." He gazed at Mrs. Weyland and Rose. "I don't want to be in the way during your special dinner tonight. Maybe I can hide out in the basement or somewhere else while you have company. I hear there's a bed downstairs?"

"We'd really like you to join us for dinner," Rose said. "It would mean a lot to all of us to have you there. And you can continue sleeping in the living room, you know. The basement might be a little cold right now. I think the vents are closed. It might take it a while to warm up."

"I just don't want to intrude on your family dinner, Rose," Tony said.

"But you *are* family to us," River said. "I already told you that. Besides, you made me a promise, remember?" She wanted him there—no, needed him with her. Tony kept her grounded, and tonight was going to be hard. She was certain he knew that, but he wasn't certain if Rose and Mrs. Weyland felt the same way she did. Obviously, that concern had just been laid to rest.

He looked down at her. "Okay. I'd be happy to be there. If I can help . . ."

"Don't be silly," Mrs. Weyland said, rising to her feet. "I've got everything well in hand." She frowned at him. "You look a little peaked. I imagine the EMTs last night told you to rest today, right? I have a niece who was in a fire and inhaled smoke. That's what they told her to do."

Tony looked a little sheepish. "Yeah, they did."

"Why didn't you tell me that?" River asked.

"I don't know. I feel okay, and I assumed they tell everyone that."

River shook her head. "Why don't you lie down in my room? There's a blanket at the foot of the bed. Pull it up over you."

Tony nodded. "Thanks. I am a little tired. I'd like to talk to you first though, River."

"Sure. Why don't you go sit down in the living room, and I'll bring you a plate. I'll make both of us a sandwich, okay?"

Tony nodded, but instead of walking away he said, "Thank

you. All of you. And Rose, thank you for welcoming me into your home."

"Oh, Tony. We're all glad you're here," Rose said, smiling. "My daughter is right. You really are a part of the family. I'm very glad you're in our lives."

Tony nodded and left the room. River could see that he was moved. She went over to her mother, leaned down, and then kissed her on the cheek. "Thank you, Mom," she said. "That was so nice of you."

Rose patted River's hand. "I meant it, sweetheart. I'm so happy you moved here. I know it might not have been what you wanted to do, but I'll always be grateful."

River glanced over at Mrs. Weyland, who smiled at her. She was certain they were both relieved that Rose seemed okay today. If only she was this way tonight. But sadly, neither one of them could count on that.

THIRTY-EIGHT

After River and Tony finished their sandwiches, River took their plates into the kitchen. Mrs. Weyland gave her a plate of cookies, which she took back with her.

"Tony, have you called your parents and your sister yet?"

He sighed. "No. I'll do that here in a bit." He looked down at Watson, who was staring at him without moving.

"What does he want? Is he hungry?"

Tony shook his head. "No. He knows something's wrong. I'm sure he misses his home too."

"He just wants to be near you."

Tony reached down and rubbed Watson's head. "I know. I can tell he's worried about me." Tony straightened up and looked at River. "I wanted to talk to you about what happened. Have you thought anymore about the person who threw that Molotov cocktail into my apartment?"

"I have," River said. "But I'm not sure who was behind it. I mean, my first reaction is that it's the person who threatened Nathan. I have a problem with connecting him to Kevin's death though. I mean, throwing a Molotov cocktail is cowardly. If the same person wanted us out of the way, why not shoot us the way he did Kevin? Something doesn't add up."

"I agree. I'm also wondering about Arnie's phone call."

"I'm not sure what to think about the note the police found. To be honest, I still have to wonder if it was real. I hope it was."

"Do you really think it was some fan trying to stir things up?"

"It's possible," River said. "People do strange things. And right now, we simply don't have enough information. Unless the police can match the handwriting or come up with some kind of proof she was in the room, all we can do is guess." She sighed. "I'm a little conflicted about Jeffrey. After all, he is her father. I think if it was my child, I'd want to be kept updated no matter. Should we call him?"

"Not her father. Her stepfather."

"I'm not sure that makes a difference," River said.

Tony frowned at her. "Maybe not."

"If I were missing and you found out I might be alive—if you kept it to yourself—even for a little while, I'm not sure my mother and brother would ever forgive you."

"I hear you," Tony said, "but we're not completely sure he's not involved some way in her disappearance. Let's give the police just a little more time to come up with something first before we tell Nathan or Jeffrey anything. Besides, the police may contact Jeffrey on their own."

"Okay," River said. "If that's what you think is best."

River's phone rang. "Wow. Arnie. Are you sure he's not listening to us? He has the strangest timing."

Tony chuckled as River answered the phone.

"How's he doing?" he asked.

"He's fine. And he's charging his phone so you can call him directly next time."

"Good to know, thanks," Arnie said. "Hey, just got a call from the police in Terre Haute. Nothing in the room that points to

April Bailey. Housekeeping cleaned the rest of the room before starting to change the sheets and then found the note. We might have found something on the glasses in the room, but they'd been carted to the kitchen and left with a dozen others. They're checking fingerprints on all of them, but it will take a while. We've also called in a handwriting expert, but he won't be able to give us an opinion right away. He's out of town on another case." He sighed. "Switching gears for a moment, you can tell Tony that the fire inspector has confirmed that the fire in his apartment was caused by a Molotov cocktail."

"That's what we expected. I'll tell him." River noticed Tony gesturing at the phone. "Seems like Tony wants the phone."

"Okay."

"Hey, there," Tony said when he took the phone. "Fill me in on what you told River?"

He listened a moment and then said, "Oh. Okay. Not a surprise, but thanks for confirming that. Anything on that motel room?" Again, he was quiet for a while. "Hey, we've been discussing something. Should we tell April's father about the note? And what about Nathan?" Tony looked at River while Arnie responded. Finally, he said, "Okay. I hear you. Thanks, Arnie. And yes, we'll be careful."

Tony clicked the phone off and put it down on the coffee table. "Arnie says we might want to call Jeffrey before the police in Terre Haute do."

"Okay. We were right in thinking they would contact him directly," River said. "I think about this as our case, but it doesn't belong to us solely, does it?"

"No, I guess not."

"Are we certain we shouldn't let the police handle it?" River asked.

"That just doesn't feel right," Tony said. "If we find out he really is just a concerned father, we're going to feel awful about not taking the chance to give him a head's up before he gets a phone call from the police. That can be really disconcerting."

"Okay. Do you want me to call him?"

"Well, I was going to take a nap . . ."

River rolled her eyes. "Oh, please, please let me handle it." She grinned at him. "Did you pick up the card he left for us at the office? I didn't get it."

"Yeah, I think it's in my wallet." Tony stood up and pulled his wallet out of his back pocket. He opened it and then riffled through it before pulling a card out and handing it to her. "I almost left it on my desk but grabbed it at the last minute. It was a little hard to have compassion for the guy. What I read in his body language was anger."

"And fear," River said. "His eyes were wide, and his fingers shook when he put the card down."

"I didn't notice that. I think I was too ticked off." Tony stared at her for a moment, his eyebrows knit together. "I wonder just what he was afraid of."

CHAPTER
THIRTY-NINE

Jeffrey Bailey hung up the phone and immediately dialed a number. He quickly told the man on the other end of the phone about the call he'd just received from River Ryland. "It's time to put a stop to these two," he said.

"And just how do you propose I do that?" Jeffrey retorted.

"The answer is to get rid of your so-called daughter. The doctor gives her a shot, and she goes to sleep. Poof. Our troubles are over."

"No," Jeffrey said, his heart racing. "I told you that I won't let that happen. I mean it. I'll go to the police myself if you hurt April. You're going to have to handle these detectives yourself."

Jeffrey disconnected his phone, his hands shaking so hard, he almost dropped it. Then he called the hospital and asked for Dr. Marnet.

"I'm sorry, sir, but he's seeing patients right now. Can I take a message?"

"I want to talk to him immediately. It's an emergency. You tell him it's Jeffrey Bailey, and if he knows what's good for him, he'll get to the phone right this minute."

There was silence on the other end for several seconds, and

250

then a click as he was put on hold. A couple of minutes later, Alexander's voice came over the phone. He was clearly angry.

"I won't allow you to order my staff around," he said, his words like small bursts of staccato explosions. "The last thing I need is for them to be any more suspicious. Since we brought your daughter back to the hospital, I'm getting some very strange looks."

"I don't care about that. Your job is to keep April sedated. What did you tell them about that nurse?"

A heavy sigh came over the line. "I told them that Audrey removed April from the hospital against my advice and she was fired. That she told me she was going back home to Georgia and that she didn't want to talk to anyone. A couple of the other nurses were her friends. I'm not sure they bought it."

"You better make sure they do. I'd like to know why she smuggled April out of there in the first place. Can you explain that to me?"

There was a long pause. Finally, Alexander said, "I believe she heard me talking on the phone to you the other day. When I told you I couldn't keep this up indefinitely. That we needed to find a more permanent solution. I think she thought I meant we wanted her dead—which isn't what I was saying at all. I didn't realize Audrey was in the hall outside my door. I believe that, in her mind, what she did was an act of compassion."

"You'd better be careful before something else happens. I warned you about that."

"Look," Alexander said, "you haven't made a payment in over a month. I'm only doing this because I was desperate for money. If you don't pay up . . ."

"You'll what? You'll tell the police that you've been drugging my daughter for months? And that because of you, your nurse is dead?" Jeffrey laughed. "Sorry. You've gotten yourself in way too deep. There's nothing you can do except to keep your mouth shut and do what you're told. And you'd better find a way to keep your staff in line before something else happens."

"Why did you call? Just to hurl more threats at me? Sometimes I think you forget who I am."

"Who you are? A doctor at a second-rate hospital who needed a place to hide out because he made so many mistakes. Don't be ridiculous. You need me and my money. You do exactly what I tell you to do, or you're going down." Jeffrey took a deep, shaky breath, trying to calm his nerves. "Look, the other person involved in this thinks the easiest thing would be for April to die. I won't allow it. If anything happens to her, you're done. I mean it."

"I don't get it," the doctor said. "You can't possibly love this girl. If you did you wouldn't keep her here—so drugged up she doesn't know where she is or even who she is."

"Shut up!" Jeffrey said loudly. "How I treat my daughter isn't your business. You just concentrate on your job. If this goes south, you'll end up spending the rest of your life in prison. I'm pretty sure your beautiful wife and those three children of yours won't want anything to do with you when they find out the truth. *You* chose to drink and harm your patients. *You* gambled away your money. *You* got yourself into a hole so deep your only hope was to make a deal with me."

"I didn't realize it was a deal with the devil," the doctor mumbled.

His comment shocked Jeffrey. Was he right? Had he become the devil? "You just remember what I said." He hung up and stared at his phone. *You can't possibly love this girl.*

A memory of a little girl's arms around his neck popped unbidden into his mind. Dancing lessons with her small feet on top of his. *I love you, Daddy. You're the best daddy in the whole world.* In the beginning, he'd only put up with April because of her mother. She was rich and he wasn't—until they were married. But as time went on, he began to care for his stepdaughter. He even adopted her so that she'd have his last name. When Katherine died, April clung to him. It changed him on the inside. He wasn't sure he loved her more than he cared about her money, but he couldn't get rid of the memories. As she got older, April began to pull away. Began to look at him with suspicion. The police hadn't been able to prove that he'd killed Katherine, but it was clear that April had doubts. Still, he couldn't let her die. Maybe his heart was hard, but there was one soft spot—and it belonged to April. If he hadn't taken so much money from her trust fund, he might have tried to be a different man. Might have tried to become the kind of father that April wanted. But it was too late for that. He knew that keeping April alive in the hospital couldn't last forever. But he wasn't ready to let her go. At least not yet.

TONY PICKED WATSON UP and put him on River's bed. Then he covered himself with the folded blanket at the foot of the bed while Watson turned around several times and lay down. Tony stroked his soft fur for a bit before he put his head on the pillow and stared up at the ceiling. The fire had upset him more than he'd let on to anyone. His home was gone. He couldn't even allow his mind to take an inventory of the possessions he'd lost. He was grateful that he and Watson were okay, but ignoring the losses he'd suffered was impossible. Photos with his family, awards from the academy, the Bible his parents had given him when he graduated from high school.

"Stop it," he said quietly. "They're just things. None of them are worth Watson's life—or mine." Still, there was a deep hurt inside him, one that he would have to deal with at some point. He turned his head when he heard someone knock softly on the door.

"Come in."

The door opened, and River stepped into the room. "I wanted to check on you before you go to sleep. I heard you coughing."

Tony had been coughing on and off since last night but really hadn't been paying much attention.

"Sorry. The EMT said it might last for a while. I think it's getting better."

"You mentioned at lunch that you had a headache. I brought some aspirin."

Tony sat up. "Thanks. Another symptom of smoke inhalation, I guess."

"Maybe you should have gone to the hospital," River said. "Had them check you out."

He shook his head. "Not necessary. Really. I'm fine."

She handed him the aspirin and a water bottle. He quickly swallowed the pills and put the bottle down on the table next to the bed.

"So, are you nervous about tonight?" Tony asked.

River sighed. "To be honest, with everything going on, I haven't had a lot of time to think about it."

"Yeah, that was my plan. The fire was just my attempt to keep you occupied so you wouldn't have time to worry about your dad coming."

"Wow," River said. "That's a lot of dedication. Starting a fire in your apartment complex just to make the confrontation with my dad easier. You really went above and beyond."

Tony nodded. "Yeah, I thought you'd be impressed." He felt something on his leg and looked down to see Watson moving up closer to him. Tony moved his hand and patted Watson's head.

"You're silly," River said. "When I allow myself to think about tonight, I do feel nervous. Even a little sick to my stomach. But I know this is going to happen, and I have to face it. It's been so long, and I've resented my father so much . . ." She sighed. "It's like you said, there are scars. It might not be easy. I might feel afraid, but I know God will get me through this. I can't allow feelings to dictate my life." She hesitated a moment, then said, "I want you to know that having you by my side . . . Well, it means more than I can say. I plan to draw on your faith—and your strength." Her eyes searched his. "Thank you, Tony."

"You're welcome."

Watson wiggled up close to River and licked her hand. She laughed. "Sorry. With you and Watson by my side."

Tony laughed at the goofy dog's antics.

"You still haven't called your parents, Tony," River said, her tone serious.

"I know. I'll phone them when I get up."

River frowned at him. "Is there a reason you're putting this off?"

"Yeah. Telling them there was a fire in my apartment after what my dad went through? The burns he endured after saving that little girl all those years ago? I guess I'm afraid it will bring it all back."

"But you're okay. They'll be so happy to know that."

He smiled at her. "We both understand triggers. Don't you think this will be especially tough on them?"

River sighed. "You're right. I've been dense. I should have realized it." She put her hand on his arm. "I guess we're all going to have to face our fears today."

"At least we won't be facing them alone."

River nodded and gazed into his eyes. Tony saw something in her expression that chased away his concerns and made him feel that he could do almost anything.

FORTY

Jeffrey was startled when his phone rang. He frowned when he saw who was calling. Dr. Marnet? Was April okay? His heart felt as if it had jumped into his throat, and he had a hard time finding his voice.

"Yes?" he said when he answered.

"Audrey Cox, the nurse who took April, was just found dead. She was inside her car. Supposedly it went off the side of a steep embankment. She wasn't wearing a seatbelt, and the police think she died of her injuries. But it's being investigated, Jeffrey. First of all, they could easily figure out that she was murdered. If they do, they're going to end up at my doorstep, asking questions. Trying to find out if I know of any reason someone might want to kill her. I didn't sign up for this. Not only have you put me in the line of fire, Audrey was a good nurse. A good person. I liked her."

"You need to keep it together. Seriously. There's nothing to connect you to her death. You had nothing to do with it. Just relax and act normal. I mean it."

"Act normal? There's nothing normal about this. Nothing. I . . .

I can't take this anymore. Listen, I want April out of here. Now. I mean it. And don't threaten me. You can't turn me in without ruining yourself. Take care of this. She's out of here by tomorrow or . . . or I'll do whatever I have to." With that, the phone was disconnected.

Jeffrey tried calling the doctor back, but it kept going to voicemail. Maybe taking April out was the right answer. He could find someplace else. Out of the country. Someplace safe. But as soon as the idea popped into his head, it drifted away. It would never work. First of all, April wouldn't allow it. And finding another doctor like Marnet would take time. Time he didn't have. Was he going to have to let her go? Everything in him screamed no. He needed Alexander to settle down. Keep the plan going for now. If the doctor wouldn't listen to him, maybe he'd listen to the man who'd put this plan into place. The man who had as much to lose as he did.

He picked up his phone and clicked on a familiar number.

THE HOUSE WAS EXTREMELY QUIET. Tony was still napping, and Mrs. Weyland had gone to the store. River used the time to call Nathan and check on him. He was home and felt secure with someone there. She and Tony had planned to wait awhile before telling him about the note found in the hotel room, but since they'd shared the information with Jeffrey, it made sense to let Nathan know as well. If Jeffrey told him first, he'd feel betrayed since he was their client.

When she told him, as she'd anticipated, he was excited.

"Nathan, I think we need to tread carefully here," River said. "So far, there's no trace of April in that room. Until the police come up with something that makes us certain she was there, we have to wonder if one of her followers is playing a game."

"Why would anyone do that?" he asked, his voice indignant.

"Attention. Excitement. Even misplaced concern for April. Wanting to make her case public so the police will work harder to find her. We saw this happen several times when we worked for the FBI. I really don't want to discourage you, but like I said, let's wait for the police to give us a real reason to hope."

"I hear you," Nathan said, "but I believe April wrote that note. She'd definitely think of something like that."

"I hope you're right, I really do. We'll keep you updated. I also wanted to tell you that we've been able to use April's notes to solve several of her cold cases. Your girlfriend is very impressive."

"Yes, she is." His voice cracked and he quickly cleared his throat. "I miss her so much."

"I know you do. I'll check in with you soon. You be careful and do what the police tell you to do, okay?"

"I will. Jared, the officer who's staying with me, is really nice. I feel completely safe."

"I'm glad."

After River said goodbye, she turned her attention to the dinner that she both anticipated and dreaded. If someone had told her even a year ago that she'd be willing to speak to her father again, she wouldn't have believed them. Now, here she was, not only facing him, but determined to forgive him. It was only by the grace of God that this meeting was taking place. God's power to change people was something hard to understand. It was truly miraculous.

"Father," she whispered. "I need You to help me tonight. Fill me with Your love and Your strength. I pray whatever happens will glorify You. And please, please help my mother. Preserve her dignity. Keep her . . . calm."

River realized that she was actually more concerned about

Rose than she was about herself. Her father's betrayal had caused so much pain.

JEFFREY WAS PACKING A BAG. He needed to get April out of the small hospital and take her far away. He was sorry he'd ever started down this road. April was in trouble because of him. This was all his fault. He'd been certain he could sacrifice her for his sins, but when it came down to it, he couldn't. All he could think about was the way she used to look at him. The way she'd adored him and called him *Daddy*. He'd spent a lot of the trust fund, but there was still enough to get them both out of the country and to keep them safe for quite a while. For now, that would have to be good enough. He'd called the doctor and told him to get her ready. He'd have to keep her drugged at first, but once they were safely away, he'd wean her off the medications. He could only hope that there was a way he could explain everything. If he wasn't able to . . . well, he couldn't think about that now. He'd never be able to tell her the truth about her mother. Never. That was a secret that would have to die with him. She'd seen her mother's body underneath the tree in their backyard before it was moved to another location and the knife wound was replaced by a bullet. Somehow, she'd turned it into a nightmare, her mind not allowing her to remember that it was real. He was grateful for that. If she hadn't hidden it away in the recesses of her mind, he wasn't sure what he would have had to do.

He was finally ready. He took the suitcases out to the SUV and was loading them into the back when he felt the first sharp pain in his back. He straightened up to see what was wrong, when he heard the second pop. He was suddenly on his back, looking up at a sky full of dark clouds, when he saw the person standing over him and realized that he was never going to see his stepdaughter again. As he waited for the final bullet that would end his life, all he could think about was her.

IT WAS ALMOST SIX. Tony was up and dressed. He'd helped Mrs. Weyland set the table. River quietly thanked God that he was here with her. She wasn't confident in herself, but she knew God and Tony would get her through what was one of the most difficult things she'd ever had to do. She'd never hated anyone as much as she'd hated her father. Only God could have orchestrated this moment.

Her mother looked beautiful. She wore a dark blue dress that accented her still-youthful figure, and although she didn't wear much makeup, River had used just enough to accent her great features. She couldn't completely push out the thought that she wanted her father to see what he'd thrown away on someone as selfish and cheap as CeCe. However, River knew tonight wasn't about that. She needed to stay centered on God's will. His reason for bringing a fractured family together.

She, Tony, and Rose were sitting in the living room, waiting for the doorbell to ring. The tension in the room was palpable. Tony was trying to relax them, but it wasn't working. Thankfully, her mother seemed to be fully aware of what was going on. River noticed she was twisting her hands in her lap. River got up and sat down next to her on the couch. She took one of Rose's hands in hers.

"I'm so proud of you, Mama," she said. "I can only imagine how difficult this is for you."

Rose's eyes filled with tears. "For you too, honey. But you need to know that I made mistakes too. It wasn't all your father's fault. I didn't deserve what he did, and neither did you. But God's love and forgiveness makes this necessary." She squeezed River's hand. "Promise me that if I . . . if I get confused, you'll get me out of the room. Please? I know it sounds vain, but I just can't look foolish in front of your father. I couldn't bear it."

"Oh, Mama," River said, her voice breaking. "You're not foolish. What's happened to you isn't your fault. Please, please don't ever think about yourself that way. I love you, Mama."

"Oh, River." Rose reached up and patted River's cheek, the same one she'd slapped the night before. "I love you too. I'm so sorry for not being the kind of mother I should have been. I want you to know how much I regret it."

"I let you down too. I should have been more understanding about what you were going through. I guess there's enough blame to go around. To be honest, I even resented Dan for leaving when he was eighteen. I guess we all need a fresh start, don't we?"

"Yes, we do." Rose leaned over and whispered in River's ear. "Please don't let Tony get away, okay? I don't want you to live with regret. It's not the way to live your life."

River looked into her mother's eyes and smiled. Then she nodded.

When the doorbell rang, she felt Rose jump. She looked over at Tony. What she saw in his eyes calmed her. Her mother was right. River had just assured her mother that she wouldn't ever let Tony leave her life. It was a vow she intended to keep.

FORTY-ONE

Mrs. Weyland had made a wonderful dinner. A prime rib
roast, garlic mashed potatoes, glazed carrots, a fruit cup,
and a green salad. River was impressed. But the real star of
the show was Rose's famous peach cobbler. She hadn't made it in a
long time. It used to be her father's favorite dessert. Mrs. Weyland
had overseen her efforts, but she hadn't made any mistakes. As
it was being kept warm in the oven, the aroma wafted through
the house. The dining room table had been laid out with Rose's
white lace tablecloth and a winter centerpiece with a large glass
bowl containing a white candle surrounded by frosted pinecones.
Everything was perfect.

River was surprised by her father. He was still handsome. In
fact, he looked the same except his brown hair had turned to
silver. She'd expected something different after all these years,
but except for his hair, he was the same man who'd walked out
on them so many years ago. Although it probably wasn't very
Christian of her, she'd kind of hoped her father had aged badly.

So far, their conversation was stilted and formal. At one point,
Dan blithered on and on about almost hitting a deer on the way
into town. He'd pointed out that even though there were more

deer in Colorado, where he lived, he'd never come close to running into one until tonight. His attempt to start a dialogue finally seemed to run out of steam, and he fell silent. Rose hadn't said much at all. River wondered if she was afraid to speak. Afraid she'd say the wrong thing.

Her father asked River what she was doing now, and she'd spent a few minutes telling him about her former job with the FBI and why they'd decided to open a private investigation firm.

"At the BAU, we spent most of our time writing profiles for law enforcement," she said. "But now, we can use those skills and do the investigations ourselves. I really enjoy it."

"She's really good at it," Tony said.

"I thought most PIs looked for people who'd skipped out on their debts or cheated on their spouses," her father said.

"That's true, but with our training, we're concentrating on criminal cold cases."

Her father frowned. "How do you get clients? Do you advertise?"

"No," River said. "Tony is friends with St. Louis's chief of police. They were together at the academy. His department has a lot of cold cases, and he wants to send some our way. The police have so much to deal with, they don't have the manpower to spend time working on all of the cases that weren't solved. True, we just started, but I think Arnie, the chief, is beginning to put a lot of trust in us. We may have started slowly, but we're confident things will pick up."

Her father put his fork down. "I'm sorry. I didn't mean to make it sound like you're not successful. I'm sure you will be . . . I mean, you are . . ."

"Please, relax," River said. "We all know this is rather . . . stressful."

Joel sighed loudly. "Stressful. Yeah."

"Dad, it's okay," Dan said.

River shot her brother a look. She loved him and was glad to see him, but she still wished he hadn't forced them into getting together with their father. It would have been better if they'd worked as a team to set something up. Of course, she could have been the first to open the door to reconciliation, and she hadn't. Still, it felt as if Dan had forcefully kicked it open without her permission.

"No, it's not okay." Her father stared down at his plate. "Look, I need to say something. I planned to wait until after dinner, but everyone's obviously uncomfortable."

"I wonder why," River said, trying to keep the anger out of her voice. She looked at Tony and saw caution in his expression. He was right. She needed to keep herself calm. Her mother was fine. She was the one who was struggling. It seemed her feelings were at war with her resolve. She was so thankful that Tony was here. She really did need him. "I'm sorry, D . . . Dad," she said. It was hard to get the word out. He didn't feel like her father. Maybe biologically, but not emotionally.

"It's okay, sweetheart," he replied. "I understand. I don't deserve anything from you, and I'm not asking for anything. I just wanted to tell your mother . . . and you . . . that I'm sorry. So very, very sorry." He took a deep breath. River could see how hard this was for him. "I had everything, but I didn't realize it. Didn't appreciate it. CeCe made me feel younger. Free. A lot of it had to do with the way I saw God. I saw Him as harsh and judgmental. Someone I could never please. I felt so . . . trapped. Leaving with CeCe was my way of running away from God. Running away from the person I didn't think I could be. After she left me, I needed God more than I ever had before. To my surprise, I found out that He wasn't who I thought He was. That he still loved me, even after all the awful things I'd done."

"That's when he called me, sis," Dan said. "At first, I didn't want anything to do with him. But he kept calling. When I finally decided to hear him out, I realized that he'd changed. Really changed. I had to forgive him, River. It was the right thing to do. You know that, right?"

"I hope you can find it in your heart to forgive me too," Joel said with tears in his eyes. "Even though I don't deserve it." He turned his gaze toward River's mother. "But the person I need forgiveness from the most is you, Rose." Until that moment, it was as if he was afraid to look at her. Rose, who had stayed quiet except for a few noncommittal grunts, cleared her throat. River began to silently beg God to keep her mother's mind clear.

"Joel, I realize I wasn't a perfect wife. I'm sorry for making things hard for you. It doesn't excuse what you did, but I forgive you. It happened a long time ago. There's no sense in carrying a grudge forever." Rose stood to her feet. "I need to go to my room. I'm sorry to miss out on the rest of our dinner." She smiled at Dan. "I hope we'll have some time together before you leave. I've missed you so much." Then she turned her eyes to River. "When you look back on your life, you think about the people who loved you. Who really loved you. River, when I needed you, you were there for me. You've been so good to me, and I love you very much. We know that as time goes by, I'll probably forget more and more things—and people. But please know this now, my darling girl. No mother . . ." Her voice caught and she cleared her throat again. "No mother ever had a better daughter. I'm so proud of you."

As Rose left the room, Mrs. Weyland started to get up to go after her.

"Please," River said. "Stay. I'll go."

"Okay, honey," the elderly woman said with a smile. "While you check on your mama, I'll get dessert."

"Thank you." River stood up and looked at her father, her heart pounding in her chest. "You're forgiven, Dad, but after you have a piece of the fabulous cobbler our mother made, I really think you should go. Mom doesn't want you to see her struggling. She still has some pride. Please respect her enough to give her that, okay?"

Joel nodded. "I understand. The truth is, I'd like to stay and help your mother through this, but if that isn't what she wants, I'll leave town. I don't want to hurt her any more than I already have."

"Thank you for coming, Dad," River said. "It took guts. I respect that."

"That means a lot to me, honey," Joel said. "This was harder than you'll ever know, but I knew I had to do it. Your forgiveness means the world to me. I can't fix the past, but maybe we can build something new. I hope you'll give me the chance to do that."

River smiled at him and then walked down the hallway to her mother's room. Rose was sitting on the bed. River went over and sat next to her, taking her hand.

"Are you okay?" she asked.

"I'm fine, honey," Rose said. "Thank you for being here for me." She turned her tear-stained face toward River's. "I'm not afraid, River. I know that no matter what happens, God will walk me through it. Sweetheart, I don't want you to give up your life for me. Please. Your father and I have already taken so much from you. More than anything in the world, I want you to be happy."

"Oh, Mom. I want to be here. Don't you see that spending time with you—being here for you—is giving me so much? I feel like I have a mother again, and that makes me very, very happy."

Rose laid her head on River's shoulder. At that moment, even knowing all the hurdles they faced, River felt incredibly blessed.

CHAPTER

FORTY-TWO

an and her father stayed for dessert but left soon after. Although River wasn't able to forget what her father had done, she knew she'd forgiven him and was determined to put the past in the past. It was something she had to do. God would have to heal the pain and show her how to develop a new relationship with her father. She knew she couldn't do it on her own. And yet, she already felt as if a great burden had been lifted. There was joy and peace filling up a place in her soul that had held nothing but anger for many, many years.

She sent Mrs. Weyland to bed, telling her she'd take care of the dishes. It was the least she could do. Dinner had been so good, especially her mother's peach cobbler. After getting Rose settled, she'd gone back and had dessert with everyone else. Her father had gotten a little emotional when he took his first bite. Although he didn't say anything, River knew why he'd reacted that way. He remembered when Rose used to make the same dish for him. River suspected it was Rose's way of telling him she was trying to move on from the past.

Tony had offered to help with the dishes, but she'd turned him down. She needed some time alone to process the evening. He seemed to understand and was in the living room getting the couch ready for another night. For now, he was keeping his clothes and other belongings in the hall closet, but River could see that the sooner they could get a room set up downstairs, the more comfortable he would be.

As she put the dishes in the dishwasher, something kept bothering her. Tugging at her mind. Like a dream she couldn't quite remember. She attempted to dismiss it. Maybe she was just emotional after seeing her father. And of course, there were challenges in front of her that had to be faced. Although she tried not to worry about them, sometimes a voice whispered in her head that things could go horribly wrong. But this wasn't that. It was something different—and it wouldn't leave her alone. This had happened to her more than once during the past few days. What was it this time? "Holy Spirit, are you trying to tell me something?" she whispered. "Please make it clearer."

She sighed as she loaded up the last of the dishes. Then she turned on the dishwasher, wiped down the cabinets, and was getting ready to leave the kitchen when she remembered. It was something her brother had said. She stood there, shocked by the memory. How could she have missed it? How could Tony have missed it too? Before doing anything else, she had to double check something.

It was then that she remembered that she'd left her notebook and her laptop at work. She needed them now. Right now. She went into the living room to talk to Tony but found him sound asleep. She thought about waking him up but decided against it. Even though he felt he had to drive her everywhere, a quick trip to the office and back wouldn't take long. He needed his sleep and there simply wasn't any reason he should have to get up and take her there. She was pretty sure she knew who had killed Kevin. She was almost certain she remembered the conversation clearly, but they'd talked to a lot of people, and she'd made a lot of notes. Getting the proof was important. It couldn't wait. Surely, even Tony would understand that.

She quickly wrote him a note and left it on the coffee table. Then she got her keys and her coat. She didn't like disarming the security system, but she'd be back right away. The office was only about fifteen minutes away.

Thankfully, she got green lights almost all the way. She had to unlock the main door, but it was set to automatically lock behind her when she entered. The only vehicle in the parking lot was a truck near the front door, but it belonged to the maintenance guy. A couple of months ago, that would have worried her, but now she wasn't concerned about that. She rode up the elevator, opened the door to their office, grabbed her laptop and her notebook, and started to head downstairs. At the last second, she went back in and opened her laptop. She quickly typed a name into the search engine. When the name brought up several articles, she read through them quickly just in case they would bring her any further understanding. Unfortunately, she didn't see anything that helped her hypothesis—but nothing led her away from it either.

She was just starting to close her laptop when she noticed that one of the articles had a picture. It caught her attention, and she carefully scanned the image. It was then that she noticed something. Something she'd seen before. It was at that moment that everything came together. All of it. From April's disappearance to Kevin's murder and the fire at Tony's. She closed her laptop, and realized she didn't have her phone. She found Tony's personal address book and picked up the office phone they rarely used. Then she made a quick call. Feeling as if she'd done everything she could, she locked the office door behind her and hurried downstairs. She'd really wanted to stay and work on her suspicions a little longer, but concern for what Tony would say made her get back in her car as quickly as she could and head home.

HE WAS PARKED OUTSIDE HER HOUSE. He'd warned them. Told them to back off. Jeffrey had been dealt with. The male investigator, Tony, was definitely here. He found out what Jeffrey had done after he told him to leave things alone. It was the final straw. Jeffrey's attempt had failed. Tony was still alive. Thankfully, they were both here together. The only good result from Jeffrey's stupidity. He'd decided to use Jeffrey's method to end this. That way it would look like the same person had used the identical method in both endeavors. It should help to lead the authorities away from him. Maybe St. Clair had survived the first attempt to silence him, but tonight would be different. Tonight, everyone inside this house would die.

He started to get out of his car, but lights hit his rearview mirror. A car. He realized it was slowing down, so he put his own car in gear and drove a little way down the street. He'd have to wait a while before striking. As he watched someone stop and then get out of the other vehicle, he realized it was her. River Ryland. She hadn't even been home. He thanked his lucky stars that he'd waited. She would have gotten away if he'd moved too soon. Now he could take care of her permanently. Then he'd be completely safe. Well, almost. After this, he'd deal with Marnet and April Bailey. He'd called the doctor a couple of days ago to tell him he needed to get rid of April, but he'd refused to do it. The doctor and his patient had to go. Then he'd be able to live his life without looking over his shoulder. He'd finally be free.

RIVER PARKED HER CAR and hurried into the house. She quickly armed the security system and then checked on Tony. Thankfully, he was still asleep. She knew he'd be upset when he found out what she'd done, but she still felt she'd made the right decision. This was something that couldn't wait. Besides, she was safe, and everything was fine.

After hanging up her coat and making herself a cup of hot tea, she carried her laptop and notebook to her room. Once there, she sat down at the desk and opened the laptop. While it loaded, she quickly thumbed through her notebook, but what she wanted wasn't there. She pulled up April's notes, but she was certain that wasn't where she'd seen it. It was then that she remembered she'd actually heard him say it. She hadn't written it down because it hadn't registered as being important at the time. She still felt stupid for not recognizing how important it was. She wondered if he'd realized later what he'd said. But even though he'd slipped up and told her what would lead to his downfall, she didn't need anything besides what she knew. She was confident the police would find a way to back it all up.

River wrote down the details and then got ready for bed. She had just slipped under the covers when she heard a noise from outside. It sounded like a car door slamming. It was probably just one of the neighbors, but she couldn't take any chances. She opened the drawer in the table next to her bed and picked up her gun. Her clips were on the top shelf in her closet. She never left her gun loaded inside the house. It was too dangerous, especially with her mother's condition. She quickly grabbed the small footstool in front of her chair and moved it to the closet so she could reach the back of the shelf. She got the box with her clips and removed two. After putting one clip in her gun, she put the other one in her pocket. Then she turned the light off in her room and walked quietly down the hallway. She stopped by her mother's room and slowly opened the door. Rose was sound asleep. She checked on Mrs. Weyland, who was also sleeping.

Her last stop was Tony, who was actually sitting up. When he saw her, he started to say something, but River put her finger to her lips. She came closer to him and whispered, "I think I heard something outside. It's probably nothing, but I'm going to check. Stay here and be quiet, okay?"

"Not on your life," he said, standing to his feet. "What's going on?"

"Like I said, I'm probably being paranoid, but I noticed a car outside the house when I got back, and I think I just heard a car door slam a couple of minutes ago."

"When you got back?" Tony said. "Got back from where? You're not supposed to go anywhere without me."

"You know that the Strangler's partner is probably nowhere near us," she said. "Besides, we've got the upper hand. So don't overreact."

"Overreact? Are you kidding me? What . . ."

"Would you hush?" River said. "I'll explain everything later. You'll understand why I left. But for now, can we deal with what's happening now?"

"I guess," Tony grumbled, "but this isn't over."

He walked down the hall to the closet and pulled out his duffel bag. Then he grabbed his own gun. River took the extra clip out of her pocket and handed it to him. If this was just the neighbor getting home after a night on the town, this could end up being very embarrassing.

She went over to the window and pulled the drape back just enough so she could get a clear look at the dark car parked outside. An SUV like Tony's, but a different make. It was the same one she'd noticed earlier when she drove up. She could see that someone had gotten out of the car. He opened the door to the back seat and pulled out a bag. Her stomach turned over when she realized what was probably in the bag. She turned to Tony, who stood next to her.

"He's going to do the same thing here that he did at your apartment if we don't stop him."

"You stay here and protect your mom and Mrs. Weyland. I'll stop him."

"Tony, you know I'm a better shot than you are."

"We'll both go," Tony said gruffly.

When Tony made his mind up there was no arguing with him. She really was a better shot and felt she was the logical choice to take charge. But they didn't have time to stand around and argue.

"All right," she whispered.

River disarmed the security system using the keypad next to the front door. Then she and Tony moved through the kitchen to the door that led to the backyard. River wanted to come up behind this guy. Walking through the front door wasn't the way to do it. Tony didn't argue, so he was probably thinking the same thing she was. They had to move quickly. If he was going to do what she thought he was, they had to be perfect. They had to stop him before it was too late.

She crept around one side of the house while Tony went the other way. As the man approached the yard, he removed something from the bag. The front porch light was on and there was a streetlight nearby, but he wore a dark coat with a hood and a scarf around the lower part of his face. Obviously, he didn't want to be seen. Their mounted outside camera wasn't a threat to him. He intended to burn everything down. In his mind, nothing would be left to incriminate him.

River quickly walked out into the yard. "Stop right there," she said loudly, stopping him in his tracks. "If you take one more step, I'll shoot you where you stand. I'm serious."

He looked at her and raised his hand. It was then she saw that he was armed as well. She didn't hesitate. She took aim and had her finger on the trigger when a shot rang out and he fell. She was confused. Had she taken the shot or had Tony? She looked over at him as he came into the yard from the other side of the house. He looked as confused as she was. Suddenly, the yard was flooded with light. Two police cars were parked on the street, and two officers were standing on the sidewalk, their guns drawn.

"Chief Martin told us you might need help," one of the officers said.

River was about to thank him when the man who'd been shot struggled to his feet and turned toward the police. Before they could stop him, he held up the object he'd taken from the bag and lit it. Exactly what River had suspected. A Molotov cocktail. He drew his arm back to throw it when both officers fired again. River yelled at them to stop, but she wasn't fast enough. The man fell again, and the bottle exploded. In only seconds, he was engulfed in fire. River prayed he was already dead. She wouldn't want her worst enemy to die by burning alive.

His body writhed on the yard, but it was probably involuntary spasms caused by the intense heat. One of the officers came up to them, while two others ran over to the man lying in the yard and tried to put out the flames.

"You need to tell them that he might have another bottle filled with gasoline in his bag," River said. "They need to stay back. He's already gone."

The officer yelled for the other officers to get back. They immediately put distance between them and the man who was still burning.

It suddenly began to snow. It was as if God was putting out the fire Himself. Unfortunately, it would take a lot of snow to accomplish that. Just then a fire truck pulled up behind the police cars. Firefighters jumped out and pulled out a long hose. Instead of using water, they began to spray foam over the fire and the body. It was the best way to fight a gasoline fire. Water could have actually spread the flames.

Tony put his arm around River and led her back inside the house. "I have a feeling you owe me an explanation," he said.

She smiled up at him. "I'm absolutely certain I do."

FORTY-THREE

Tony sat at the kitchen table with River. Mrs. Weyland had finally gotten Rose back to bed. She'd heard the sirens and woke up confused, afraid someone was breaking into the house. Once she was settled, Mrs. Weyland went to her room. Now that the house was quiet, Tony wanted answers. He was still upset that River had left the house alone, but he was even more confused as to what had just happened outside. Did River's errand have anything to do with the death of the man in her front yard?

"First of all, as I'm sure you know, the incident outside had nothing to do with the Strangler," River said. "I'm convinced it was the person who killed Kevin. He may have set the fire at your apartment, but I'm not sure about that yet. He might have copied what happened to you to throw suspicion on someone else. That's just a guess. We may not ever know the truth about that."

"And how do you know all of this?" Tony asked.

River took a deep breath. "Okay, let me start from the beginning. I know you're angry with me for leaving, but I hope you'll understand once I explain."

"It would take the explanation of a lifetime for me to understand that."

"One thing you need to realize is that if I'd gone to bed earlier, I wouldn't have seen that SUV outside. And I might not have heard his car door slam. This could have turned out much worse. Can you see that?"

"You're trying to handle me," Tony said. "Knock it off."

"What I'm saying is true, Tony. But let's move past that." She leaned forward in her chair. "We were having supper and my brother said something about almost hitting a deer on the way here, do you remember?"

"No, not really," Tony said.

"Anyway . . . . I was doing the dishes when I kept going back to our conversation. I knew there was something bothering me, but I couldn't put my finger on it. That's when I remembered what Dan said. And then I recalled something else. I just wasn't certain where I'd heard it. I started wondering if it was on April's podcasts or in her notebook. I also wondered if I'd made a note about it in my own notebook. But I'd left it, along with my laptop, at the office. I had to have them, Tony. Because if I was right, it would reveal the person who killed the hitchhiker, Cheryl Armitage. I do have to add that he had help. At this point, I'm not sure who did what, although they're both to blame."

"I'm not following, but keep going," he said.

"As I was saying, I needed to prove that he'd said it." She held her hand up before he could say anything else. "Just listen. Anyway, he'd mentioned something I should have picked up on right away. To be honest, I have no idea why he even brought it up. I'm sure he didn't mean to. I think he probably used it as an excuse back then to cover his tracks and he repeated it to me without thinking. Because of who he was, no one thought to challenge him. Or if anyone was suspicious, they were too afraid of him to say anything. I have no idea if he realized later what he'd revealed. He might not have. I just can't be sure. Then last night, while I was at the office, I did a quick search under his name. I wanted to know if he'd crossed the line before. You know, done something that would make my suspicions look credible. It was then that I noticed it. The nail in his coffin, so to speak. Although right now, that might be a little too literal."

River turned her laptop toward Tony. He gasped when he saw the photo. "You've got to be kidding. How could it be him?"

"Two reasons. On the night that Cheryl Armitage died, Detective Vincent Porter said that he'd hit a deer on the way to the crime scene."

"That's not really enough to make you think he ran over Cheryl. People hit deer quite a bit in Missouri—although it does give me pause."

"That's only the first thing that turned me on to him. Now look at his ring."

Tony looked closer at the photo. Porter was wearing some kind of signet ring. It looked very familiar. Where had he seen it before? That's when it hit him. "It's the same ring Jeffrey Bailey wears."

"Right. I looked it up. It's some kind of Masonic thing. I can't prove it, but I'm sure Detective Armbruster will be able to track it down. It made me suspect that Jeffrey and Porter knew each other."

"Which leads me to my next question," Tony said. "How did the police show up so quickly tonight?"

"I found Arnie's number in your address book. By the way, most people keep their phone numbers on their phone, Grandpa."

"He's called you. His number is on your cell phone."

River didn't say anything, but her cheeks turned slightly pink.

Tony shook his head. "You left this house alone, unprotected. And you forgot your cell phone?"

River looked sheepish. "Let's not focus on the negative, all right?" She frowned at him. "That vein in your neck is throbbing."

"You think? We're going to have a long talk later about the

chances you took tonight. And don't tell me again how every-thing turned out okay because you weren't in your room when Porter showed up."

River didn't say anything for a moment. She must have realized he was upset and decided to back off.

"Anyway, I called Arnie from the office. I guess he decided we might be in danger. I thank God he sent two patrol cars and the fire department over here. If he hadn't . . ."

Tony reached down and patted Watson's head. "I don't want to think about that. I take it that burning pile of . . . whatever . . . outside is Porter?"

River nodded.

"So, now Porter's dead. We need to find Jeffrey and look for answers."

"I've tried calling him, Tony. He's not answering his phone."

"It's really late. He's probably asleep."

"Maybe," River said slowly, "but I've got a bad feeling."

"You're thinking Jeffrey Bailey and a crooked cop were work-ing together? Why? Just because of the ring? So where's April?"

River shrugged. "I can't be sure, but I can guess. I have to wonder if they were covering for each other. Jeffrey knew what Porter had done, maybe he told him, I'm not sure. I think Jeffrey had a secret too. I'm guessing it has something to do with April's trust fund. My guess is that Jeffrey's been helping himself to it. So, they keep each other's secrets as *brothers* or whatever, because of their secret club."

"I know people who are Masons. They don't act like that."

"I'm sure you're right," River said. "These two seem to have taken it to extremes."

"Okay, how does April fit into your hypothesis?"

"Well, Porter was afraid April was going to uncover his secret through her podcast. Maybe he told Jeffrey he needed to get rid of her. But then Jeffrey made a deal. I think he promised he could keep her quiet so Porter wouldn't kill her." She sighed. "It's all conjecture at this point, and I don't know if we'll ever learn the entire truth. I doubt either one of them wrote anything down. They were probably both too paranoid. Oh, and one other thing. Jeffrey lied when he said he didn't hear Nathan's voicemail telling him he'd visited us. He heard it. That's why he started sending us those warnings. He had to lie, or we would have realized it had to be him." She shook her head. "We should have picked up on that."

Tony took a deep breath and let it out. "I need some sleep. This has been a very busy night."

"That's an understatement."

"Hey, I realize with everything else going on, this may not be the first thing on your mind right now," Tony said, "but I really want to know how you feel about your father's visit. We haven't had a chance to talk about it."

"I'm satisfied . . . for now anyway," River said. "I think we can finally start mending our relationship. I intend to work on it."

"Good." Tony yawned.

"Let's get to sleep," River said. "You're barely able to stay awake."

"My body may be tired, but my mind is racing."

"I understand," River said. "But I think someone else is more than ready to snooze out." A sudden loud snore from Watson made them both laugh.

Tony was still upset that River had taken off on her own, but he wasn't surprised. She had her own mind, and when she was following a lead, she was like a dog after a juicy bone. The thing that worried him was that her independence and stubbornness would someday get her in real trouble. The odd thing was that it made him love her even more. Would the day ever come when he could tell her?

"Good night," River said.

"Good night."

River got up and headed toward her bedroom while Tony and

Watson went into the living room. Tony lay down on the sofa bed, but he didn't fall asleep for quite a while. His mind wasn't on the events of the day. Instead, all he could think about was the diminutive girl with the green eyes who had completely captured his heart and soul.

CHAPTER
FORTY-FOUR

t felt a little odd to be back in the office. They'd taken Monday off so they could both relax and recuperate a bit. So much had happened, and they still hadn't located April. River was worried about her, and she knew Tony was too.

She could tell Tony was also concerned about the Strangler's accomplice, but strangely enough, she wasn't. She was ready for this to finally be over. She was tired of this maniac's threats hanging over her life. But for him to be stopped, she needed to be in the office. Tony knew that was true, but he was clearly tense. He wasn't leaning back in his chair, a sure sign that he was worried. Although he was trying to act like he was just fine, there was no doubt in her mind that he was afraid that something could go wrong.

"I really appreciate your dad and your brother offering to move things around in the basement so I can stay down there," Tony said suddenly, "but you really don't need to put me up. My insurance will pay for a hotel."

"I know that, and I'm glad you have great insurance, but we need to stay together right now. And after we take care of our Strangler problem, I still don't want you in a hotel. I really think you'll be comfortable in that room downstairs. It was built to be a bedroom. My mom's never used it for that, but all of Dan's bedroom furniture was stored down there. I think she was toying with the idea of turning the space into a guest bedroom. She just never got around to it. There's also a small bathroom that I'll clean up and stock. I even ordered a new mattress for the bed." She waved her hand at him when he started to say something. "Don't even go there. I'm not going to be able to sleep thinking of you down there on some old, lumpy mattress. That thing's so ancient, it's not fit for anyone to sleep on. Besides, once you go back to your apartment, we'll finally have a guest bedroom. Dan's said he'll visit more often. He can stay down there, so really, having you at the house has turned out to be a blessing in many ways."

"I appreciate that, but I'd like to at least reimburse you for the mattress."

River shrugged. "You don't need to. Happy birthday."

"My birthday isn't for two months."

"Okay, happy early birthday. Now hush up."

Before he had a chance to respond, his phone rang. While he answered it, River took her laptop out of her tote bag and put it on her desk. She plugged it in and turned it on. Then she started checking their emails. She was happy to see several requests for meetings. Most of them were references from Arnie, but River was confident that eventually they'd get even more business by word of mouth.

When Tony finally disconnected his call, he stared at her with a strange look on this face.

"Something wrong?"

"No, actually just the opposite. If you weren't already sitting down, I'd tell you to."

River frowned at him. "Okay, I'm intrigued. Tell me."

"A doctor named Marnet in Illinois contacted the police.

He had quite a story to tell them. Seems that about a year ago, a man he knew offered him a lot of money to accept his daughter into his small, private hospital for patients deemed mentally disturbed in a small town near Terre Haute. Since he was almost bankrupt because of his gambling debts, he accepted the deal. His instructions were to keep the girl sedated, unable to leave. But then one of his nurses helped the girl escape. The police are certain she's the one who sent Nathan the notes telling him April needed help. Another man, someone working with the father, found them hiding in a motel. The girl was returned to the hospital, although the man who brought her back wanted the doctor to kill her. Give her an overdose. The father wouldn't allow it. But when the nurse who'd tried to help the girl was found dead, Dr. Marnet decided he'd had enough. He called the police. When they arrived, they arrested the doctor and moved the girl to a hospital in St. Louis where she's being monitored."

River tried to blink away the tears that filled her eyes. "Please tell me you're talking about April."

Tony nodded. "Arnie was alerted, and he called Nathan, who's on his way to the hospital."

"Wow. That's . . . that's amazing." She frowned. "But why didn't the nurse just call the police?"

"Seems she was afraid of the man working with April's father. Afraid he would kill her if he found out she'd told anyone. Something else—when the police went through Porter's house, they found his laptop. A quick look revealed that he was Lamont Cranston. They also found a note they think Jeffrey Bailey wrote saying he knew April's login information for her podcast and that he'd shut it down. Since he cleaned out her apartment, my guess is he found it in that planner Nathan told us about."

"Well, that makes sense," River said.

"Porter was trying to shut April down from the beginning, afraid that she'd uncover his secret. Like you thought, he's the one who struck and killed Cheryl Armitage. He hid the damage to his car by saying he'd hit a deer. No one followed up on him because he was a respected police detective. Seems he was drunk the night it happened and didn't notice her. Cheryl must have seen him though. That's why she whispered 'three little piggies' while she was dying. Porter and a couple of his cronies had encountered her before. I guess they weren't very nice about it. That was her nickname for them. Once they found out Porter was dead, one of his old police buddies came forward with that information. Guess he was too afraid of Porter to say anything before."

"You know, I just realized something else," River said. "When I talked to Porter, he told me that Cheryl's husband couldn't have taken April because he was dead *when April went missing*. But I didn't tell him when April disappeared. He knew because he was involved in her kidnapping. Another thing I missed."

"Don't beat yourself up about it," Tony said. "I didn't catch it either. We both assumed a respected detective wouldn't be involved in something like that." He shook his head. "Seems Porter was walking on the edge of a cliff, and he was afraid April was the one who would finally push him over.

"Something else about Jeffrey Bailey. Now that the police realize he was working with Vincent Porter, they're going to look into April's mother's death again. The dream April had as a child about seeing a woman dead under a tree? They're wondering if Porter actually killed her and then staged her death somewhere else. You remember that Jeffrey was cleared of her murder because he had an alibi?"

River nodded.

"If they can find something that connects Porter to her death, it could mean that Jeffrey really was behind it. I hate thinking that

April may have to deal with something like that, but I believe she needs to know the truth."

"I do too," River said. "You said there were two things you needed to tell me. Was that the second thing?"

Tony chuckled. "It's another story about someone in law enforcement. However, I can guarantee you'll like this one a lot more. Not long ago, a woman who was having car trouble pulled over to the side of a road that wasn't very well traveled out near Kimmswick. A man stopped and asked if he could help. Then he attacked her. Turns out the woman was an off-duty police officer. She took him down. Guy never stood a chance. When other officers arrived, they found a bag with silk dogwood flowers in his car."

"Are you telling me that they caught the guy who killed Shelly Evans and Ted Piper?"

"Yeah, and because you noticed those flowers, they believe they'll be able to tie him not only to their deaths, but also the others Arnie told us about," Tony said.

"That's incredible."

"Doesn't that mean that all of April's cold cases are closed?" Tony asked.

"Yeah, except for the man whose body was found next to the railroad tracks. I wish we could have done something with that."

"I do too, River, but to be honest, not all crimes are solved. This is one we'll just have to walk away from."

"I guess so." She shrugged. "I can't complain, I guess. I would like to know what happened to Jeffrey Bailey. It's obvious he and Porter were connected and keeping each other's secrets."

"I'm convinced he's dead, River. I think Porter killed him. Even though the police haven't found his body yet, I'm sure they will."

"Yeah, maybe," River said. "But isn't it possible he might have just taken off? Decided to run away?"

"Anything's possible, I guess. Arnie said that in his own way, he cared about his daughter. He spent a lot of the money from April's trust fund trying to keep her alive."

River snorted. "Yeah, sure. Who keeps their daughter drugged up for months? Sorry, but Jeffrey Bailey deserves whatever he gets . . . or got. I know I'm supposed to be compassionate toward people—remember that God loves them as much as He loves us. But sometimes it's really hard."

"Yes, it is." Tony sighed.

"You okay?"

Tony shook his head. "No, I was thinking about Watson. Wondering if I should have brought him with us today. He's been sticking close to me ever since the fire. I know he was traumatized by it."

"Traumatized? Are you kidding? He's having a blast with all the attention he's getting. Mom, Mrs. Weyland, and Scutter are all crazy about him. He's soaking it up like a sponge." She smiled at him. "Seriously, Tony. He's doing great. He was a little confused and insecure the first couple of days, but he's got so much support now, I think he's over it."

"Maybe you're right." He stared at her for a moment before saying, "I'm so grateful Porter was stopped before he bombed your house. If you hadn't gone to the office . . ."

"It's okay. I usually try to do what you ask me to do, but sometimes . . ."

"Sometimes you're smarter than me?"

She grinned at him. "I wasn't going to say that. I was going to say that sometimes God is smarter than you."

Tony leaned his head back and laughed, which made River feel better. They still had a major obstacle in front of them, but God had proven to be exactly who He said He was. A help in time of trouble. A loving Father. A protector. She had faith that everything was going to be okay.

THEY HUNG AROUND THE OFFICE the rest of the day. At five o'clock, they got up from their desks. Tony walked up next to her and put his hand on her shoulder.

"Let's pray first," he said.

"You know it might not be today."

"I know," he said. "But we're giving him a chance. I think he's been waiting for it."

She nodded. "I agree. I'd appreciate that prayer."

Tony took a deep breath before praying, "Father, Your Word says that you give Your angels charge over us to keep us in all our ways. That no weapon formed against us will prosper. Father, we believe that since River has set her love upon You, that You will protect her. You've promised to be with us when we're in trouble—to deliver us and honor us. We believe Your promises. Thank You for being with River and . . ." Tony took a deep, shaky breath and choked out the rest of his words. "Thank You for giving us success in this endeavor. I know You'll keep her safe, Father. She means so much to me . . ."

River looked up into his tear-filled eyes. Before she realized what she was doing she reached up and put her hand on his cheek.

"I'll be okay, Tony. We both will. When this is over, there are things to be said."

"I'm tired of waiting," Tony said, his voice husky with emotion. He leaned down and put his lips on hers. She felt something so powerful when they kissed that it took her breath away. When he moved away, all she could do was stare at him.

"I believe you'll come back to me," Tony said, "and you're right, when this is over, we'll sit down and talk. But I don't want you doing this thing until you know how much I love you."

River tried to speak, but Tony put his fingers on her lips.

"Not now," he said. "When you're ready."

She wanted to tell him that she loved him too, but she was too emotional to speak. As they headed for the door, River was filled with peace. At the same time, she was overwhelmed by the love she felt for the man who had changed her life and taught her what love actually was.

FORTY-FIVE

I t was one of the hardest things he'd ever done. Driving away and leaving River in the parking lot. They'd set it up, but would he take the bait? Tony drove several blocks away and then turned onto a side street, where he took out his phone and called Arnie. Although they couldn't be certain, Tony felt in his gut that tonight they would finally stop the Strangler's accomplice.

"She's there alone," he said when Arnie answered him.

"We're already tracking him," Arnie said. "He's still at the office. You know we can't confront him until he takes her."

"I'd feel better if she was wired," Tony grumbled.

"He's too sophisticated. He would have found it, and River would have been in immediate trouble. Besides, she has her phone on. She's recording him. We'll get what we need from that."

"You'll tell me when he leaves the parking lot?"

"Yes, but you've got to stay out of the way. If he sees you . . ."

"I know, but I can't just sit around and wait."

"Okay, he's on the move," Arnie said. "Stay where you are, and I'll tell you where he stops. You've got to wait, Tony. We need to take him down before you meet up with us. You got it?"

He sighed, frustrated by waiting, yet he knew Arnie was right. "I've got it. Promise you'll call me immediately?"

"I promise. I've got to go."

Arnie hung up, and Tony sat in his car, the motor running. Every second felt like an hour.

RIVER WATCHED TONY DRIVE AWAY. Although she was nervous, she was also excited. Trapping the man who had tried to kill her and Tony would give her so much satisfaction. But at the same time, she couldn't get the feeling of Tony's lips on hers out of her mind. She almost wished he hadn't kissed her now. That he would have waited until this was over. She was distracted, and she couldn't afford to be. She took a deep breath and forced herself to focus on the task at hand. She looked around her but didn't see anyone. His car was still in the parking lot. She fumbled around in her purse as if she were looking for her car keys. No one came out of the building. Finally, she got into her car. Maybe tonight wasn't the night after all. She wanted to get this over with. She, Tony, and Arnie had worked this out to the last detail. She was confident their plan would work. She fought frustration. *Please, God*, she prayed. *End this man's evil reign once and forever.*

She drove home slowly, checking behind her to see if he was following her, but she couldn't tell. It got dark early in the winter. There were cars behind her, but she couldn't be sure if any of them belonged to him.

When she finally got home, she got out of her car and started to call Tony to let him know it hadn't worked. She was waiting for him to answer when she felt the barrel of a gun pressed into her back.

"Stay quiet and get into my car," he said, his breath turning to steam in the icy cold. He grabbed the phone from her hand and threw it on the ground, stomping on it. It broke into pieces. River stared at the shattered phone. She'd planned to keep it on.

Record his confession. Now it was useless. Her mind raced as she wondered what she should do. But she was an ex-FBI behavioral analyst. Her testimony would be credible. Besides, as a narcissist, he wouldn't be able to deny his genius. He'd proudly proclaim what he'd done once he was captured. Everything was all right. All she had to do was wait for Tony and Arnie to come. Their plan would work.

"You won't get away with this," she told him. "The police are watching my house, and there are cameras recording us right now."

He laughed softly. "It doesn't matter. The police aren't here now, and the two old ladies inside probably don't know how to check the camera. Besides, by the time anyone sees the video we'll be long gone. No one will be able to find you in time, and I'll have vanished again after you're dead."

He pushed her hard, and she almost fell.

"Now, get inside the car. If you call out or try to run, I'll shoot you. And then I'll go in the house and kill your mother and her friend."

River had no intention of following his instructions. Surely Tony would be here any minute. Where was he? Where were the police? When she didn't move, he grabbed her and pulled her around to his passenger-side door. Then he forced her coat open, tearing the buttons off. He ran his free hand over her body and inside her blouse, searching her carefully. There wasn't a hint of anything sexual in his movements. He was looking for something that might make it possible for someone to trail them. When he was satisfied she wasn't wearing a wire, he shoved her inside his vehicle and slammed the door shut. While he was walking around to his door, she quickly reached down and made a quick move that he didn't see. She wasn't sure it was necessary since they had a plan in place, but her run-in with the Strangler had taught her to be overly cautious. She wasn't certain she could record him, but at least it was a chance. One she was willing to take. She glanced up and down the street, trying to spot cars that didn't belong or anyone who might be watching. The neighbors' cars were parked up and down the street, but they were empty, and she didn't see anyone. It was so cold, everyone was inside their homes, staying warm. For the first time, she felt afraid. This isn't what they'd planned.

When he climbed into the driver's side, he locked all the doors. She was certain he'd used his child locks to make it impossible for her to get out.

"Why are you doing this?" she asked.

"Shut up." He put his car into gear and started down the street. The falling snow was illuminated by the streetlamps, which had just flickered on. The beauty of the crystalline white flakes was in direct contrast to the evil emanating from this man. Of course, she knew who he was. There were a lot of things about him she didn't understand. But she wanted to. Needed to.

"If I'm going to die, I should be able to ask a few questions, don't you think?" she asked. She wanted him to tell her what he'd done before her time with him was over.

"I told you to shut up," he growled.

Then he reached over and hit her in the face with his gun. River felt an explosion of pain and then felt herself drift away.

BY THE TIME TONY TRIED to answer River's call, she'd hung up. What did that mean? Did she hang up because the man they were stalking had approached her? He tried to call back, but his calls went straight to voicemail. He was getting ready to call Arnie when his phone rang. Relief flooded him. River. But when he looked at the phone, he saw that it was Arnie.

"Meet us at this address," he said, his words clipped and fast. Something was wrong. "What's going on?" Tony asked.

"Just get here." Arnie hung up.

Tony took a deep breath. He felt faint. Then he remembered their prayer. "I'm trusting You, Father," he whispered. "You're all she has. You have to protect her." He put the address Arnie had given him into his GPS and drove as quickly as he could to the location. It was hard to think straight, but he kept going over and over Scriptures about God's protection.

Finally, he saw Arnie's car as well as several police cars up ahead, but this was a residential street. Not the kind of location he'd expected—unless it had been River's house. They'd discussed that possibility, although the parking lot seemed like a better option for him to confront her. But from there he should have taken her somewhere near the river. What was going on?

He pulled up behind Arnie's vehicle and got out. Arnie came walking up to him. He held his hands up like someone trying to stop traffic. When he reached Tony, he quickly brought him up to speed on what was happening.

"It's all my fault." Tony slammed his hand against the door of his car.

"That won't help," Arnie said, putting his hand on Tony's shoulder. "There was no way to know he'd switched the tracker."

They were standing outside the home of a very frightened real estate agent whose office was in the same building where their detective agency was housed. Of course, being questioned by the St. Louis chief of police would intimidate anyone. Trying to explain the mix-up certainly hadn't helped the situation much. Maybe mentioning that they were tracking a dangerous serial killer had been a mistake.

"Our killer knows," Tony said. "He's aware that we know who he is. That just makes him even more dangerous."

Arnie's phone rang and he quickly answered. He grunted a couple of times and then said, "Try to reassure them that everything's okay." Then he hung up.

"What?" Tony asked.

"River's car is parked in front of her house. The driver's door is open, and her purse is on the passenger seat. Her phone's on the ground, smashed to pieces. Her mother and her caregiver are extremely upset. I told Jimmy to go inside and try to reassure them." He sighed. "So, what do we know? He's driving a dark blue late model Buick. He's parked somewhere near the river, probably no farther than thirty minutes from here. And . . ."

Just then, a detective got out of the car across the street and jogged over. "We've got his license plate number," the detective said. "What do you want us to do now, sir?"

"Put out a BOLO on the car and the suspect. Also, add River Ryland to the order. I want squads to check parks, pull overs, anyplace along the river within a twenty-mile radius."

"Lights and sirens?"

Arnie looked at Tony. "I don't think we have a choice. I know it's a gamble. If he hears us coming, he might decide to move faster."

"You mean kill her right away." Tony's statement was said as a fact, not as a question.

Arnie didn't respond to his statement. "We've got to get going."

Tony just nodded. His mind raced, trying to find a way to save River's life, but without divine intervention, he couldn't see any way for River Ryland to survive the night.

FORTY-SIX

When she came to, she looked out the window of his car. He was turning onto a road that led toward the Mississippi River. Parks were popular places during the summer, but in the winter, they were almost completely deserted. He pulled into a parking area and then got out. He opened her door and grabbed her by the arm, yanking hard. Unfortunately, her seat belt was still fastened. His arm drew back, the gun in his hand.

"No!" she said loudly. She quickly fumbled with the belt, her fingers trembling with the cold and mounting fear. When the latch finally clicked, he pulled her out so quickly she almost got caught by the belt wrapping around her neck.

Once she was free, she looked around them. The parking area was deserted. Where was Tony? Why hadn't he followed them?

Swearing loudly, he began shoving her toward the river. She slipped twice on the snow, but both times he roughly pulled her to her feet.

"Knock it off," he yelled.

"I'm not slipping on purpose. The ground's icy and you're pushing me."

They finally reached a group of trees near the water, where he stopped. There were lights on poles back in the parking area, but here they were mostly in the dark. He let go of her but kept the gun leveled at her chest. Her face hurt where he'd hit her, but she had no intention of letting him know that.

"So, now you can ask your questions," he said. "I would enjoy answering them." His grin was demonic. Taunting.

"Is Joseph Baker angry that he didn't kill me? Did he order you to finish the job?" River was upset that her voice shook, but she couldn't help it. It wasn't just the icy temperature. She was attempting to fight the fear that was trying to wrap its arms around her. She was holding on to God's promises with all the strength she had. It seemed that He was the only one who could save her now.

His harsh laugh cut through the frigid air, his warm breath surrounding them like some kind of eerie smoke from a horror movie.

"You don't get it, do you? Joseph Baker isn't the Salt River Strangler."

As soon as the words left his lips, River finally understood. Once she and Tony realized who the man standing in front of her was, there'd been one question they couldn't answer. But now that she knew the truth, she became painfully aware that they should have figured it out sooner. Much sooner

"I thought you were both trained FBI profilers," he said in a low voice. The lights from the parking lot highlighted his features, making his face look like a Halloween mask, created to generate feelings of terror. It was working. "You blew it. And now you're going to die because of your failure. Not so cocky now, are you?"

"You're the Strangler. Baker is *your* minion. That's why he allowed himself to take the fall."

"Don't be mistaken. He killed his fair share of women—but

only at my direction. When I told him my plan, he went along with it. He'd die before he'd let me down. Of course, now it doesn't matter anymore."

"But why? Why save us, David? You could have let Tony and me die."

He grinned. "You believed there was only one killer. I wanted you to know how wrong you were. Destroying your self-righteousness was a pleasure."

River kept glancing back up toward the street and he noticed.

"Ah, you're watching for your friend Tony . . . and the police? I'm sorry, my dear, but they won't be coming. Did you think I wouldn't find the tracker you put on my car? Right now, your friends are chasing some poor schmuck who runs a real estate agency. I slapped your tracker on his car. It was parked next to mine in the parking lot. You don't seem to be wired, but even if you were, it wouldn't do you any good. You won't be found in time."

She wasn't wired. They'd been afraid he would check for that—and he had. Still, she couldn't stop watching the road behind him, praying that she'd see lights.

He laughed again. "Seriously, you can quit looking for your backup. No one's coming."

Suddenly, River began to feel a sense of peace. The prayer Tony had prayed seemed to grow inside her. She could swear she could hear him talking to her. Reassuring her. No matter what, God was with her, and she trusted Him. Knowing she wasn't really alone as she stood next to the massive river helped her to confront the terror that was trying to eat at her faith. She would be okay. Even if she left this life, she'd step into the next one, where she would find herself in the arms of her Savior. No one, not even the Salt River Strangler, could take that away from her.

"So, you accomplished what you wanted. You shook our confidence. Let us find out there were two killers instead of one. So why murder me now?"

"I played with you for a while—the way a cat toys with a mouse before he kills it. But I have other goals. I want to ramp up my body count. Become a legend. I had to wait for you. For this. But now it's over." He laughed. "And before you ask, yes. I killed your friend Jacki, after she told me what I wanted to know. She's still in the river. Too bad you'll never find her."

She had already suspected Jacki was dead, but her eyes filled with tears at hearing him confirm it.

She could barely make out his features now, but she could see his face twist into a frown. "One thing I have to know. Just when did you realize who I was?"

"You did a great job of changing the way you look. The glasses, colored contacts, the beard and mustache. We didn't recognize you at all until we talked in the parking lot. You were upset about the trash near your car. You forget that we watched you testify. Spent time with you. Watched the way you move. The way you talk. You have an odd way of pronouncing the word debris. You add an 's' to the word. You said it that night. And when you walk, you favor your right leg. I suspect you were injured at some point in your life?"

"I broke my leg when I was a kid. Or, I should say, my mother broke it when I didn't eat the moldy bread she ordered me to ingest when I was seven."

"So you blame your mother for your twisted psyche? I know people who've gone through worse things than you can imagine but overcame them. I don't feel sorry for you."

He hesitated a moment, probably trying to control his rage. David Prescott wanted to kill her—but he had a plan. He wouldn't allow her to upset him and destroy his carefully constructed agenda. If she could just ignite his anger, she might be able to overcome him.

"And then of course we realized that the name of your company—TSRS—were initials for the Salt River Strangler, not the Thomas Sullivan Recovery Service."

"Why didn't you just call the police? I have to say, that would have been the smarter choice."

At that moment, she was thinking the same thing. "We wanted you to admit who you were. We had no evidence, and Baker won't rat you out. So we decided to set a trap. One where you would try to kill me. Where you would admit to your crimes. Just like you are now."

"And then your police friends would swoop in and save you? And arrest me?"

"That was the idea. We know how you think. It wouldn't take long for your narcissism to make you confess to everything you've done." She frowned at him. "My turn. How did you find out about the tracker on your car?"

He laughed again, but the sound of it gave her shivers. "Pure luck. Some guy who works for a graphic design firm a few doors down from my office saw Tony under my car. Asked if I was having car trouble. I found it odd that he would be messing with my car, so I checked it out. Found your tracker." He sighed. "It is really cold out here, and it's getting dark. Let's get this over with, shall we?" He reached into his pocket and pulled out a zip tie. "You know the drill, right? Hands in front of you."

River hesitated.

"Obey me now, or I'll shoot you in the leg and do it myself. That choice would be much more painful for you."

River held her hands out in front of her, and he put the tie around her wrists. Then he pulled it so tight she cried out.

"Shut up," he barked. He pushed her down, grabbed her legs and then yanked another tie from his pocket. She watched as he put his gun down, pulled her ankles together, and zip-tied them as well. Was there some way to get his gun? Were the police and

Tony relying on the tracker, or had they actually followed David's car? It was beginning to look as if no one was coming. Or if they were, that they might not get here in time.

The funny thing was, at that moment, what she wanted more than anything else, was to tell Tony St. Clair how much she absolutely loved him. She'd had the chance and hadn't taken it. Would she ever get another opportunity?

FORTY-SEVEN

A s she lay on the ground, snow falling on top of her, River prayed. It was all she had left. She asked God to remind Tony about something that could save her life. Would he remember? This morning, she'd felt led to slip her extra phone into her boot. In the car, before Prescott got inside, she'd reached down and switched it on. If Tony remembered, the police could track her whereabouts. Why hadn't she mentioned it to him earlier? Probably because she didn't want to worry him. Didn't want Tony thinking she was still afraid. And she was—but not like the first time. This was different. She wanted to live, but she wasn't terrified.

As she prayed, something flowed through her. Like liquid love. She felt such peace. Did it mean God was going to save her? Or did it mean she would be with Him soon? Either way, evil would lose, and God would win. She kept her eyes on the snow falling from the sky instead of the man who plotted her death. The beautiful white flakes danced around her, creating beauty in the midst of darkness. Just like God's love in the presence of her enemy.

She heard something behind her and flipped her head around. Prescott was dragging an old chest out of the trees. Icy fear clutched at her chest, and she gasped. It wasn't from fear of dying. It was from fear of dying like *that*. In the river again, unable to move, choking on the water as it filled the trunk. *Oh, God. Anything but that. Please. Don't let me die like that!*

Even though she'd known somewhere deep inside this was the Strangler's plan for her, she'd ignored it. Was afraid to acknowledge it. For some reason she began to think about the Apostles. How each one of them died. Peter, crucified upside down because he didn't feel worthy of dying the way Jesus had. Andrew, also crucified, but preaching to his murderers until the life left his body. Matthew slain with a sword. Matthias and Barnabas stoned to death. Some of their deaths were so gruesome, her mind couldn't go there. She'd read about a man who'd become a Christian after reading of their deaths. Not one of them renounced Jesus. The man was convinced that unless they'd seen the resurrected Lord, they would never have endured these terrible deaths and not turned their backs on Him. She reasoned that if they could suffer the way they had, surely she could go through whatever she had to with dignity and faith.

"A nice coffin for you," Prescott said, a contorted smile on his face. River looked into his dead eyes.

"David, God loves you. You may not believe this, but He wants to forgive you. He gave the life of His Son for you. Jesus paid the price for all of your sins. Past, present, and future. He really wants to help you. You can have a brand-new life. A new start. You'll have to live it in prison, but even though your body is confined, your soul will finally be free."

For just a moment, Prescott stared at her with an expression that even she couldn't read. Was it remorse? Surprise? But in only seconds, it became clear that whatever thoughts had occurred to him in that moment, they quickly turned into rage. He walked up next to her and kicked her hard, several times. River cried out in pain. She wasn't certain he was going to stop, nor was she sure she wanted him to. Maybe it would be better if she died before she went into the water. She considered pushing him harder, causing his anger to flare up so he would end her life now. Yet she was surprised to discover a small flame of hope still burning inside her. And there was nothing David Prescott could do to quench it.

Prescott leaned down and put his hands under her armpits. Then he dragged her over to the chest. River wanted to fight back. Kick him away, but the pain in her body was too much. She felt the darkness approaching again, encouraging her to pass out, but she couldn't let that happen. She fought to stay conscious. No matter what, she wasn't going to give up. River wanted a chance to live for God. To reach others with His love. She wanted to make things right with her earthly father, spend time with her mother, and tell Tony that she loved him. "I need more time," she whispered. "Please, give me more time."

Would He answer her prayer, or was she getting ready to meet the God she'd grown to love with everything inside her?

TONY'S PRAYERS WERE FERVENT, almost violent. It was all he had left. There was no path that could lead them to River in time unless police officers searching near the river found them before it was too late. The search area was so large, it would take a miracle. But God did miracles. Why wouldn't He do one for River?

He jumped when Arnie walked up next to him and said, "Don't give up. God is watching out for her."

Tony stared at him in surprise. "Don't think I've heard you say anything like that before."

Arnie shrugged. "Maybe you're rubbing off on me."

Tony kept looking at him but didn't say anything. Finally, Arnie sighed.

"Okay, maybe I started going to church. People in our job either lose faith or gain it. Some of the things we see defy explanation. Either evil is real—and God is too—or nothing makes sense."

Tony blinked away an unexpected rush of tears. Maybe it was the stress of the moment, but there was something about seeing the change in his friend's life when another friend's life was on the line that simply overwhelmed him. This was God. Able to bring good out of devastation. It didn't make sense to the mind, but it made a lot of sense in his spirit.

"Don't get emotional on me," Arnie said, his voice getting husky. He started to say something else when his phone suddenly rang. He held his breath while Arnie listened silently. Finally, he said, "Okay. Keep looking." As he hung up the phone, Tony's heart fell.

"Not yet, but they're still searching. All we need is to spot the car. Remember that people aren't out tonight because of the weather. His vehicle will stand out. We'll find them."

Tony didn't respond. It wasn't that the car couldn't be found. The question was whether or not it could be located in time. Prescott wasn't stupid. He knew he needed to move quickly. River understood his narcissism. She'd stroke his ego. Try to get him to reveal his brilliance as a delaying tactic. But he wouldn't allow her to keep him occupied too long. Not if he wanted to get away, which Tony was certain he did.

"There's still time," Arnie said, confirming Tony's thoughts.

"He'll take some time preening before he kills her, but not so long that he puts himself in danger."

"Let's stay positive." Arnie sighed. "If only she had her phone, we could have tracked her."

It was then that Tony felt Someone whisper to him. It was so clear he turned to his right to see who was standing next to him. No one was there.

Tears filled his eyes again and this time he didn't blink them away. He grabbed Arnie's arm.

PRESCOTT OPENED THE LID to the chest. "Get in," he ordered.

River shook her head. "I'm not going to do it. If you want to kill me, do it now. I won't die that way. I just won't."

He grabbed her and turned her around, then he shoved her toward the trunk. It was old and smelled musty. It reminded her of the other one, and she was determined not to get inside.

"This is your last chance," he said, pointing his gun at her. "Get in!"

River stood her ground. She wasn't going inside that trunk. Not for any reason.

Get inside. Trust Me.

She started to tell Prescott to go ahead and shoot her when she realized he hadn't said the words she'd just heard. She took a quick involuntary breath. Every fiber of her being screamed that she shouldn't obey, but she'd heard a soft whisper that was stronger and more forceful than her fear of dying in the water. A deep sob ripped through her as she pushed herself to her feet, sat on the edge of the trunk, and swung her legs inside the old chest. It was difficult with her ankles bound.

"All the way," Prescott ordered.

River forced her muscles to move, and she knelt down. Then she put her head down, her chin resting on her bent legs. It made it hard to breathe.

"I win," Prescott said loudly. His laugh was obscene. "I beat you and your partner. He may not be dying tonight, but he'll die inside when he pulls your body out of the river."

"You've won nothing," River said, her words muffled by her position and the knowledge that Tony would be crushed if Prescott succeeded.

"If I die here, God will take me home to be with Him. So you lose, David. No matter what you do, you still lose."

Before she had a chance to prepare herself, pain exploded in the back of her head. He'd hit her again with his gun. She fought to stay conscious, but she felt herself slipping away. The last thing she heard was David Prescott cursing God's name.

When she regained consciousness, she couldn't see anything. It was dark and cold. And wet. She gasped loudly when she remembered where she was. In the Mississippi River, drowning.

"God, please," she cried out. "Please don't let me die here. I'm not ready. I haven't told Tony that I love him. Please, Father."

She stopped as she felt water in her mouth. She choked and gagged. Remembering the last time she was inside a trunk, she wiggled herself onto her side so she could get a few more breaths of air before the chest was completely submerged. She recalled begging for her life back then. Promising God she'd return to Him, but then turning her back once she'd been rescued. This time would be different. If she died, she would die praising Him for His love. For giving the life of His precious Son for people who hated Him. Who reviled Him. Even for people like David Prescott. It was the kind of love that was impossible to understand.

She tried to turn on her back, attempting to keep her head elevated, but she couldn't. Suddenly, a song filled her mind, and she began to sing. The cold made her body tremble and her lips quiver. As well as she could, she sang, "My God is an awesome God, He reigns from heaven above . . ." She stopped as water filled her mouth and nose. It seemed that this time no one was going to pull her out. No one would save her. It wasn't what she wanted, but if this was what was going to happen, it was okay. Fear was gone. She was getting ready to see the face of her Savior. The One who loved her more than anyone else.

She held her breath as long as she could, but she finally had to give up. She was so cold, it was as if she couldn't control her muscles anymore. She felt herself drifting away. Then there was warmth, and she found herself standing in a field of flowers. She was amazed to see hues of color beyond anything she'd ever imagined. As if there were colors human beings had never seen. A warm breeze moved the flowers, and they sang. It seemed that everything around her was made of music. All of creation was praising God. There were no words in the English language to describe the beauty she beheld.

Suddenly she realized that Someone was walking toward her. He was made of light. She couldn't clearly make out His features because his face was too bright. Somehow, she realized that she didn't have the kind of eyes that could see His face. Not yet, anyway.

"Lord?" she whispered.

He came up and took her hands. "It's not time for you to be with Me," He said. "But you will be someday. I want you to always remember how much I love you. Never doubt it for a moment. You are my beloved daughter, and I am well pleased with you."

River looked down at His hands and saw the scars on His wrists. She tried to tell Him how much she loved Him, but her vision grew misty, and He began to fade. The last thing she heard was "Don't be afraid. I am with you."

Peace flowed through her. Peace so strong, she realized that it was what she'd read about in the Bible. Peace that passed understanding. She smiled and drifted away.

FORTY-EIGHT

River was suddenly aware of a bright light that surrounded her, but it didn't feel like the light she'd seen before. She felt warm, but it was different too. Where was she?

"Lord?" she whispered. Her throat hurt and she was confused. There wasn't supposed to be pain in heaven. What was wrong?

"You can call me Tony," a voice said.

River forced her eyes to focus. Someone was standing over her. "Where . . . where . . . ?"

"You're in the hospital, River. You're going to be okay."

She blinked several times, trying to clear her vision. The light was from the fixture overhead and the warmth came from the blankets that covered her. She could finally make out Tony's face. "What . . . ?"

"Just save your voice," Tony said. "You've had a tube down your throat. It will be a little sore for a while. When we found you, Prescott had thrown you into the river. We almost got there too late."

"My phone?"

Tony nodded. "River, I swear God reminded me about that phone. I'd completely forgotten about it. Then, when we realized

Prescott had found the tracker and we had no idea where you were, suddenly I could hear you telling me about that stupid phone. I remembered the number, even though I'd never written it down. I should have. It was stupid of me. I'm convinced it was God taking care of you. Arnie had your phone tracked and we found you. If we'd gotten there even a few minutes later . . ." He cleared his throat. "It's a miracle the doctors brought you back."

"Brought me back?" The pain in her throat brought tears to her eyes.

Before Tony could answer her, someone else came into the room.

"I heard you were awake." An older man with gray hair stepped up next to River's bed. "Do you know your name?"

River frowned at him. "Of course. I'm River Ryland," she croaked. "And who are you?"

The man's bushy gray eyebrows shot up, and he grinned at her. "Perfectly good question. I'm Dr. Schell. I've been treating you since you were brought in. I know your throat hurts. We had to give you oxygen through an endotracheal tube. We also gave you fluids to warm you up. You had hypothermia and inhaled water from the river. If it wasn't for Mr. St. Clair, I don't think you'd be with us."

"What do you mean? What happened to me?" River said, her voice barely audible.

"I'll let Mr. St. Clair tell you about that. We had to treat him too, but thankfully, he's just fine." The doctor went around to the end of River's bed and picked up a clipboard. He read it over and smiled. "You're doing very well. If you keep it up, we may be able to send you home tomorrow."

"I'd rather leave now." She put her hand to her throat as if that would somehow help.

Dr. Schell laughed. "I guess I shouldn't be surprised. From the stories I've heard about you, I should have expected that. Let's wait until tomorrow though, okay? I want to make certain we don't have to stick you back in here, and I'm sure you feel the same."

"How . . . how long . . . ?" she croaked.

"Have you been here?" the doctor asked.

River nodded.

"It's been three days since you were brought in. We had to keep you unconscious for a while. Warm you up slowly and keep an eye on your lungs. I feel safe in saying you're going to recover completely. Some patients who are brought in with your symptoms are never the same. You're a very lucky young lady."

"Not . . . not lucky," Tony said. "Blessed."

She felt Tony squeeze her hand. Her vision was clearing, and she looked up into his eyes. What she saw there filled her with joy.

"I stand corrected," the doctor said. "I think you're right. 'Blessed' is more accurate. Let's see if we can get a little food inside you. I'm sure you'd enjoy that more than your IV."

River suddenly realized how hungry she was. "Sounds good," she whispered.

"Try resting your throat," the doctor said. "I'll get you some ice chips and something for pain." He turned and left the room.

"What . . . what . . . ?"

"Stop," Tony said. He let go of her hand and walked over to a chair in the corner. There was a small table next to it. He picked up a spiral notebook and brought it over to the bed. After flipping the pages several times, he handed it to her. He'd turned it to a blank page. Then he reached into his pocket and took out a pen. He put it in her hand. "Write it," he said. "Save your voice so it can recover, okay?"

She nodded and wrote, *What did the doctor mean when he said you saved me?*

Tony picked up the notebook and read what River had written.

His cheeks turned red. He only did that when he was embarrassed.

"Look, when we got to the spot where Prescott took you, he'd already put you in the water. The chest was almost completely submerged. That river is huge and has strong undercurrents. There wasn't much time. I had no choice. I . . . I jumped into the water."

River reached out for the paper and pen. *You shouldn't have done that!!!!*

She handed it to him. He chuckled when he read it. "Well, we can put you back in if you want."

River held her hand out for the notebook.

He shook his head. "No, not yet. Before you fill the pages of my notebook with angry retorts, hear me out. You would have done the same thing for me, and you know it. The truth is, I went in the water and grabbed onto the chest. There were two other officers who followed me in and the three of us were able to get you to shore. I couldn't have done it by myself. They deserve the credit. If you want, I can track them down and you can write nasty comments to them too."

Despite herself, River smiled. Then she shook her head. This time when she reached for the notebook, he gave it to her.

I almost didn't make it?

He took it back. "Yes, that's true. I performed CPR after we got you out of that chest and on the shore. Kept it up until the ambulance showed up. That's when the EMTs took over. You . . . you had no pulse for a while. By the time they got you to the hospital, they'd revived you. Then you had to be treated for hypothermia. They were very concerned because you'd stopped breathing for a while. The doctors were also worried about brain damage, but I told them you'd always been a little off."

So, seeing Jesus wasn't a dream. It was real. Tears filled her eyes and dripped down her cheeks.

"I'm sorry. I wasn't being serious."

Tony looked so stricken, River fought back a laugh that definitely would have hurt too much. She shook her head. And wrote *Something happened to me after I stopped breathing. I'll tell you about it later. It was wonderful.*

"I was so frightened at first." He took her hand again. "What if I'd lost you?" he said. "I prayed like I'd never prayed before. But then I remembered the Scriptures we'd quoted before you left. And I felt so much peace."

River smiled at him and wrote, *I did too. God was with me the entire time.*

"I know He was."

River reached for the notepad again and wrote, *Did they get him?*

Tony took the notepad. "Yes," he said. "They did. He took out a gun and pointed it at the police and they shot him. Thankfully, he didn't die. I want him to spend the rest of his miserable life in prison."

River grabbed the notebook. *Prescott is the Strangler. Not Baker.*

Tony nodded. "We know. He's pretty proud of himself. About how he fooled us—until he didn't. Thing is, now he'll have a long time to think about how we beat him. How he lost. With his ego, that will cause him more suffering than anything else." He frowned at her. "We'll have to testify. I know you probably don't want to do that."

River grinned and took back the notepad. *Are you kidding? I can hardly wait. I want to see his smug face when he realizes he's going to spend the rest of his days thinking about us.*

After reading what she wrote, Tony said, "I keep telling myself that God loves him too. We need to remember that. Maybe we should . . ."

"Not yet," River said, her voice cracking under the pain and the emotion. "I know we have to forgive him, but I'm gonna have to work on that a bit."

"That's only fair," Tony said. "Now stop talking."

River grinned and took the notepad back. *When we get back to the office, I want to see if we can discover the identity of the man who was found dead next to the railroad tracks, okay?*

When Tony read what she'd written, he laughed. "Why don't we see if April wants that one. If not, I'm all in."

She took the pad from him. *Maybe we could work on it together. If April's interested, I think we should hire her. What do you think?*

When he took the notepad, he nodded. "I think that's a great idea, but I'm not sure we can get another desk in that office. We may have to move to a bigger space. Arnie says that after it gets out that we caught the Salt River Strangler, we'll be turning business away. I think we can afford a building of our own. Is that okay with you?"

River nodded. Then she put her hands out for the notebook one last time. She wrote, *When I woke up, I wanted nothing more than to tell you how much I love you. I may not be able to talk right now, but there is something else I can do.*

Tony read her words and smiled. "I think I know what that might be." He leaned down and kissed her gently. "We have a lot of years to talk, I guess."

"And a lot of years for this too," River whispered. Then she pulled him close and kissed him again.

NOTE FROM
THE AUTHOR

Dear Reader,

I hope you've enjoyed this book. I try hard to write stories that will entertain you, but even more importantly, I pray that something I've written will touch your heart. If you find yourself relating to my characters who struggle with fear, loneliness, and sorrow, just like the rest of us, I want to give you some good news. God has the answer to every problem you face, and He loves you with a love that is deep, eternal, and boundless. If you've never asked him into your life, you can take care of that today. John 3:16 says "For God so loved the world that He gave His one and only Son, that whoever believes in Him shall not perish but have eternal life" (NIV). Below is a prayer you can use to change your life forever.

"Lord Jesus, I turn to You in my time of need. I believe that You are the Son of God and that You died on the cross to pay the price for my sins. Lord, I receive You as my Savior, and I want You to be my Lord. Wash me clean with Your blood, and fill me with Your Holy Spirit. Help me to follow You the rest of my life. Amen."

If you've prayed this prayer, will you let me know? You can contact me through my website, NancyMehl.com. Please find a good local church where you can become part of a family that will help you on your journey. May God bless you abundantly.

ACKNOWLEDGMENTS

My thanks to the amazing Jessica Sharpe, who makes my books better. I'm so glad you're my editor.

Thank you to Susan Downs, whose wisdom guides me through each and every book. Thank you for your years of support and encouragement.

Thanks to Kate Jameson, who catches my mistakes and keeps me out of trouble. I appreciate your kindness and patience.

To Donita Corman, who helped me through *Cold Threat*. Thank you for introducing me to Burlington, Iowa. It was a great place to set that story. I couldn't have written it without you. I'm so glad we're friends. You inspire me.

Thank you also to Supervisory Special Agent Drucilla Wells (Retired), Federal Bureau of Investigations, Behavioral Analysis Unit. Without your help, none of these profiler books would have happened.

My appreciation to Retired Police Officer Darin Hickey. Your help is invaluable to me.

Most of all, my thanks to God, who allows me to write. I pray You will speak to the people who need You through my books. I love you. You are everything.

Read on
for a sneak peek at
the first book in

THE
ERIN
DELANEY

SERIES.

Available March 2025.

CHAPTER ONE

Erin stood in the street outside a large, dirty brick building that housed too many people in small rooms with mold-infested walls. *Human beings should not live like this.* And tonight, some no longer were.

She felt something on her shoes and looked down. The street was beginning to flood. The nearby streetlight flickered, and she suddenly realized she was standing in blood—dark, thick, gooey. She wanted to run, but her feet were stuck. She couldn't move.

"Erin!" someone yelled. "Erin!"

She looked up and saw her partner, Scott, standing several yards away. She could barely make him out through a strange fog that swirled around them, but it was obvious he was struggling. He held his arms out toward her.

"Erin, save me. You're my partner. You're supposed to have my back."

She watched in horror as the same crimson flood that held her fast swept him away. She fought as hard as she could to reach him, but it was impossible.

"Scott," she called out to him. "Scott!"

And then he was gone.

As terror seized her mind, she became aware of someone else standing below the streetlight, a dark shadow in the shape of a child. The only feature Erin could make out were her eyes. They glowed with a strange inner fire, and they were locked on Erin. She tried to look away but couldn't. She was still frozen in place, unable to control her body or move her gaze from the child who stared at her with smoldering hate.

ERIN GASPED AND SAT UP IN BED, sobbing, her face wet with tears and her sheets soaked with sweat. She swung her legs over the side of the bed and put her face in her hands. When would these nightmares end? Would she ever heal from that night?

She looked at the clock next to her bed. Three thirty-three in the morning. Again. How could she wake up every night at the same time? It was eerie. Made her shiver.

She got out of bed and walked over to her closet. After sliding open the door, she glanced up at the locked box on the top shelf. Her gun. She hadn't touched it since . . .

Every morning when she woke up, her feet led her to the closet as if they had a mind of their own. She was drawn to the gun and yet repelled by it. It wasn't the one she'd used that night. She'd turned that one in—along with her badge—when she quit the force. Erin stared at the box as the clock on her nightstand ticked too loudly in the quiet room, a reminder that her life was ticking away.

She shook her head and closed the closet door, then made her way to the kitchen. Maybe a cup of chamomile tea would help. Her doctor had prescribed sleeping pills, but they remained untouched on her nightstand. She was afraid to open the bottle. Afraid she . . .

"Stop it," she said to herself as she flipped on the kitchen light.

She finished brewing her tea and thought about going back

to bed, but her sheets were still damp, and she didn't feel like changing them. She wasn't sure she had any clean ones, anyway. She hadn't done laundry for a while. She'd finally hired someone to clean her apartment, though it embarrassed her. She was basically unemployed, had nothing else to do, but she couldn't take care of the relatively small space where she lived.

Correction—where she existed.

She used to pride herself on being able to do everything. Cook, clean, take down bad guys. But now she spent her time watching too much TV and trying to dodge calls from her editor, who wanted more books. She wasn't sure she had another book in her. She'd only written the first one because she needed something to do. A way to focus on anything besides that night. Her novel was created as a way to release the dream she'd had inside for so many years. A dream that died the same night Scott had.

She sat at the kitchen table and looked out the window at the falling rain as it streaked the glass. The light on her deck caused the rivulets of water to shimmer and dance. She continued to stare outside while she finished her tea. Then she went into the living room and lay on the couch, turning on the TV.

What should she watch? No cop shows. It was too painful. Strangely, comedies made her angry. Seeing people laugh felt so wrong. Scott was dead. Her career was over. And she was lost. Utterly and completely lost. The life she had now was unsustainable. The only time she'd felt alive was when she was writing that stupid book, and that was fiction. Not real.

She glanced at her coffee table. *Dark Matter* by Erin Delaney. She'd been able to live vicariously through her protagonist, Alex Caine. Alex was the FBI behavioral analyst Erin would never be. Alex lived out Erin's dead dream. The FBI certainly didn't want a broken ex-cop. The book had made a lot of money and even shot to the top of the *New York Times*' bestsellers list. But it hadn't made her happy. All it did was make it clear how empty her life had become.

Erin knew how to write. She'd taken creative writing courses in college—along with her real interest, criminal justice. Straight out of school, she'd had a couple of novels released by a small publisher. She hadn't made any money. It was just for fun. But *Dark Matter* had caught the interest of a large publisher, thanks to the retired FBI behavioral analyst who had been her source—and had become her friend.

Erin had hoped writing the book would be cathartic. She'd written about an FBI profiler who watched a colleague gunned down in front of him. The rest of the book followed his mission to hunt down the deranged serial killer who had taken the life of his friend. But working on the book hadn't healed the trauma. She was still haunted by that night.

Now her editor wanted three more books. Not only did she have nothing else to say, she was afraid of facing additional pain. Why did her editor keep calling? Her agent understood and had remained silent. But her editor wouldn't take no for an answer. Was it the money? The prestige? Erin didn't care about any of that.

She jumped when her cell phone rang. There was only one human being who knew she woke up at the same time every night.

"Hello, Kaely," she said when she answered the phone.

"Now you've got me waking up at three thirty," Kaely said.

Kaely Quinn-Hunter had walked Erin through the details of *Dark Matter*. Without her, she couldn't have written the book. As they shared things that only those in law enforcement could understand, they had bonded in a way no therapist could comprehend. Erin knew this for a fact. She'd been through three already. None of them had helped.

"Sorry. I'm sure Noah doesn't appreciate that."

Kaely laughed. "Noah sleeps like a log. Nothing wakes him

up." She hesitated for a moment before saying, "You still having that same nightmare?"

"Yeah. It's like some kind of dysfunctional friend who won't go away."

"Not sure it's your friend," Kaely said, then paused again.

"Okay, spit it out. I can tell you have something on your mind."

Kaely sighed loudly. "I hope the day doesn't come when I really need to keep something from you."

"Why would you want to keep something from me?"

"You're taking this too literally. I...I want to propose something."

"If this is another invitation to visit you, you're wasting your time," Erin said. "You know I can't leave my apartment."

"Erin, you can leave your apartment. You just choose not to."

"Says you."

"Yeah, says me," Kaely said. "I'm not asking you to come here, but I am asking you to leave that apartment. You can't spend the rest of your life holed up in there."

Erin really did want to venture out, but she couldn't stand the idea of being in a situation she couldn't control. She was safe here. She'd gone out a few times—but just to the doctor or the therapist. She could have groceries delivered, and she knew all the restaurants that would bring her food. She'd even bought a new car online and had it delivered. Life had certainly changed over the last several years. Now anyone could cut themselves off from the world. It was relatively easy.

"So what are you asking me to do?" she asked, certain she wasn't going to do it.

"Just get into that nice new car you bought and drive to the Smokies. I have a friend who owns a cabin in a town called Sanctuary."

"You're making that up."

Kaely laughed again. "No, I'm not. That's really the name of the town. Anyway, I'm proposing a week in an isolated cabin, just you and me. We can talk, cry, yell, do whatever we want with no one to bother us. I'll even pick up our groceries, do whatever I need to. All you have to do is be there. The area is gorgeous. You'll love it. What do you say?"

Erin searched for an argument, but as she gazed around her kitchen, realizing how tired she was of looking at the same walls, she heard herself agreeing to go.

After getting more information from Kaely, Erin hung up and wondered what she'd just done. She wanted to call Kaely back and explain why she couldn't go, but suddenly the image of that box in the closet flashed in her mind. She had the distinct feeling that if she didn't meet Kaely at the cabin, one of these nights she might finally unlock it.

Nancy Mehl (NancyMehl.com) is the author of more than fifty books, a Parable and ECPA bestseller, and the winner of an ACFW Book of the Year Award, a Carol Award, and the Daphne du Maurier Award. She has also been a finalist for the Christy Award. Nancy writes from her home in Missouri, where she lives with her husband, Norman, and their puggle, Watson.

Sign Up for Nancy's Newsletter

Keep up to date with Nancy's latest news on book releases and events by signing up for her email list at the link below.

NancyMehl.com

FOLLOW NANCY ON SOCIAL MEDIA

Nancy Mehl Fan Page   @NancyMehl1

More from Nancy Mehl

Former FBI profiler River Ryland suffers from PTSD from a serial killer case gone wrong and has opened a private investigation firm with Tony, her former colleague. Their first job is a cold case, but when they race to stop the killer before he strikes again, an even more dangerous threat emerges, stirring up the past and plotting to end River's future.

Cold Pursuit
RYLAND & ST. CLAIR #1

Former FBI behavioral analysts River Ryland and Tony St. Clair are asked to assist on a profile to catch the Snowman, a serial killer who has stayed hidden for over twenty years. As the killer's pattern emerges and danger mounts, River and Tony are in a race against the clock to catch a killer before he catches one of them.

Cold Threat
RYLAND & ST. CLAIR #2

When authorities contact the FBI about bodies found on freight trains—all killed the same way—Alex Donovan is forced to confront her troubled past when she recognizes the graffiti messages the killer is leaving behind. In a race against time, Alex must decide how far she will go—and what she is willing to risk—to put a stop to the Train Man.

Night Fall
THE QUANTICO FILES #1

◈ BETHANYHOUSE

 Bethany House Fiction

 @BethanyHouseFiction

 @Bethany_House

 @BethanyHouseFiction

 Free exclusive resources for your book group at BethanyHouseOpenBook.com

 Sign up for our fiction newsletter today at BethanyHouse.com